# LESLEY HOWARTH

## WALKER BOOKS
### AND SUBSIDIARIES
LONDON · BOSTON · SYDNEY · AUCKLAND

# Contents

## MapHead

# MapHead 2

# Catshake

The reason Powers'd liquefied the cat in the end green-house first is it asked for it. It was a scrawny grey number with pleading yellow eyes and sticking-out hip bones, like it'd swallowed a box or something. It came mewling around at the slightest niff of food. It'd even beg for tomatoes when it knew it couldn't eat them.

One evening, after a film, Powers turned his eyes on the scrawny grey cat. It was bad news for the cat. Under the power of Powers' eyes it quailed and fell down. It must've heaved in its skin a full ten seconds before its organs reduced. Then there was draining and disposal. And about two pints of catshake. "Enjoy," said Powers. Boothe grinned. He'd only been Boothe ten minutes. Really his name was MapHead. But already he felt the new name bite.

The end greenhouse was home, for the while. It was the largest of five great glasshouses on the tomato farm – and the furthest from the bungalow. Evenings, they usually wandered up the track and sat in their hollow place in the hedge. It was the ideal angle to catch the telly in the bungalow living-room. They always felt like munchies when they got back. It was just the cat's bad luck.

The film that night was *The Emerald Forest*. They both watched closely, but they saw no emeralds. They didn't really get it, at all. They'd been watching the film anyway when they spotted the name Powers Boothe in the credits and liked it so much they split it between them, Powers for father, Boothe for son. "When in Rome," said Powers.

"Sorry?" said Boothe.

"A saying," explained Powers, back in the greenhouse. "When in Rome, do as the Romans do. Now we're here, we'll have a proper name each."

"Romans?" said Boothe. Boothe was big on Romans. "Can we play Circus Maximus?"

"No. No more Circus Maximus today."

Boothe sighed. It was only a game. But still. He drained his catshake, eyeing Powers over the top of his can. Powers wouldn't change his mind. He didn't know how.

"Hey," said Boothe. "Hey. What's protein status, catshake?"

"Where's your speech rhythms?" asked Powers sternly. "You should make it flow. Make it more natural."

12

Boothe paused. "Hey, Dad, what's *in* a cat?"

"Better," nodded Powers. "Much better."

Powers considered the catshake. He made some quick calculations. "I'd give it around fifty-eight per cent usable protein. Quite a bit of rubbish in a cat."

Only fifty-eight per cent. Boothe whistled. He liked the effect. He whistled some more. "Hey," he said again. "Hey."

Then he got up. He wandered down the tomato rows until he found a real killer. Postbox red and big as a fist, it plumped in his hand like a gift. He held it up, for a joke.

"Look. The tomato that ate the world."

Powers looked blank. "How could it?" Powers took everything literally.

The tomato plants filled the greenhouse in endless leafy lines with walkways in between. They grew straight up, twelve feet or more, in the wheezing glass roof. But the roof didn't stop them. If no one let down their strings to give them room, they just doubled right over and grew downwards. Nothing could stop them. Even if the stem cracked, or you stood on them, they grew. They grew like madmen, all season. In between them zigzagged enormous powdery bees. They went from flower to flower transferring pollen. They were unstoppable too.

Boothe sank his teeth in his killer tomato. It bombed his chin with juice, but he didn't mind at all. Powers watched him eating. He didn't bother with tomatoes himself any more. Instead he drank the special growth fluid that fed the plants, sucking it straight from the tubes connecting every rootball to a meaty feeder pipe along the centre of every row. More logical, said Powers. All tomatoes did was change it into sugars. Powers'd eat anything. He'd even tried a bee or two.

Boothe wiped his chin. He'd been Boothe fifteen minutes. He wasn't sure he liked it, now.

"Can I not be Boothe?"

"You *are* Boothe."

"I mean, can I *not* be?"

"You can't be MapHead," said Powers sharply. "MapHead isn't a name."

"I don't want to. Be Boothe."

"Speech rhythms. Why not?"

"I don't prefer."

"But Boothe's natural. It's a name."

Already MapHead was blushing a map of his home terrain over his domed head, the contour figures slipping and sliding over his skin, down his neck, the way he did when he was stressed.

The fact was, he wasn't going to get natural overnight. Powers was natural. He fitted in pretty well. But Powers had visited this neck of the woods before, once or twice. Once, at any rate, some twelve years ago – else he, MapHead, wouldn't even be here, would he? Not unless his father had visited his mother in the beginning. No visit, no MapHead. Simple really.

14

Now they'd come back. That was simple too. No return visit, no known mother. She was the reason they'd come. As far back as MapHead could remember, she'd never been around. Powers had a story about how he'd met her. Sometimes he'd tell it, sometimes he wouldn't. Whenever he would, MapHead liked to hear it.

The last time he'd told it was on MapHead's birthday. MapHead had turned twelve in a grove of meagre trees on the plain of the Indus river. All that afternoon he'd watched a ghostly caravan of sumptuous long-dead princes swing ponderously over the plain. Every place he visited, MapHead saw everything everyone else saw and quite a lot else besides. Sometimes there were ghosts. Sometimes hidden watercourses way underground would tug at his arms so they twitched like a dowser's rod. Wherever he went with Powers, he sensed the secrets that every bluff and valley wore under its everyday face. It was a view that fitted snugly round the real world like a skin on an orange; a subtle world in which Powers flashed from place to place as casually as a tramp might hitch a ride – a world that MapHead had grown up with.

They'd left the Indus shortly after MapHead's birthday. Powers had grown impatient. And here he was, twelve and one month exactly, in the land of the killer tomatoes.

"All right." Powers sighed. "*Be* my MapHead, then."

MapHead grinned. Learning to speak naturally was

one thing, losing your name you'd grown up with, something else again. It was all very well for Powers. Powers' real name was Ran, but he had a host of other names, and not one of them fitted him more than any other. Powers was indescribable and untaggable. He changed who he was, to fit wherever he was, as easily as he changed his heartbeat.

But MapHead was who he was, no matter how he learned to speak. And he *was* learning. Reading was one way. MapHead had learned to read, sitting on a rock in a cave by a waterfall in California, back when Powers had bothered scavenging storybooks for him. Their home in the cave had been lonely and damp; but the storybooks had opened out the walls and crowded in fantastic characters that MapHead had come to know as friends. Reading wasn't the same as talking, though. It wasn't the same as joking, sharing, batting back thoughts as they came. Natural speech was a hard nut to crack, said Powers.

"Meaning?" asked MapHead suddenly. "Hard nut? To crack?"

"A saying," explained Powers, "meaning an intractable problem."

"Huh?" said MapHead.

"Good," said Powers approvingly. "Huh. Very natural."

"Answer my 'Huh'," said MapHead.

"Intractable," said Powers, "means: that which cannot be brought under control."

"Like me," said MapHead happily. Powers flashed up the dictionary definition over his scalp by way of emphasis. MapHead blushed up a map of the immediate area, by way of a signal he understood. He specialized in maps. Maps were all he did. Usually he said everything he needed to say with his head. Words were so much clumsier. But now he was twelve he would need them.

Twelve, said Powers, was an important age. The name of the twelfth year was called Dawn of Power. Hadn't he himself drawn strength from his parents at twelve and blazed away from them, whole? Hadn't he, Powers, gathered and completed himself in a way that MapHead couldn't without his mother? Now that he was twelve he must meet her. Strength through certainty, said Powers. Look at the plants. How would the growing tip unfold without drawing strength from its roots? Everyone needed to know that much. Even tramps have mothers.

Powers and MapHead were tramps, of a sort. They ranged through lonely places, wherever wilderness remained. The deserts were theirs, and the mountains. They didn't rub shoulders with people too much. Too much effort, said Powers. Fitting in with people would be a first for MapHead. They usually based themselves around plants of various kinds, mainly for the vibes, which were good. Waterfalls were good too; Powers had a weakness for waterfalls – cascades he liked to call them – but plants were better. Greenhouses, garden nurseries, even conservatories – they were all good. And the tomato farm was ideal. Ideal was the buzz word on the tomato farm. The workers used it a lot. And it was, said Powers. For them the set-up was … ideal.

MapHead yawned. Then he toyed a bit with Circus Maximus. It was only a game of beetles and stones – a little space in the gravel, over against the clonking great heating pipes that ran all the way down the track from the central boilerhouse and back.

Sometimes Powers joined in, then it was better. The way MapHead did it, the beetles had to be pushed a bit. But Powers'd zap 'em round twenty crazy laps a minute with his eyes, just by looking. The real Circus Maximus in ancient Rome had held a hundred thousand people for the chariot races, later three hundred and fifty thousand! Three hundred and fifty thousand people! The chariot teams were named by colour – the Purples and the Crimsons, the Blues, Greens and Whites. First there were acrobats. Then the main event. Teams of four horses, open-back chariots. Death or glory were the watchwords. Not much else was known.

When he was six MapHead'd seen a film called *Ben Hur* through a caravan window in a trailer park somewhere in Arizona, USA, he'd forgotten exactly where. But he'd never forgotten the chariot race sequence. There was one man dressed in black who got dragged beneath the horses – he was cheating anyway, with knives on his wheels, so he deserved it. Ever since then

MapHead had been big on Romans. Especially the chariot races.

When Powers zapped the beetles round, MapHead could see it all – the coloured ribbons, or favours, in the crowd, the savage turn, the Greens storming home between the painted poles with the lead horse streaked and broken. Or the lead beetle, depending on how much he'd pushed it. Some of 'em didn't take too kindly to Circus Maximus. Some kinds of beetles had legs that dropped off. Sometimes the one he thought would win won, and sometimes it didn't. But whichever the winner, it was always the Greens to MapHead.

There'd been a family in the caravan in the trailer park where he'd seen *Ben Hur*, he remembered. A proper family, with a mother who told her kids: "Turn that teevee down will ya, I'm try'na talk to your father." He wondered what his own mother would say if he turned up outside the window when she was talking over the telly. *If* they ever found her.

"When we find her, how will we know?" he asked, fiddling a new beetle out from under the polythene and setting it down.

"Don't worry," said Powers. "We'll know."

"How will we?"

"She's your mother," said Powers heavily. "Isn't she? We'll know."

MapHead pulped his beetle. A non-starter, if ever there was one. Only the best would win. Only the fittest. The maps crossing his scalp bled freely into one another.

"She might not want to know," he whispered low over the beetle-mash so none but beetles should hear. "She might not. Ever. Want to. Know."

# No Waiting

"You're not going to book me, are you?" asked the young woman incredulously. "I've only been a moment."

Fore Street, Rubytown. Outside the bank, MapHead watched, fascinated. It was true. She'd dashed into the bank and dashed out again. Forty seconds by his reckoning. But forty seconds was enough. The traffic warden clicked her Biro. She brought out her little book of tickets. She hardly looked at the young woman at all.

"But there's other cars parked here—" said the young woman wildly.

"That's my business."

"But I've parked here a moment before."

The traffic warden eyed the number plate and completed the ticket with a flourish. "This makes up for all the other times I haven't been around then, doesn't it?"

The young woman looked tearfully up and down. She had an interesting shape, thought MapHead. An interesting bump. He knew he probably shouldn't, but he looked inside it anyway. Her baby was almost ready. He looked again. A girl.

"Is this going to cost me a lot of money?" She was crying openly now.

"It's going to cost you thirty pounds." The traffic warden ripped off the ticket. She tucked it in the pregnant woman's hand. Then she found a records form and began to complete it.

The young woman looked hopelessly at the ticket. "You just deprived my son of his school shoes. I hope you're proud of yourself."

"Only doing my job," said the warden, with relish.

"You don't have to do it like *this*."

The warden stepped back. "Morning," she nodded, to a passer-by. As if to say: I'm normal, me. This is a normal kind of thing to do. Isn't it?

The man in the crinkly black shell-suit hardly missed a beat. "Haven't you *died* yet?" he snarled, passing on. There had, thought MapHead, been a whole pot of poison in his voice.

The traffic warden blanched. She looked around for someone else to greet. The young woman had screwed up her ticket and slammed into her car. She looked up.

"What a wonderful contribution to society you do make," she said bitterly, "don't you?"

MapHead watched her car weaving away down Fore Street. He was sorry for her. But it had been an interesting exchange. Haven't you died yet? Haven't you. Died yet. Drop dead. Why don't you.

The warden eyed him unpleasantly. "Got a problem, sonny?"

MapHead tilted his baseball cap and considered the question. Had he got a problem? Speech rhythms were always a problem. And what did they do with problems? Run round 'em, like water round a stone. Where *was* Powers, anyway? A long time coming out of the supermarket, that was for sure. Anyway. It wasn't so much what she said, it was the way she said it.

"Yes," said MapHead politely. "I have a problem with horrible."

The warden scribbled fiercely in her tight little book. She snapped it shut. "I'm only doing my job."

"Only," repeated MapHead, "doing. Your. Job."

She scanned Fore Street like a gunfighter.

"That's what I said. This your parent's vehicle?"

MapHead took in the blue car next in line. KEEP YOUR DISTANCE, said a sticker on the blue car. BABY ON BOARD. He moved back a little.

"Wait," he answered carefully. "My parent said wait."

"She did, did she? In that case I'll—"

"He. My parent. Said wait."

She looked twice at MapHead. She fished out her book. "No waiting between nine and six. That sign over there. I'm booking your father."

Booking your father. Booking. Your father. MapHead ran over it twice, three times. Powers liked books. Books were ideal. But somewhere there was a threat, he was sure.

Suddenly he laughed sardonically. "Hey," he said, mimicking the acid tones of the man in the black shell-suit. "Hey. Get a life, why don't you?"

"Excuse me?" She dotted a full stop and narrowed her eyes. "You kids these days. You want to have a bit of respect."

"Respect," brayed MapHead. The tension was getting to him. The threat was still there, somewhere. It had grown to include him, now. "Respect. Spelt: R-E-S-P-E-C-T. Verb, transitive. Meaning—"

"Meaning," cut in Powers behind him, "regard with deference; pay due regard to; due consideration or appreciation." He smiled disarmingly at the warden. "Someone like yourself to look up to. An object lesson to an unformed mind. What weather. Shan't know sunshine when we see it, shall we?"

Powers looked down at MapHead. See? That's the way people talk. That's natural, that is.

"This your vehicle?" asked the warden coldly, indicating the blue car.

"I wish," said MapHead.

"I regret but it isn't," said Powers ungrammatically, as though he'd own it if he could, to please her. "Can you supply me with local schools information?"

"I'm not the Tourist Information Board. Your son

told me this was your vehicle. Now you're telling me it's not?"

"Correct," said Powers, delighted to be in agreement. "I wondered, is this the catchment area for Stonewalls Primary? My son," he said, "he needs a good education."

"I'll thank you and your son," ground the traffic warden, "to *kindly* stop wasting my time."

And she turned on her heel and left. The very flower baskets outside the supermarket seemed to wither as she passed.

Powers tore out a slice of the pappy white supermarket bread he'd queued for. He handed it to MapHead thoughtfully. They didn't eat pap for the carbohydrate. Nor for the protein, such as it was. They ate it for the preservative. Powers had deduced that the preservatives in pappy supermarket bread supplied some vital need or other. Powers' ideas were often ahead of his time.

"Schools information, why would you ask, not our car is it? Why would you?" blurted MapHead, muddled and wishing for peace and bare feet. The hum of the tomato house. Less pavements, people and hard, hard shoes.

"I know your mother's round here," said Powers through his pap. "I know she's got a child. Children go to school."

"Can I?"

Powers swallowed. "Can you what?"

25

MapHead swallowed twice, in sympathy. Under his hat his scalp was buzzing. Grid references swam on his neck. A line map of Rubytown Industrial Estate flushed by, quickly followed by the Stonewalls area, scale: one inch to the mile. He glowed like a cuttlefish.

"Can I. Go. To school."

Powers mentally scrolled through the Education Act. He dallied on clause three. Then he searched for the right thing to say. He finished his slice of bread and tore out another.

"Why not?" he said at last.

# An Ideal Team

*"Coo–woar!"* The peacock paused. Then it called again. *"Coo–woooar!"*

It picked its way jerkily over the scrap wood outside the chipping shed, stop-go, stop-go, like a character in a bad cartoon. The wood pile was treacherous. It completely blocked the track to the bottom greenhouse, and it was never the same two days running. Every day it slipped and altered a little. The wood pile was food for the chipping machine in the shed. Every day it fed the dreadful chipping machine with odds and ends of timber, and every day the chipping machine fed the boiler with the mound of wood chips it coughed up; and the boiler grew ruddy and heated the pipes which snaked into every greenhouse to warm and cosset the tomatoes.

The little black bantam hen had skipped the wood pile as lightly as a grasshopper. She fluttered ahead down the track to the bottom greenhouse. The peacock followed, stop-go, stop-go. Silly great thing was at least five times as big as the little bantam hen. His pulpy purple leg alone was larger. But he'd lost his mate the year before and had mooned hopelessly after the bantam ever since. The little black hen busied herself in the grass. She allowed the peacock to mince right up and lay his head in front of her. Then she gave his head a good pecking.

Inside the bottom greenhouse the pickers were at work. There were two tomato pickers, Mo and Jan. They made an ideal team. They understood one another perfectly.

"How many trays we got left?" asked Mo.

"'Bout six," said Jan. "I'll go up and get some more."

"We'll have coffee break, shall we? Then we'll get some."

"Ideal."

"How tight are you picking?" asked Mo – meaning, how far from ripe?

"I'm picking 'em almost green," said Jan, "aren't you?"

Powers and MapHead were sunning themselves just outside the big double doors, drying off MapHead's poultice. Not that the pickers could see. Powers had lowered their – his and MapHead's – light refraction capacity to zilch. This meant they absorbed light instead of reflecting it. Without reflected light, no one could make them out. Also, he'd tweaked the pickers in a special way he had, so they couldn't look directly at Powers and MapHead. And if they did, they didn't see.

The poultice covered MapHead's scalp completely. It hung down in a thick welt just above his eyes, to take in his eyebrows as well. Powers' poultice had things in it too foul to mention. Fetid tomato leaves featured strongly.

The fact was, said Powers, it was a lot easier killing hair than making it grow. Making it drop out was easy, you weakened the keratin near the scalp. But getting it to grow – especially after stopping it so long – was a bit ticklish. You could stimulate the follicles a bit. But for speed, said Powers, you couldn't beat a good savage poultice. MapHead ran over it a few times. For hair, you needed a poultice. For school – said Powers – you needed hair. His heart hammered a bit. Powers, he knew, had been to see the school.

"How did you say again?" asked MapHead.

"*What* did I say," corrected Powers. "I said, we're travellers. We're passing through. My son needs a good education."

"What did Schoolhead say?"

"The head teacher said, 'Bring him in for the day. See how he likes it.'"

"They're not twelve. Are they?"

"No, not twelve like you. Ten and eleven, however."

"I want twelve."

"You wouldn't be natural in secondary school," said Powers. "You can't keep up. A child like your mother's goes to primary school. Young children in this area go to Stonewalls Primary. Their mothers meet them – Have a good day? – when they come out."

Powers poked the poultice speculatively. Still wet. He could have baked it solid at a glance, but it was better to let it dry naturally. His son would just have to wear it for the rest of the day.

The peacock harried his bantam down the path towards them. He looked a bit the worse for wear. His crest hung down on one side of his head. A very small head, thought MapHead, for such a big bird. He tuned in, peacock-level. Nothing. Only a dull bleep. It was pretty stupid, all right. He calculated its brain surface area would just about cover his foot.

Powers produced a carrier bag. "I got you these. Jeans, T-shirt, pants, sweater." He produced a box as well. "And these."

"Not," said MapHead, "more shoes?"

"School shoes," said Powers grimly.

A crust of bread pitched at their feet. It came from inside the greenhouse. The peacock cocked his head, but the bantam hen was quicker. When she finished the crust she pecked her way into the greenhouse for more.

Mo and Jan were enjoying their hard-earned break just the other side of the open double doors.

"Sales were on when I went to town," said Jan, over vacuum-flask coffee.

"You don't want to park in town," said Mo, over tea.

"No?"

"That traffic warden's in like a knife."

"I parked up Barrack Street car-park," said Jan. "Handy for the sales."

"Get anything then?"

"Nice white blouse. I wanted to get some bits for the kids, but if your girls are anything like mine, they'd go, 'Why'd you get that?'"

"That's what mine say," said Mo. "Mine say, 'That's *sick*.'"

Sick. That's *sick*. MapHead tried it a few times, under his breath. It took his mind off his itching scalp.

"See that programme last night?" asked Jan. "One about UFOs?"

"What time's that, then?"

"It was on about eight. There was a woman on, she'd been in a UFO and met 'em and everything, little pale bald people. They took her in space, then they brought her back. There's hundreds of people've seen cigar-shaped spaceships. One man saw a big dark triangle in the sky and it swallowed planes."

"My neighbour saw one," said Mo darkly. "She was out in her garden. Great long thing with lights round it up in the sky."

Powers and MapHead listened round the door. MapHead hugged his knees. Cigar-shaped spaceships. Do me. A favour. He could hardly keep from laughing out loud.

Mo threw out the end of her Wagon Wheel. She

31

aimed it at the peacock, but the bantam seized it greedily. The peacock watched her eat it, eyeing the situation from every possible angle.

"Shame, too," said Mo, peering round the door. "That bantie never lets him have nothin', does she? They want to get him another peahen."

Inside his knees, MapHead shook with laughter. Bits of poultice dropped off round the back of his neck. Unidentified Flying Objects. Aliens from outer space. He hadn't got over it yet. It always cracked him up.

"Where's that little grey cat?" asked Jan suddenly. "I don't recollect seeing that little grey cat, days now."

MapHead jerked upright. He looked across at Powers, but Powers was unconcerned. MapHead pictured the catshake cat's pleading yellow eyes. The look in those eyes had haunted him for days. There had been something more than trust in the grey cat's skinny frame. Fellow-feeling, that was what it was. "Please," those eyes had said, "please. Aren't we creatures, all? You and I alike?"

MapHead swallowed. He'd always liked animals. Why had he drunk them so often? Why had it taken a pair of trusting yellow eyes to wake him up to himself? What about the beetles he'd squashed? Weren't they creatures, too?

It wasn't too late to change. He wouldn't squash beetles and he wouldn't drink cats. He wouldn't drink anything that could drink or eat or crawl. He looked at

32

the spot by the greenhouse door where the grey cat would plead to come in. He remembered its thin and reedy cry; the way it would wind itself round his legs; its poor, heaped body asleep in the corner, thrilling with dreams. Aren't we creatures, all?

MapHead looked at Powers. He looked at his horrible hard school shoes. He didn't feel much like laughing any more.

# MapHead Goes
# to School

"Today we welcome Boothe," said Mr Bandy. "He won't be with us very long – so to speak – so we're going to make him feel at home. Aren't we?"

The class groaned and settled. Everyone looked at MapHead, up front with Mr B. MapHead was uncomfortable with his shoes, his clothes, his name, with just about everything. But there it was. He was in school, along with everyone else.

"All right, top class," said Mr Bandy. "Get out your projects."

He turned to MapHead. He smiled wryly, as if to say, would you like to deal with this lot? MapHead grinned.

"So. Where do you come from, Boothe?" asked Mr Bandy conversationally.

"From the Subtle World, Mr Bandy."

"The what, Boothe?"

"The Subtle World. Where I come from."

"I meant, what place?" said Mr Bandy patiently. "You don't come from round here, do you?"

"Yes," said MapHead simply. "Round everywhere. That's where I come from. All around."

Mr Bandy gave up. He looked at MapHead a full minute. He looked especially at the boy's peculiar hair. It was excessively short. It looked, thought Mr Bandy, like nothing so much as the sort of fluffy-looking mould that grew on oranges too long in the fruit bowl.

"Well, Boothe," he said. "You'd better sit down."

MapHead spent a glorious morning on The Romans. School was everything he'd hoped for, and more. Mr Bandy had given him a green folder. He'd given him a label saying ANCIENT WORLD PROJECT. MapHead quickened when he understood what was required of him. He asked, could he do the Romans for his Ancient World Project? Yes, he could do the Romans. The Romans or the Greeks or the Egyptians. Everyone had chosen, said Mr Bandy. The Egyptians were popular, but the Romans were favourite.

Andy Steed, a thick-set individual in a nasty acrylic jumper, took MapHead to the library. The library was wonderful. MapHead brought back a book large enough to carpet and live on.

He paged through it to the First Empire. There was even a diagram of Circus Maximus. For the first time in a long while, MapHead was completely happy.

There was a mid-morning break when he wasn't. When they crowded out into a tarmac yard, when his classmates said nothing, when MapHead said too much, because he was trying too hard; when he had no crisps like everyone else and no one offered him any – then he wasn't happy at all. He wasn't at all sorry when a bell rang and they crowded in again.

After a while, Mr Bandy came over. "How's it going?" he asked.

How. Is it. Going. MapHead swallowed. He must be natural, at all costs.

"Huh?" he said carefully.

Mr Bandy sat down. "Any ideas for your model yet? We're all doing models. Anything you like."

"Yes," said MapHead. "I've got an idea." Mr Bandy waited to hear what it was. But MapHead was reading again, unselfconsciously, just as though Mr Bandy weren't there. Not for the first time, Mr Bandy gave up. Strange child, he thought. Strange eyes.

"Good work," he said, moving on.

At eleven fifty-five Mr Bandy stood up. He cleared his throat. "Yes," he said, "you at the back. *When* you're ready."

The noise subsided. Several sat down. Mr Bandy cleared his throat again. Then he said: "As you know, this afternoon we have a special guest. Mrs Wellbeloved will be coming in to talk about road safety and the Highway Code, directly after lunch. So I'd like you all in quickly and quietly. We'll pack up now. Alex. Wait for it."

The bell rang and they tumbled out, Anxious Alex

Hayes last of all, thanks to Mr Bandy. Anxious Alex Hayes was a pale and nervy item much given to jumping the gun before the bell rang. Andy Steed showed MapHead where to queue for dinner and ran off. MapHead put his dish of cottage pie thoughtfully on a chair. Then he wandered off with an apple. After the apple he drank a lot of water. It wasn't bad. He drank a lot more. Then he wandered back to his dinner. Amazingly, no one had sat in it. He ate all the cold potato and left the rest.

In the playground after, he wondered what Mrs Wellbeloved would be like. Would she talk like Mr Bandy? Would he, MapHead, have to talk back? Then he wondered what Powers was doing. He sat down and took off his shoes. He tried asking anyone near him if their mothers had ever been struck by lightning? At any time? But no one came near him much. Especially after he asked.

Then there was an accident. A smallish boy near MapHead performed an extraordinary manoeuvre at the fence. He seemed, thought MapHead, to have thrown himself down.

"Chris!" called a larger boy. "Chris! You all right?"

But Chris wasn't. He had a bloody graze and a smashed watch. MapHead initiated bodily contact. He thought it was appropriate. But Chris smacked him off.

"Get your 'ands off, you," Chris picked himself up. He listened to his watch. He tapped it and shrugged.

MapHead chose his moment. "Was your mother struck by lightning? I mean, ever?"

Chris reacted stolidly. "That's Kenny you want." He whistled piercingly. "Kenny! Hey, Kenny!"

Kenny approached. He was chunky, blond, with a radical haircut. He must have been ten or eleven. MapHead had noticed him in class. "Yours was, wan't she?" bawled Chris.

"Was what?"

"Struck by lightning."

"My mum was, yeh," said Kenny. "Who wants to know?"

"I do," said MapHead.

"Yeh," said Kenny proudly, "my mum got struck by lightning once. Never burned her nor nothing, but she lost her memory. My nan was worried sick. She never knew where my mum was for months."

MapHead glowed. With an effort he kept his scalp quiet. *This* was he. This Kenny. The son of his mother, his half-brother. Through Kenny he would find her. How pink he was. Was he like her, at all?

"My nan's comin' in later," went on Kenny carelessly. "It's my nan's doin' the talk."

"Talk?"

"The road safety," explained Chris. "Mrs Wellbeloved's his nan."

"Anyway," said Kenny cagily, "how did you know?"

"Know what?" asked MapHead.

"About the lightning. I mean, how did you know to

ask? Funny thing to ask."

How did. You. Know to. Ask. Suddenly MapHead was floundering. He so much wanted Kenny to like him. Too much.

"Hey," said MapHead desperately. "Hey. Hang loose. Little buddy."

"Yeh," said Kenny, "right." He backed off. Chris followed.

MapHead watched them go, sadly. He had not been natural enough. Unnatural, that was what he was. A freak. A not-natural, map-flashing, beetle-shoving freak.

When the bell rang they filed into the hall. Three classes together, smallest at the front. MapHead took a keen interest in proceedings. He looked forward to seeing his grandmother for the first time. He might be a freak, but he was a freak with a grandmother. A grandmother who gave talks. If Mrs Wellbeloved was Kenny's nan, she was, after all, his nan as well.

At last Mr Bandy came in. He said, "Will you all stand," importantly. They all stood. Then he turned to face the door. "They're all yours, Mrs Wellbeloved," he said.

In came Mrs Wellbeloved. MapHead felt as though his brains would burst. In the first shock he waited for the real Mrs Wellbeloved to come in behind her. But she didn't.

The real Mrs Wellbeloved, his very own grandmother, was already in front of him, pig-ugly eyes scouring the back rows, orangey-white hair parted martially under her official cap. The traffic warden folded her arms and smiled.

# MapHead Moves Some Molecules

It ought to be, *had* to be, possible. MapHead screwed up his eyes. He'd seen Powers do it. He knew the principle. What you did was, you vibrated the keratin molecules. This weakened the hair at the base. With any abrasion it would drop out. Over the top of his classmates he brought the full power of his concentration to bear on his grandmother's head.

They'd galloped through road safety. The road safety hadn't taken very long at all. Most of the questions seemed to be about obscure road signs. It was, said Mrs Wellbeloved, a talk with special reference to no-waiting restrictions. A message, said Mrs Wellbeloved, for their parents. How often did they go to town? And where did they park when they did?

"What," asked Warden Wellbeloved penetratingly, "does a single yellow line tell us?"

Tells us you're pig ugly inside and out, thought MapHead.

"No waiting, six till nine," he volunteered.

"No waiting between the times specified," agreed Mrs Wellbeloved. "And a double?"

No one answered. MapHead was busy. He had movement in the keratin molecules, no doubt about it.

"Come on, top class," urged Mr Bandy. "What do double yellow lines mean? Boothe. Take a guess."

"No waiting nine till six?"

"No waiting ever, at all," burst Andy Steed.

"Correct," said Mrs Wellbeloved. "In effect, Boothe is right as well. The additional yellow line tells us we can't wait *at any time*, round the clock."

"Not even for a minute?" The pregnant lady had wept, remembered MapHead. She'd actually wept.

"A rule isn't a rule if it can be broken for one reason or another," said Mrs Wellbeloved acidly, "is it?"

Then MapHead hated her. She was inflexible and entirely hateable. He whacked up the power through her hair. Under her ruthless hat, things were cooking all right.

"Well," said Mrs Wellbeloved, "I feel a little warm, so we'll stop there." She turned to Mr Bandy. "I think we've covered most things?"

Mr Bandy jumped up and proposed three cheers for Mrs Wellbeloved. She received them graciously, sweating the while. At last they lined up and began to file out.

Mrs Wellbeloved stopped MapHead at the door.

"Don't I know you from somewhere, Boothe?"

MapHead shook his head wordlessly. He was encouraged to see puffs of orange hair on the back of her navy collar. It was coming out already.

She handed him a slim booklet. *A Child's Highway Code* said the cover. Everyone had one. "Study and learn," she said. "Next."

MapHead looked at his present. It would be natural enough to say thank you. But he wasn't natural, was he? Instead he shuffled out.

He reached the door. He turned. "Get a life," he said, "why don't you?"

The boy next in line lifted his *Highway Code* from Mrs Wellbeloved's unconscious hand. Her jaw dropped. She watched MapHead's back disappear in the crush.

When the three-fifteen bell rang, MapHead missed Kenny. When he streamed down the path to the school gate with the others, he missed Kenny again. School was out. Where was he?

Powers was waiting among the mothers. He'd had plenty of time to examine them all. *She* wasn't among them.

"Powers, I did Romans and it's Mr Bandy and I—"

Powers held up his hand. "Please," he said, "I have to ask you, first." He drew himself up and put on a smile. "Have a good day?"

"I *did* and I found him," ran on MapHead, "isn't *she*

waiting? I found him, he's Kenny, only I can't see him now—"

"She's not here," said Powers. "What's this?"

"It's a book of rules," said MapHead, handing over the *Highway Code*. "From my – " he couldn't quite bring himself to say grandmother – "from the traffic warden. She did a talk."

All the way back he explained. He explained about the school day, about the model he was going to make, about how you had crisps for break. He explained how he'd put the lightning question to Kenny – and what Kenny had said to him back.

"It's him," said Powers. "No doubt about it. All we have to do now is find where he meets his mother."

"*My* mother," said MapHead.

They walked on a bit in silence. "Tell it again," urged MapHead.

"When I met your mother? You know I don't explain it very well."

MapHead stopped. "Tell it, please," he said.

Powers hung his head. They walked on. "The sky was grey," said Powers, "the hill was green. I was enjoying a thunderstorm. I saw your mother hurrying home over the hill. She carried a red umbrella. I saw the lightning strike the tip of the umbrella, I saw it flash blue down the handle; in less than a nanosecond she'd be shocked dead – so I took her up."

"You took her up."

"I saved her. I took her with me travelling. She said

she loved the freedom. She said – yes – she loved me. It was months before she started pining for the old life. Then nothing else mattered *but* the old life. I took her back. She left me you. Then I made her forget. Everything. It was kinder that way."

"Doesn't sound very kind to me," said MapHead. "None of it."

"You don't know," said Powers. "You don't understand what it is to be natural."

"No," said MapHead, "I don't."

That evening they lazed on rock wool slabs with the greenhouse humming behind them. The rock wool slabs were spongy blocks sheathed in polythene, each the length of an arm. Three neat holes would be slit in each, and three tomato plants popped on. There was no goodness in them at all. They were simply there for the plants to set their roots in. There was always a good stack of spares in the corner. They made a fine settee.

MapHead passed the glucose drip to Powers. The bees bumbled in their boxes behind him, settling down for the night. They lived in little wooden boxes at the end of every aisle. Attached to every box was a bottle of bright glucose, or sugar solution, for the bees to feed on. It was the bees' sugar solution that MapHead was drinking. He'd binged the bottles dry lately. The bees' food was very pink and very, very sweet.

Powers was lost in the *Highway Code*. He took its

mysteries seriously. He shut his eyes and tested himself on hazard signs. MapHead lay thinking and thinking. The vents overhead wheezed shut automatically as the temperature-sensitive system sealed the house for the night. How warm it was. How peaceful.

A weedy little kitten wandered in. Powers looked up. He put down the *Highway Code*.

"Fancy a snack?"

"No," said MapHead quickly. "I'm not hungry."

"Looks good to me," said Powers. He watched the kitten pick its way towards them. Its little triangle tail stood straight up behind it. Powers narrowed his eyes.

MapHead started up. "No," he said. "Don't kill it."

"Why not? It's natural."

"No, it's not."

"Things kill other things. It's the natural order."

"It isn't natural for *me*," said MapHead. "And I'm not drinking *cats* any more."

Powers flung down the glucose bottle. Abruptly he turned his back, shielding his eyes with his arm.

The kitten wobbled over. MapHead tweaked it up by its tail. Its tiny black legs flailed. Its startling pink mouth opened and closed. "*Meeee*," it said. "*Meeyou*." He tucked it under his arm.

"And," said MapHead, shaking now, "I want to know. How they knew my mum got hit by lightning. If you made her forget."

The bees drowsed, the house hummed. The kitten was warm in his arm. At last Powers stirred. "They found her red umbrella," he said softly. "Her scorched red umbrella, you know."

"I don't believe it happened like you said," cried MapHead in a passion. "And I don't believe she ever would have left me."

Powers turned. His eyes were blazing. "Believe what you like," he said.

# The Prazey Effect:
## Part 1

"He's weird," said Kenny. "And he hangs around after me, days now."

"He's new," said Kenny's mother. "He's trying to fit in. No skin off your nose, is it?"

"He lives down the tomato farm. And he's called Boothe," finished Kenny, witheringly.

"Boothe what?"

"How do I know?"

"P'raps he'd like to come over, one night after school?"

"No," said Kenny. "He wouldn't."

She was pretty, thought MapHead, from the hedge. His mother was fair as a Dutch doll. The sunlight flashed her bobbed hair bright as she pegged and stooped and pegged some more. T-shirts, football shorts, a sweater, a couple of big navy skirts – and socks. Lots and lots of socks. She spun the rotary line. Under her quick fingers the washing straggled out in the brilliant Saturday sun.

She was just ten feet away through the hedge. Just ten feet, and a world. It was tempting to rush out and fling it all down: "It's me, your son. Really. Know me, will you? Love me. Can't you?"

But that, MapHead knew, would be pointless. She wouldn't know him at all – much less love him. Love him? Certain deep wells, said Powers, would have to be drawn on for that. It was no use trying just now. Still, he was tempted. Except that it was pointless, he'd do it.

What wasn't pointless, was Kenny. There was only one way to get Kenny on his side. He would have to reveal himself as he was. With hair, it would be tricky.

MapHead slid carefully down off the hedge. Tucking his box of tomatoes under his arm, he ducked round to the gate. VIEWTOWN said the name of the house on the gate. He clicked it shut behind him.

He pictured Powers' reaction if he knew. Powers was in the dark about Viewtown, Ruggy Lane. That was because MapHead hadn't told him. *And* he'd put up a block in his head, so Powers wouldn't see what he knew. Powers had grown impatient the last three days. A bunch of faceless mothers at the gate. No Kenny, nor a whisper of *her*. Where *was* the boy? he grumbled. Was there another school gate? Where did he live? Why couldn't MapHead ask?

MapHead had. He'd asked Chris. "Kenny?" said Chris. "He's the end house, Ruggy Lane." It was only over the hill. But he hadn't told Powers a thing. He wasn't sure why himself.

He gave his box of tomatoes a last shift round. They were good rich ripe ones all right. He'd left the stalks on properly, the way the pickers always did.

Pressing his poor head quiet, he climbed the cottage step. Then he banged twice on the door. He waited, taut as a kite-string. He wouldn't – would *not* – fall down.

Where were they? No one stirred. They were out the back, of course. He'd started down and round when Kenny snatched the door.

"Yeh," said Kenny, "what?"

MapHead hurried back. He fronted his tomatoes nervously.

"My dad sent these for your mum."

"He never."

MapHead swallowed. "He did. Hey. You don't know. Or why did I come?"

"Because," hissed Kenny, "you're jus' hanging round, you are. You c'n stuff your old tomatoes an' bog off."

"Who's that?" called Kenny's mother. Then she brightened the door – and he, MapHead, was really looking at her. And she was looking at him. Really his mother, really looking. At him. He almost fell down.

"Oh. Are you all right?" she said. "Is he all right, Kenny?" she said.

"I brought you these," said MapHead. "My dad's got

more than – more than he can eat."

"Are you Boothe?"

MapHead nodded, too full to trust himself.

"From the tomato farm?"

MapHead nodded again.

She took the box wonderingly. "More than he can eat, I should think he has. It's very nice – isn't it, Kenny?"

Kenny shrugged. "Don't like 'em much, anyway."

"We're just off out to Prazey Savers," said MapHead's mother brightly, "or we'd ask you in, Boothe."

MapHead sagged. He made a final effort. "My dad's going out. My dad said, if I could stay. He'd be happy if I could."

"Are you sure? You're welcome to come."

MapHead nodded again. Then he held her eyes. He tried hard to show how he felt. Kay, her name was, he knew – same as the boy the Snow Queen stole in the story, the boy with the splinter of ice in his heart, the splinter that made him forget. It was a story that had struck a deep chord in MapHead. The boy Kay in the story had forgotten everyone he ever loved – and his, MapHead's, mother had forgotten, too. It's me, he thought meltingly. But she wouldn't remember. How could she?

"We'll just nip round and check with your dad."

"You can't," lied MapHead weakly. "He won't be back till three."

"Well, if he knows where you are," she said, "we'll leave a note."

And that was how they went, off out to Prazey Savers, MapHead and Kenny together. And she, their mother, drove them. Her bright head in front was inches from MapHead's own. Her bright eyes checked him in the mirror, more than once.

Back on the farm, Powers ground his teeth. He scanned around for MapHead, and he knew. He knew without looking, distrust was abroad. Mayhem and MapHead, together.

Crazy Prazey Savers. The craziest place MapHead'd seen in twelve whole here-today-gone-tomorrow crazy years in this world or any other.

The first thing he noticed was peacocks. Plus moorhens – he thought they were moorhens – big ducks and small, swans and Canada geese, the works; and all on a pond the size of summer. Over and round it on one side hung ornamental conifers. The other side, nearest the tremendous car-park, was given over to patio furniture and swing-bed garden settees, some with puffy almost-OK upholstery, some not, all sizes and combinations – and all in white plastic. White plastic, that was it.

What Prazey Savers was, was a monster cut-price store, the biggest for miles around. Prazey Savers drew bargain hunters and cheapskates of every kind, like a rash. Some didn't even know they were bargain hunters till they got there. Then the Prazey Effect took hold and they tranced through the store while the day spun away, whole families of 'em, emerging crossly at the far end ready to tear each other's heads off, loaded to the teeth with crazy Prazey things they didn't really need but couldn't resist. The Prazey Effect was characterized by a killer headache, coming on just as Dad crashed the gears on the exit to the dual carriageway outside.

The whole place was done up in lumpy alpine-style stucco, or plaster. It wasn't even real stucco. It was stucco-effect. Gargoyles and grotesques capped all the main doors. They looked, thought MapHead, as though they might chuck at any moment on the happy punters flooding in below.

"Curtains, curtains, curtains," said Kay, checking the giant direction arrows on the main stair. "Curtains – that'll be Furnishing Fabrics. Straight up and left."

She paused halfway up, against the flow. An overheated family with an overheated baby dodged around her. The baby grizzled miserably all the way up.

"Do you boys want to wander while I look? Meet you by the car in half an hour?"

"An hour, I s'pect, Mum," said Kenny. "Be real."

"All right, an hour. Say about twelve-fifteen. Got your money, I hope?"

They watched her disappear into the crowd. Then Kenny turned scornfully on MapHead. "You heard," he said. "The car, at twelve-fifteen."

"Can't I come with you?" asked MapHead.

"No," said Kenny. "Stuff off."

He started purposefully through ground floor Motor Parts & Tools, without looking back. MapHead took it all in his stride. Soon he came alongside. Kenny dodged right, through Garden Accessories. MapHead countered with a swift move through DIY, which brought him up smartly at Carpets & Underlays at precisely the same time as Kenny.

Kenny sighed. "All right. Where to now?"

"Wherever you're going," returned MapHead, enjoying the game immensely.

"I'm going CDs," said Kenny. "Then I'm going Gifts & Stationery. Now you know, you might as well come."

MapHead went, enjoying himself more than ever. He was gaining with Kenny, he knew. In CDs they found more than a little common ground. Especially when it came to the Cut-Price Classix. After, they browsed happily through Gifts & Stationery. MapHead looked through fake-leather diaries. Appointments said some, at the top of the page. MapHead wondered what it would be like to have appointments. Then he came to the road maps. He scanned the southern counties, committing Dorset, Somerset and Wiltshire to memory in less time than it took to shout about it. Then he looked around. Plenty of people – but none looking his way.

"Hey," he said. "Hey, Kenny."

Kenny looked up. "What?"

"See. This map. Well, look." MapHead held up the road map. Then he flashed a line-for-line copy on his face. He phased the lines a little, so the map slid over his nose. He closed his eyes so Kenny got the trunk roads clear and easy, extending all the way up through his, MapHead's, hair.

"Whaa…!" said Kenny. "How'd you do that? Trick book, is it?"

"No," said MapHead. "Watch."

Then he went to town, spinning a dozen or more maps over his face, all the dear old places – even Takoma Falls. Especially Takoma Falls. Hadn't he lived there the best part of three years?

He stopped. Kenny's mouth hung open. He sucked in some dribble. "Tattoos, is it?"

"Not tattoos."

"What, then?"

MapHead shrugged. He shrugged again. It felt right. "What you see."

"What are you – mapface?"

"No," said MapHead. "MapHead."

"Wow," breathed Kenny. "Wow."

After that, things got really crazy. They whooped through Furniture & Bedding like madmen, bounced on all the suites, left the salesman with a face like thunder, took off through Children's Clothing and finished, breathless, by the checkout. It was a funny kind of checkout where they checked out receipts from things you'd bought earlier. And stamped them. They were big on stamping receipts at Prazey.

Kenny fished around. He put his purchases on the desk. He fished around some more. He'd only need three receipts. One for the CDs, one for a poster, one for the bumper Sellotape MapHead had wanted. He found only two.

The man in blue checked them against the goods. Then he stamped them solemnly. He waited. Kenny looked nervous.

"CDs?" said the man in blue flatly. "Got the receipt?"

"I have, yes, somewhere." He really had lost it. The woman behind him piled a set of enamel pans pointedly on the desk. The queue behind pressed her forward. "I *did* pay," said Kenny. "Can't I just go through?"

The man in blue shook his head. MapHead tuned in, suddenly. He understood this situation. It was inflexible authority again. Warden Wellbeloved all over. He would have to take a hand.

"Receipt, please," the man in blue was saying. "For every purchase I've got to have a…" A blank look came over his face. "What are we talking about?"

"The weather," said MapHead. "Nice day."

"Oh, right," said the man. "It is. Don't forget your goods, now."

MapHead and Kenny slid out. They kept it dead straight as far as the outsize pond with the mandarin ducks and the peacocks. Then they cracked up.

"How did you do that?" asked Kenny.

"I made him forget," said MapHead carelessly. "I can do it sometimes, a bit."

"It's ten past twelve," said Kenny, checking his watch. "Better head for the car. So what are you, an alien or something?"

MapHead exploded. The ducks and peahens scattered. An alien? Him?

"Boys!" waved Kay, at the car. "Boys – come on now, will you?"

"Well," said Kenny, "*are* you?"

MapHead wanted scornful, and found it for once. He was getting more natural all the time. "What do *you* think?" he said.

# The Prazey Effect: Part 2

KING-SIZE PRAZEYBURGER & CHIPS £2.50 said the steamed-up sign by the door. The smell outside was less than wonderful. The Prazey Savers Café – The Happy Gobber, Kenny called it – was full to bursting, anyway.

"No animal protein, thank you, I'm a vegetable," said MapHead firmly.

It didn't have quite the effect he supposed. Kenny and Kay swapped a funny look. "He's got to be a turnip," cracked Kenny. "With a face like that, he's a turnip."

"Don't mind him," said Kay. "You mean, a vegetarian."

"That's what I mean," said MapHead, laughing too.

"P'raps we'll give the burgers a miss," said Kay. "Come on, we'll grab something to eat at home."

They walked back to the car. The best of the day was gone. A bunch of ugly white ducks with livid red beak extrusions over their faces hunted scraps by the waste bins. A few peahens hung around the car-park in the petrol-coloured puddles.

Kay unlocked the car. She opened the boot. The boot was almost full. Ready-made Velour Curtains, King-size Quality Towels, Coordinated Valance & Duvet Covers, Exterior Coverplus Paint…

"Sure you bought enough stuff?" joked Kenny.

"Look at that," said Kay. "King-size towels, eleven ninety-nine. Good quality, too. I wish I'd got the brown set as well." She paused, thinking. "I'll just nip back. You can't afford not to, at that price."

"Aw, Mum," said Kenny.

She bowled him the car keys. "Ten minutes. Promise," she said.

Kenny and MapHead leant on the car and teased the ducks a bit, feinting throws with non-existent food. The ducks soon cottoned on. But the peahens were stupider. There were four of them, nothing so splendid as the male birds. They were dull as a ditch, all four. The leader came close, then closer. MapHead reached out and soothed her with his hand, softly, over and over.

"Where's your dad?" he asked Kenny.

"Mum and Dad split up," said Kenny. "My nan lives with us now. I hate my nan, she's a cow."

She is, thought MapHead. But still. "I thought you liked her coming to school. When she did the talk."

"You don't know what she's like."

I do, thought MapHead. But still. "She's still your

nan," he said. And mine, he thought – and mine.

"She's a slaphead," said Kenny, "that's what. All her hair's fell out."

MapHead soothed and soothed. The peahen's head relaxed in his hand. Suddenly he scooped her up.

"What you doing that for?" asked Kenny. MapHead laid the peahen carefully in the boot. It was limp as a wet umbrella. He slid the packs of sheets and towels over the top of it, just in time. Kay was heading back behind a giant oriental-style lampshade.

"You can't do that," gaped Kenny.

"I just did," said MapHead. He was learning fast.

The journey back was hungry and hot. They strapped the giant lampshade in the front seat next to Kay. She hadn't meant to get it, but the identical one in town was twice the price, she'd seen it. Where would it go? She wasn't sure. It might go in the hall.

As soon as they pulled in at Ruggy Lane, MapHead jumped smartly out. Kenny jumped out after.

"We'll bring the stuff in for you," offered Kenny quickly. "If you want."

"I'll get the kettle on," said Kay. "Spaghetti on toast all right, Boothe?"

"No," said MapHead. "I mean, I think I'd better get back."

"Stay for dinner, can't you?"

"My dad. Left things for me to do," said MapHead awkwardly. "So that's what I have to do."

Kay smiled. "Perhaps we'll see you again, then."

You will, thought MapHead. You will. "Yes, thank you," he said. "Goodbye."

He and Kenny stacked the stuff in the hall. The peahen lay limply where MapHead had left it. "You better get it an' go," said Kenny nervously. "My nan's around somewhere."

MapHead nodded. "Hang loose."

Kenny grinned. "Don't say that, it's for nerds. Say, 'See ya.'"

"See ya."

"Monday," promised Kenny, going in.

MapHead leaned into the boot. He cupped the peahen's head in his hand. Its beady eyes shone. It was going to be awkward to carry, but he could always—

"You there. What d'you think you're doing?"

MapHead snapped out of the boot. It was a voice he knew only too well.

"I'm getting my stuff," he said, flushing. "I just got back with Kenny."

Mrs Wellbeloved advanced. Her scarf had slipped back off her head. Under it, she was almost completely bald. At least, thought MapHead, she looked like one of the family now.

Mrs Wellbeloved draped her big navy skirts on her arm. She'd rescued the washing. Now there was this boy. She remembered him now. Wasn't he the one who…

"I remember you. You're the one saying 'get a life' all the time. Well," said Mrs Wellbeloved cuttingly, "let me tell you I have got a life, I've got a very nice life, thank you very much."

She advanced a little more. MapHead moved to block the boot. He swallowed. What would happen?

"You're an ugly boy," said Mrs Wellbeloved. "Aren't you? A very ugly boy."

MapHead considered thirteen separate responses with incredible speed before he answered. Then he cleared his throat: "Seen yourself lately?"

Mrs Wellbeloved paused magnificently. Then she put her face in MapHead's.

"It's boys like you that grow up to violate parking-restricted zones. I don't like your attitude. I don't like you round my grandson. You can get your stuff and go. And don't," she added, "come back."

She drilled him full of holes with her gunfighter eyes. Then she bullied in.

"Slaphead," said MapHead after her, when he knew she wouldn't hear. Then he moved quickly. Looping the roll of Sellotape on his arm, he scooped up the peahen and ran.

He bumped along back to the farm as best he could, framing excuses for Powers. Powers had a way of knowing, whatever you said. He would have to get back and act natural.

But when he got back, he didn't have to. Powers was nowhere around. MapHead flopped the peahen in the grass. Then he tuned in, peahen-level, quickening it by degrees until he'd brought it up to functional again.

He arranged its neck a bit. It would be all right in a while, stupid thing.

Then he looked for Powers. He looked in all five greenhouses, in both sheds, behind the bungalow, in the boilerhouse, the hedges, and in all the fields around. Powers was thoroughly and completely gone. The only thing he'd left was a meal of sorts, on a box in the bottom house.

MapHead ate it slowly. Half a cucumber, three green tomatoes, a sticky bun and a pint of milk. Typical Powers. The nutritional content was calculated to a tee.

When he'd finished his meal, he turned up the box he'd eaten it off. It had definite possibilities. He remembered where he'd seen some rusty scissors. Then he found his Sellotape and worked with it awhile.

After a bit he looked around some more. He wandered as far as the chipping shed and back. There was something of a commotion by the rubbish tip. He grinned as soon as he saw.

His peahen was strutting unsteadily in circles. Around her, in wider, convoluted circles, went the grand old man himself – the hopeless peacock, hopeless no longer, courting for all he was worth. He had entirely forgotten his bantam hen. He guarded the peahen's circles smaller and tighter bit by bit. Then he laid down his head. She eyed him stupidly from several angles. But she didn't peck his head.

"*Coo–woar!*" he crowed, ecstatically. "*Coo–woar!*" It

echoed all around. The loneliest sound, thought MapHead, you'd ever want to hear. But it wasn't lonely at all. The peacocks were happy together.

MapHead watched their circling a long while. They needed each other, he thought. Everyone needs someone. Suddenly the weight of everything seemed unbearable. He got up and ran down the track.

"Powers!" he cried. "Where are you?" His heavy heart hurt inside. "Dad! I'm sorry, Dad!" he cried.

# Alone

"What would you be, if you could start over?" asked Mo.

"That's a hard one," said Jan. "A writer. What would you?"

"I dunno. Work with children p'raps. Done some writing, have you?"

"A bit. Missed the boat, now."

"Never too late. Do anything you want if you want to enough, they say."

It was Sunday de-leafing in the bottom greenhouse. Heads down, Mo and Jan snapped their way rapidly up and down the rows, stripping the lower parts of the plants completely bare of leaves. They were careful not to damage the heavy trusses, or bunches, of tomatoes. Now that the foliage round them was gone and the sun could reach them, the tomato trusses would ripen. The freshly-wounded stems looked stringy and naked. MapHead could see clear through to the other side of the house after de-leafing was done.

He crouched in the doorway and watched the happy snappers. He didn't care if they noticed him, although they never did. Powers had fixed them that way. He might have been a lump of manure for all they noticed. But he had nothing better to do. It was comforting, anyway, listening.

Already they'd covered farming and the price of lamb in the shops, holidays down West, getting help of any kind around the house – a favourite topic, this – the film the previous night, fondly-remembered chocolate bars you couldn't get any more, and the probability of the Black Beast of Exmoor being an escaped panther. It was still only half past ten. Way to go, thought MapHead.

He'd spent a miserable night. The wind had got up outside the greenhouse in the small hours. Then he thought of Powers. Powers was out there, somewhere, in that wind. In the end, he got up and went out into the tumult. The fields were wild and strange under a sickly yellow moon. The great glasshouse rattled like a tin. He found himself a dirty white duck under the hedge and brought it back for comfort. He smoothed it quiet and curled himself round it. It made a good hot-water bottle. When he woke up it was gone.

"What the so an' so's *this*?" said Jan.

"This what?"

"This here." She held up a cardboard box. The edges had been cut down and bowed round the ends to make a rough oval. "Someone stuck this bit in the middle – and put gravel all round, like a racetrack or something. Ugh." Suddenly she dropped it. "Beetles in it, see?"

Mo peered in. "Leave it go. Dirty old thing."

MapHead watched anxiously. He was relieved to see Mo and Jan lose interest and replace it. He'd meant to put Circus Minimus somewhere safe. That's what he was calling his model of the chariot races. You couldn't really call a box Circus Maximus. He hoped Mr Bandy would like his little joke.

The de-leafing went on monotonously. It would go on all morning, ready for Monday's pick. MapHead grew bored. He wandered off to the wood pile and spent a happy hour or two making a slide with some shiny cupboard doors which would presently feed the chipping machine.

At lunch time he swiped a cucumber from the top greenhouse – they grew a few cucumbers in the top house. He took it way down the bottom track and over the fence to the milkman's dairy next door. Waiting his moment, he slipped into the shuddering cold-store where the next day's milk waited in red plastic crates. He lifted a couple of pints and an apricot yogurt and left the cucumber outside by way of payment. After drinking the milk he put the bottles back, neatly. He took the cucumber absently, as well, and munched his way up to the bungalow.

He spent the afternoon watching telly from the

hedge. There was a hollow place just the shape of MapHead, he'd sat there so often and watched. The telly in the bungalow living-room had educated him more than a little. With his super-attenuated hearing, he could pick up the sound pretty well. The film that afternoon was a re-run of *Star Wars*. It made him laugh quite a lot.

By evening he was in trouble. Stress levels were mounting by the minute. The soft pulse in the centre of his scalp beat fast, then faster. Dad-dad-dad, it pulsed without stopping; Dad-dad-dad, over and over again. Maps of everywhere he'd ever been rushed over his head like dreams. He started to rub off his hair.

At nine he saw the light. It grew slowly at first in the field behind, so he ran out to see what it was. Then it brightened and burst like a wonderful dawn – and out of it stepped Powers. Powers, radiant in the glorious silver suit that he'd worn when MapHead was small; Powers, strong and clear and purposeful, with his hand outstretched for MapHead's eager face.

They dined off avocados, gladly, in the twilight. Powers had brought them with him. They washed them down with rosy-sweet and bloodwarm California wine.

Powers flashed his suit. He was silver, head to toe. "Hasn't travelled badly, has it? Remember where I left it?"

MapHead thought. "The little cave – the little drippy cave – at Takoma Falls!"

Powers laughed. "I'm surprised you remember after all this time."

How could he forget California? Takoma Falls was the last time Powers had worn his silver suit.

"Takoma Falls? You mean – you've been all the way to America and back? In less than a day and a half?"

"Took me a little longer than I thought," admitted Powers. "But I had to have my suit."

"Were you angry? When you went?" asked MapHead softly.

Powers nodded. "Yes," he said, "I was angry." He reached fondly for MapHead's neck. "But I'm not angry now."

"Me neither," said MapHead happily. "And, Dad – I know where she is."

Powers looked deep into MapHead. "I know you know," he said. "That's why I had to have my suit. I was wearing it when we met, all those years ago."

"Is it time to call her?" asked MapHead, softer still.

Powers sniffed the air. He stretched his silver legs and crowded MapHead close.

"Almost time," he said.

# Mrs Wellbeloved Gets a Life

*Neeeee-nyuk-neeeeeeee. Neeee-nyuk-nyuk-neeeeeeeeeeeeeeee.* Mrs Wellbeloved buzzed the garden strimmer one more time. Then she surveyed the lawn. Better. One thing she couldn't abide was untidy edges. She took up the shears and levelled the privet a final snip or two. Straight lines, that was the thing.

She wished Kay would do something with the heap of untidy conifer trees in the corner. They'd been on offer at Prazey – Instant Hedging: Grows Eighteen Inches a Year. It was all very well, but where would they go? And when? They'd been waiting in the corner three months if they'd waited a day. She'd half a mind to strim them to pieces and be done with it. Her eyes wandered on round the garden. She had a funny feeling she was being watched.

The business with the boy Boothe had been unfortunate. An insolent, know-it-all kind of boy, too big for his boots altogether. She wouldn't have done it on purpose, all the same. It had been unfortunate he'd put his model racetrack down just as she'd stepped back. Stupid boy should've known better than to put a thing like a cardboard model on the ground when school was tipping out. If she hadn't squashed it, someone else would've. But even Kenny had turned on her furiously. Last time *she'd* collect him from school. Kay could get him herself.

She turned her attention to the flowerbeds. Why did Kay like nasturtiums? They spilled out everywhere over the edges, floppy great pestering things. Mrs Wellbeloved sighed. Why couldn't plants grow straight, in regular shapes to start with? Everything grew everywhere, any old how. Nature, thought Mrs Wellbeloved, was so uneven, so – disorderly. There didn't seem to be any rules at all.

MapHead watched bitterly from the hedge. He'd been there an hour and a quarter. He would find out what made her tick if he had to stay there all night.

So she liked gardening, did she? She liked clipping things straight and even and tidy. What else? Why *was* she hard like a beetle, so that everything funny, warm and reasonable bounced off her? He thought of his own beetles, crushed in Circus Minimus under the Warden's well-heavy foot. She hadn't even said she was sorry. She'd said it was a stupid place to put it. It seemed she was never in the wrong.

He'd planned to fix her, anyway. She would be in the way when the time came to call on his mother. She would get in the way of everything, the way she'd stepped on his model. Hadn't she warned him off? Told him to stay away? Killing her hair off was a start, but it wasn't nearly enough. It was high time, thought MapHead, something radical was done about Warden Wellbeloved. With luck, tonight was the night. Just then, Kenny came out.

"Mum says, can you mind her conifers? Only, she's going to plant them later."

Mrs Wellbeloved eyed her grandson coldly.

"She is, is she? She wants to get on with it. If it was up to me they'd be on the rubbish heap before you could say Jack Robinson."

"Well, it isn't, is it?" glowered Kenny. "Leave them, she said."

"Nice bit of fencing's what she wants out the front. A nice bit of larch-lap fencing, never mind fir tree things."

Kenny handed her the mug he'd nursed across the grass. "I brought you a cup of tea."

"Doesn't Nan get a biscuit?"

"Yeh, all right," said Kenny. "Don't let it go cold."

He looked penetratingly at the hedge a moment. Then he went in.

MapHead settled down to enjoy himself. There was no danger in the tea, not a bit. Hadn't he checked the chemical composition with Powers? They were only tiny toadstools, after all. He'd found them behind the heating pipes in the top house. Hadn't Powers said they were largely innocuous? Largely innocuous, that's what Powers had called them – so danger was not on the map. Pop four into the teapot, said MapHead. Let 'em brew a bit. Four, said Kenny, you sure? Better go with three.

Kenny reappeared with a couple of chocolate crumbles. He hung around ghoulishly while Mrs Wellbeloved drained her tea.

"Thank you, Kenneth," she said. "I'm just going to weed the border. Like to give me a hand?"

Like fun, thought Kenny. "I'm helping Mum," he said.

Then he filtered off. He went back through the house, out by the front gate and round by the road. Until he found MapHead in the hedge.

They watched her a good quarter-hour. Mrs Wellbeloved trowelled her way ruthlessly down through the border, rubbishing weeds as she went. She didn't grow larger or smaller, like Alice. Instead she grew hotter and crosser. Nothing seemed to change with her at all.

"I thought you said she'd be different," hissed Kenny. "Looks jus' the same to me. Worse, prob'ly."

"Maybe she needs some more," said MapHead dubiously.

Kenny shook his head. "I'm not givin' her no more."

In the end they went down to the rec and duffed a ball around. Then they sat talking on the footbridge over the smelly little stream that bordered the field. MapHead was telling the Roman races:

"…and all the kids, they'd have coloured favours – that's ribbons they'd wear – and support different teams—"

"Like wearin' Tarmouth colours," put in Kenny earnestly. "Like supporting Tarmouth Argyle."

"Right, only instead of scarves and hats, they'd wear their chariot team's favours. And the Green Mantles, the Greens team, no one could beat 'em. They were the best."

MapHead drew breath. He'd painted in the chariot races with the broadest brush he could. At least Kenny knew how terrific it was, the stadium roar and the crush. And the danger, the edge at the turn.

"You're talking a lot different than when you came," said Kenny generously. "You don't make so many mistakes."

"I don't now, do I?" said MapHead. Mainly thanks to Kenny, he'd got a handle on natural speech at last. He was a quick learner anyway. But Powers, he knew, would be pleased.

"Where'd you live before? Somewhere foreign?"

"Yes," said MapHead softly. "Somewhere foreign."

They neither of them spoke for a while. The stream ran away under the bridge, and everything Kenny had wanted to ask ran away with it. He watched a crisp packet eddy by until it dived into the channel under the road. The only things that mattered right at that moment were him and MapHead and the warm, still evening carrying his questions away with the stream. Everything else could wait.

"Shame about your model," said Kenny at last. "My nan never meant to mash it."

"She didn't say sorry," said MapHead.

"That's what she's like," shrugged Kenny. "Mr Bandy liked it though, din' he? Old Bandy goes, 'Remarkable, remarkable.' So you got a good mark, all right."

"Mr Bandy liked it a lot," admitted MapHead. Then he jumped down off the bridge. "Let's see what your nan's like now."

They wandered back through the late summer twilight. Bats flickered close overhead. A warm wind blew in the trees. MapHead felt all his senses heighten. It was on just such an evening as this that he would presently call on his mother. And then she would know him at last. He looked across at Kenny. Wasn't she his mother, too? How would Kenny feel?

"Hey, Maps," said Kenny, "do our house, will you? Just once."

MapHead grinned. He was only too happy to oblige. First he flashed up the Stonewalls area. Then he zeroed in on Ruggy Lane. The lines swam over his cheeks, his jaw, his nose. He tilted his face to the moon, enlarging the scale by degrees: five miles to the inch – one mile. Then he closed his eyes. The map was complete. Viewtown, Kenny's home, sat precisely over his cheekbone.

"Wow," said Kenny. "Unreal."

At last they reached the corner. They turned in at Ruggy Lane. They mounted the steps to Viewtown. It was time to say goodbye.

But Kenny turned at the door. "Who's there?" he called, across the garden. The figure in the moonlight turned. "Nan," he called, "that you?"

Mrs Wellbeloved drifted over like a sleepwalker. Her face was profoundly changed. Hard to say how, thought MapHead, but softer and warmer was in it.

"I've been out *such* a long time enjoying the night air," said Mrs Wellbeloved softly. "I don't know why I haven't done it before. Here's this glorious garden, this wonderful evening, and we don't come out when we should. Look up there – Orion's Belt, see it? And the Pole Star, see it shining?"

Kenny and MapHead looked up in the brilliant night sky, crowded with numberless stars.

"Makes you feel small, doesn't it?" breathed Mrs Wellbeloved. "So many shining stars, so many wonderful worlds – who can say how, many?" She smiled, with a million stars in her eyes. "We should look up more often, I think."

"She *is* different," whispered Kenny wonderingly.

MapHead nodded. "She is."

It was wonderful what a good strong cuppa could do. Something told him Warden Wellbeloved had Got a Life at last.

# Lightning Strikes Twice

It was surprising, thought MapHead, the things you found on the bottom of the river. An old bicycle, several tyres, lengths of rope – even an ancient bed-frame. What kind of person tipped a bed into the river? He allowed himself to settle softly into the mud beside it. Then he looked up. Way above him, through the murk, the splendid sky broke on the surface of the river. He turned, lazily. Somewhere in the green a trout flickered by. It was time to go up, he supposed. He'd been underwater a good half-hour. He was getting low on oxygen, he knew. Half an hour was pushing it a bit.

He let the river draw him up in its own good time, pausing a little, three to four feet down, in a glorious warm patch where golden motes swam in the shafting sunlight. Then he swam to the bank, feeling the river rush over and under and through him.

He dried himself with his sweater and sat in the rusty leaves. There was more than a bite of autumn in the air. Quietly, like a closing book, the summer was slipping away. At least, thought MapHead, he had the weekly bath under his belt. He might've skipped school for once, but he hadn't been entirely wasteful with the morning. Powers would be pleased for that, if nothing else.

Powers had gone shopping, he knew. Powers had taken to shopping a lot, lately. He enjoyed the bustle and the over-the-counter banter. He spent his mornings in the Rubytown Café, catching the local gossip. The Rubytown Café was a real finger-on-the-pulse job, said Powers. The cutting edge of the culture. MapHead had his doubts. It seemed to him, Powers was getting sidetracked. He had folded away his silver suit. He was vague and shallow lately, like the edges of the river. It was time, MapHead knew, to take a dip in darker waters.

He gathered his shoes and sweater. The sun had blinked away. Overhead a leaden sheet of cloud was rushing in fast from the west. The leaden river beneath it looked suddenly uninviting. Good job he'd bathed and done with it. He'd go back and have a good read. Root out some old yellow newspapers from under the boilerhouse door. What day was it? Wednesday. He'd be home free in the boilerhouse today. It was Oddsworthy Market, Wednesdays. The van had departed early, laden with tomatoes.

MapHead felt the tension mounting in the air as he crashed up the slope through the trees. A peculiar wind tore up through the woods behind him, heavy and hot, hurrying him on with horrible urgency. The leaves whooshed up in strange little whirlwinds on either side as he went; the branches rattled nastily overhead. Something was coming, something ugly and momentous. And it was coming in fast, from the west.

He reached the rise breathless, and looked back. Way below him, beyond the treetops, the river wound sullenly on. Over it rolled the approaching storm. MapHead darted across the road and over the yard beyond. Already big rain was dashing the concrete dark. He rattled the packing-shed door, but the packing-shed door was locked. He turned for the bottom house, fast. There wasn't a moment to lose.

First time, he ran right past her. Then he ran back. A narrow figure in a wax jacket in front of the chipping-machine shed, the rain and the wind gusting her pale hair flat.

"Boothe," waved Kay, holding her coat-collar close.

"Come on with me," shouted MapHead. "Don't stand there, you'll get soaked."

She looked at him speechlessly. The rain lashed the chipping-shed door and loaded the gutters above it.

He ran up and pulled her along. "You can't stay there, come on!"

Then they were dashing headlong together down the track – in between the raindrops, joked Kay breathlessly – dodging recklessly over the wood pile and round the rubbish tip beyond, reaching the bottom house door as thunder banged overhead.

MapHead rolled back the door. "Hurry," he said. "Come in." He rolled it home with a boom. They were in. Warm and dry – and strangely shy.

The hush inside was profound. The tomato plants hung warmly down like scarves. The bees drowsed, the hot pipes talked a bit together. The rain drummed overhead, flooding down like silver on the glass.

"Take a seat," said MapHead, rustling up a dirty old chair. "You can dry off your coat on the pipes."

He draped his sweater on the hot pipes, to show her. He propped his shoes up beside. "It's OK. They're not too hot."

Kay wiped her face with her sleeve. She flinched as rain dashed the glass. She looked pretty rattled, thought MapHead.

"I'll just stay until the worst's over." She tried to smile. "I don't like thunderstorms much."

"Me neither," chimed MapHead comfortingly.

"No school today?"

"I fell in the river. I've got to keep warm."

Kay smiled uncertainly. "Nice and warm in here."

"Thirty Celsius," said MapHead promptly. "Never drops below."

"I rang last week about a part-time job," said Kay. "I tried the bungalow, but there's no one about."

"Never is, Wednesdays. They always go Oddsworthy Market."

"Trust me," mugged Kay. "I would choose Wednesday, wouldn't I?"

MapHead was glad she had. Even if she didn't know him, he had his mother to himself for a while. They would sit together cosily. They would look in each other's eyes and chat about this and that. He would wipe away the anxious look from her face and make her laugh a bit.

"You c'n sit here if you'd rather." He plumped the rock wool settee. "This is where I sleep."

"You sleep in the greenhouse?" said Kay. "Can't you sleep at home?"

"This is home," said MapHead.

But Kay wasn't listening. Thunder ripped high overhead. The rain blasted sideways and fiercer. A split-second flash lit the sky. Closer, counted MapHead. Much closer.

Kay sat down. Then she stood up again. "I shouldn't've come out this morning," she said uneasily. "I knew I shouldn't've come out."

MapHead looked round. What could he show her? He scooped the weedy black kitten he'd rescued from Powers out of its nest in the corner. It had milk round its mouth and bits in its fur. He picked it tidy and held it up.

"This is Shakey. He's about – six weeks old. I get milk for him over the Dairy—"

A terrific flash overhead lit the glasshouse top to bottom. It lit MapHead, Kay and the kitten in a blinding white freeze-frame that left them seeing spots of every colour. The thunder pealed down on its heels, so loud it seemed that the whole works would come down round their ears. The kitten writhed and spat. It was half-wild with fright. MapHead looked at his mother. She was half-wild with fright herself.

He sat down beside her and held her. She covered her head with her hands.

"It's all right," said MapHead, "it's passing off already. Look. It's goin' off, see?"

After a moment she looked. Then she ducked down again. They sat together, waiting.

"I like animals, do you like animals?" asked MapHead after a while, to take her mind off the storm.

"Yes," said Kay in a small voice. "I like animals."

"I had this gopher once – know what a gopher is?"

Kay shook her head.

"What a gopher is, is kind of like a squirrel with no tail. And they dig up people's gardens an' stuff. In America this was. Anyway, I had this gopher. I fed him bits an' he'd come when I wanted him an' everything. Want to know what I called him?"

Kay nodded.

"Nibs. I called him Nibs because that's the noise he made when he was eating. An' old Nibs, he'd bite through anything. Know what he did?"

"No," said Kay. "What?"

"One day he bit through the outside of this big thick electric cable in a trailer park. Put the whole park out, he did, an' everyone's tellies went off. And so I never went there again."

"What happened to him?" asked Kay. "Wasn't he – " she hesitated – "electrocuted?"

MapHead shook his head. "Funny thing was, he was fine. But then a while after that, he never showed up. I looked all over. I asked my dad if he'd seen him, but my dad was making dinner. My dad said, drink up, he's probably gone off with his friends some-where better. But after, I wondered what it was we'd drunk. Then a couple of days later I found a squashed gopher out on the Interstate Highway, an' that kind of made me feel better."

Luckily MapHead's tale of gore and betrayal had passed over Kay's head. She straightened slowly. She took a deep breath and looked around.

"Gone, see?" said MapHead. "Look, the sky's comin' light." This time it was more than wishful thinking; the sky was lighter altogether, with a sense of relief in the air.

Kay drew another long breath. "It's silly, I know, but I—"

"I know," said MapHead softly. "You got struck by lightning once."

Then something arced between them eye to eye – and in that moment, they met.

"I know you," she said. "Who are you?"

*It's me*, said MapHead's eyes. *Who else? You know it, deep inside.*

"I have these dreams," she whispered. "I feel so lost sometimes."

MapHead took both his mother's hands and laid them on top of his poor homeless head. It was such a strange gesture, the moment passed away. Kay jumped up, confused.

MapHead jumped up too. "Don't go yet. Please."

"I don't know where the morning's gone," said Kay. "Would you tell your father I called about the job? Will he be here on Friday?"

"My father?" MapHead looked puzzled. "You want the bungalow man."

"But don't you come from the bungalow?"

"No." MapHead shrugged. "I watch their telly sometimes."

Kay boomed open the door. The fresh bright sunlight flooded in and lit up her hair like a halo. She had a lovely smile now she was safe in the sun.

"I'm all mixed up this morning," she said. "I'll have to give them a ring."

"Wait," said MapHead. "One thing – did you ever have a red umbrella?"

"I'm sorry?"

"A red umbrella. Did you?"

He was surprised to discover how badly he wanted to check out Powers' story – the story about saving his mother. Whatever happened to trust?

"What makes you ask?" she said cagily. "I may've, I don't remember. Thanks for keeping me dry."

MapHead watched her skipping freshly-filled puddles all the way up to the wood pile. Then he turned away. He felt lonelier than ever.

"Come round," he heard her call him. "Come round any time."

MapHead found his kitten. He buried his face in its silly black fluff and rocked it a long time in his arms. He had invited his mother into his home. He had been ready to open his heart. Why had she bolted away, when a hug could have made everything all right? It was funny. The weedy black kitten wasn't wet at all when he picked it up. But when at last it struggled free, it was very wet indeed.

# Mr Bandy Gets Off Lightly

Breakfast next morning was a simple affair. Milk, with pappy bread and syrup. Powers was into syrup lately.

"So what else did she say?" he asked, coating his bread thickly using the edge of a Stanley knife.

"Not a lot," said MapHead edgily.

It was too late to take it back now. Already MapHead was wishing he hadn't mentioned his mother's visit. Once he heard what had happened, Powers' face had changed. He, Powers, had enjoyed the previous day's storm from the highest point available. He had clamped himself to the base of the telly transmitter on the wind-stricken peak of Baradon Hill. Setting his teeth, he had rejoiced in the crackling discharge of power. There was nothing Powers liked better than a violent thunderstorm.

"That settles it," said Powers. "We're calling on your mother Saturday night. And Sunday, we're out of here."

"But why?" asked MapHead. "Why do we have to leave after?"

"Because," said Powers unhelpfully, upending the syrup tin into his mouth. The strange minerals he used to fill holes in his teeth glinted metal-green and yellow as he threw back his head.

"Because what?"

"Because it's time to move on. Because after, everything will change."

"But how will it? How will it change?"

"That's up to you," said Powers. He looked at MapHead searchingly. "You're twelve now. Time to grow up."

"Yes," said MapHead. "I want to."

Powers stood up, wiping his mouth. "Got your stuff for school?"

"Yes," said MapHead miserably.

"Want me to walk you up?"

"No. I like it on my own."

"Fine. I'll catch you later."

MapHead took his usual route to school. This involved a detour along the railway tracks. There was something about the railway tracks that attracted him. There was one particular place – there'd been an accident there, he knew from Mo and Jan – there was one particular place, where some mornings he glimpsed a figure in a plaid shirt walking the path alongside. It was always the merest glimpse. Whenever he looked again, always the figure was gone. He could have gone into the whole thing a lot more if he'd wanted. But there were hundreds of places like that, where something deep had happened, sometime past. The Subtle World was full of deep places, like a river, that wanted to suck you in. MapHead was happy to skim the surface, for the present. Some things, he knew, would keep until he was older.

As he walked, he thought. He thought about what Powers had said about growing up. He was changing already, he knew. Powers had brought him to the edge of realizing himself. He must take the final step alone. For some time now, MapHead had felt a feeling growing inside him that must one day soon burst out.

There would come a time, he knew, when Powers would move on without him. Then the world would be his, and anything would be possible. Anything was possible, anyway – that was one trick he knew. One day soon he would let himself go, and take his world by the throat. Then he would be as unbounded and frightful as Powers himself. Then there would be choices! Responsibilities too. MapHead sighed. It was all too big for him yet.

He was well up on the main drag through Stonewalls village when a funky old split-screen Morris Traveller passed by. And braked – some twenty metres or so up the road. It reversed back erratically to meet him.

The nearside door swung open. "Like a lift,

Boothe?" asked Mr Bandy.

"Yeh," said MapHead. "Thanks."

He'd rather've walked, on his own. He had a lot to think about. But he thought it not polite to refuse. Besides, he liked Mr Bandy.

"So. Poorly yesterday?" asked Mr Bandy pleasantly. He checked his mirror and pulled away. "We missed you at library session. Mrs Cousins brought in some Roman artefacts."

"Did she?"

Mr Bandy changed gear and nodded. "Coins from the reign of Octavius. Bits of Samian pottery, a couple of hypocaust tiles. Mrs Cousins' sister found them in her garden. In Cardiff."

It would be yesterday, wouldn't it? He had missed his chance to touch things real Romans had touched. But somehow this morning MapHead could hardly even rise to disappointment.

"Sorry I missed it," he said flatly. He knew he was, really. He just couldn't feel it.

Mr Bandy glanced across. "Something bothering you, Boothe? Not bad news, I hope?"

"Sort of," said MapHead, suddenly close to tears. It was too bad. Crying over kittens and welling up the moment Mr Bandy asked him anything with sympathy in it at all. How old was he, six or something?

"Like to talk about it?"

"Well," said MapHead carefully, "I might not be here next week. I think we're moving on."

Mr Bandy negotiated a tight squeak with a red Sierra. *And you!* he gestured. Then he turned to MapHead. "I'm sorry to hear that, Boothe."

"Me too. I'm sorry I'm going."

"Kenny's going to miss you. We all will. Any chance you'll be coming back?"

Chance in a million, thought MapHead. Once you took a spin with Powers it was anyone's guess where you'd fall.

"Maybe," he said. "I don't know."

Mr Bandy pulled up reluctantly at the main gate to the school. They sat a moment, in sympathy. They both wished the journey were longer.

"Well," said Mr Bandy, "shouldn't be stopping here, really. I've got the school computer in the back. You couldn't take the monitor in for me while I park up properly, could you?"

"Sure," said MapHead softly. But they neither of them moved.

"If there's anything, ever, you'd like to talk to me about," said Mr Bandy, clicking out a pen, "here's my number at home."

It was almost too much for MapHead. He took Mr Bandy's number and folded it carefully away. He was framing up to get out, when someone rapped smartly on the roof.

She was MapHead's side of the car. A thick navy midriff studded with martial buttons. No need to look further. There was only one bosom like that in the history of traffic policing. She circled the car like a battleship.

"Oh, no," groaned Mr Bandy, "we're on double yellow lines." He closed his eyes, as if in pain. "Please, God, let something fall on her from a great height."

MapHead pictured something falling on Warden Wellbeloved from a great height. Something like the Town Hall.

Mr Bandy jumped out. "Morning, Warden. We're just unloading, aren't we, Boothe? Literally, just unloading – and shooting off again. It's Boothe," he added confidentially. "He's – got a problem with his leg. I like to drop him as close to the main gate as I can, I'm sure you understand."

Mrs Wellbeloved looked at him strangely. She looked a bit strange altogether, thought MapHead, as he climbed out of the car with an exaggerated limp.

"Nothing wrong with that boy's leg," she said. "Hello, Boothe. How are you?"

"Um, I'm fine," said MapHead. He straightened warily. He wasn't too sure how to play it. Why was Mrs Wellbeloved wearing a brilliant orange nasturtium in her hatband? And the wig! Brilliant orange too! It took a bit of getting used to at ten to nine in the morning.

"It's the computer, you see," said Mr Bandy, sweating a bit round the edges. "It's such a hustle – hassle – getting it in with all the bits. I know it's double yellow lines, but—"

Mrs Wellbeloved held up her hand. "That's quite all right, Mr Bandy. You take as long as you want."

"Oh. Well. I – appreciate it, we really do, don't we, Boothe? That's really very civil of you. Really very good of you indeed. And it won't happen again, you can rest assured."

"Take a leaf from my book, Mr Bandy," said Mrs Wellbeloved, leering close in a most inappropriate way. "Relax. You've got your job to do, I've got mine. We all help each other, the world's a better place. What do you say, **Boothe**?"

"Aw – right!" crowed MapHead recklessly. "Way to go, Nan!"

"Nan, Boothe?"

"Yes," said MapHead, casting caution to the winds. "You're my nan, you are." The relief was enormous. What did it matter? Wasn't he leaving soon anyway? Mrs Wellbeloved overflowed. She was in such an over-weeningly golden, milk-of-human-kindness condition, she couldn't take it in.

"Yes," she said vaguely, "there's a sense in which I'm *everybody's* nan. A marvellous sense, a sense of togeth-erness, don't you think, Mr Bandy?" Her nasturtium flower bobbed wildly in her hat. Her wig frizzed wildly under it. "Such a *glorious* morning. Can I help you in with anything?"

"I think we can manage, can't we, Boothe?" said Mr Bandy uncertainly. She really was an extremely grotesque woman. He couldn't think what had come over her. "But thank you anyway, Warden."

"That's *quite* all right, Mr Bandy. Best of the morning to you."

Mrs Wellbeloved wandered on her way, spreading happiness around her as she went, like a cloying cloud of gas that altered all before it.

"Well," said Mr Bandy. "That makes a refreshing change."

# Nemo's World ...

The hamster looked at MapHead through the bars of its cage. It had eyes like the bobbles on blackberries. Its name was Nemo, no one knew why.

Nemo, the school hamster, lived permanently in the top class's window. Weekdays, his cage was cleaned on a rota system; weekends he spent alone. Holidays, he visited with Mrs Cousins. Two successive top classes had used and abused him, but still he scraped a living in his sawdust on the window shelf between the pot plants. He didn't complain much, Nemo. Mostly, he just slept.

MapHead brought his face in closer. Nemo looked through him and past him. Nemo's rapid heartbeat pulsed his body faster than was good for him, thought MapHead. He was pulsing away his life span at a rate of knots, was Nemo.

"So. Have you worked page three yet, Boothe?"

MapHead snapped back to his desk. "Almost, I

have, Mr Bandy."

He hadn't, at all. The percentage exercises swam on the page in front of him. He couldn't concentrate at all, and he couldn't even care that he couldn't. Everything today was toneless and flat. Everything, everywhere, left the bitter taste of leaving in his mouth.

"Any problems?"

Millions, thought MapHead. Percentages didn't even figure on the list. "Not 'specially, I don't think," he said.

"If VAT is charged at 15% on an item costing £35, what will the final cost be?" asked the maths page relentlessly. MapHead sighed. Mr Bandy had gone over percentages at length. Then he'd gone over them again. Then he'd gone over them a third time with Kenny, because Kenny'd wallied off miles away in his head thinking about something else entirely the second time round.

MapHead took up his pencil. He put thirty-five over a hundred, then he made a multiply sign. Then he put fifteen over one. Then he stopped. His pencil traced on, by itself:

I want you to know how much it hurts to leave.
I've been around long enough to know your my best
teacher ever since Dad. I wish I could of stayed
and done the Prince of Thieves play. I think Andy
Steed is your best bet for Little John now.

*Tell the truth, I've been looking for my Mum. My Mum is the same Mum as Kenny's. It doesn't matter telling now I'm gone. I won't be seeing you again, my Dad has places to go. He's OK and I'm OK, I hope Mrs. Bandy is OK too. Thanks for everything you said, I hope to come bak powerful one day and say remember me ? Till then your best thing is forget I came,*

*yours kindly*

*from Boothe*

The pencil stopped. MapHead looked mistily at what he'd written. It was something, but only the half of it. He would leave it on Mr Bandy's desk last thing tomorrow. The way it looked, Friday would be his last day.

The bell for break rang shatteringly in the corridor outside. Mr Bandy looked up.

"All right now, books away. Alex. I'll see exercise five before you go. Who's on Nemo duty?"

Kenny jumped up. "Me 'n' Boothe today, Sam 'n' Kelly Monday."

"Fine, I'll let you get on."

The class rose as one and jumbled out, leaving Anxious Alex Hayes glowering over his books. He'd rushed through exercise five to get ahead, just as Mr

Bandy had known he would. For someone who liked to be first, he spent a fair bit of time being last.

Kenny fetched the sawdust chippings from the cupboard. Then he went back for a newspaper or two. MapHead got up. He unhitched the top of Nemo's cage from the tray underneath. "Nemo," he whispered. "Hey, Nemo. Wake up."

The hamster blinked out from its nest. It wobbled around a bit, searching dimly with its nose for whatever might descend on it next. MapHead tuned in, warming to the world inside the cage. It was only about thirty by twenty centimetres – way too confined for a travelling animal. Around about six hundred square centimetres, that was Nemo's world. Animals very like hamsters, he'd read, covered miles on the Russian Steppes. That was where they'd come from.

In place of the Russian Steppes Nemo had a red plastic wheel, the spout of his drink-bottle, a brown plastic feeder crammed with hamster-mix, and a whole mess of chippings, plus assorted droppings of his own making. And a food-store in the corner. He was very particular about his food-store. Anyone would think he was laying in food for a siege. Now, in cleaning it out, they were about to rubbish his little world completely. Poor old Nemo, he wasn't too bright. Any disturbance, and he crammed his pouches with peanuts. It was sick, said Kenny. You could feel 'em under his skin.

At last Mr Bandy released Anxious Alex from the

rigours of exercise five with a nod and a big red tick. Then he cleared out for coffee. "And I don't," he said in parting, "want chippings on the floor."

They scraped out the tray into the dustbin outside. Then they refreshed it with bitter new sawdust. They clamped on the cage. They fed the feeder and filled the drinker. His cage was spotless and foreign. Nemo wouldn't know himself.

Kenny cracked out his crisps. "Haven't you got none today?"

MapHead shook his head.

"Want some pizza flavour?"

MapHead shook his head again. He ran Nemo wordlessly over his hands. Then he popped him back, pegging his door closed securely.

Kenny shrugged. He stuffed a few pizza-flavour crisps between the bars of Nemo's cage. Nemo was partial to crisps.

"Where were you yesterday?" he asked.

"I got cold. I fell in the river."

"Oh, yeh," said Kenny sarcastically. "Right. I'm always fallin' in."

MapHead watched the hamster make its bed. He wondered where he'd make his own bed, Sunday, when they left. Beside a mournful Scottish loch or Andean cataract? Beside the mighty Ganges, where the holy men were blessed? In deep and tropic highlands where monkeys beat their chest?

"Hey, Maps. You got a lot to say this morning,"

observed Kenny. "Don't talk so loud."

"The thing is," said MapHead heavily, "the thing is, I might be—"

"Anyway," interrupted Kenny, "my nan's havin' a party. A real big one. She was on about it last night."

Mrs Wellbeloved?! Having a party?! MapHead pictured Mrs Wellbeloved. Having a party. Then he pictured her as she'd been that morning. The flower in the hat. The freaky orange wig. The way she'd let Mr Bandy off lightly. A sense – what had she said? – a marvellous sense of togetherness. Now he thought about a party, it didn't seem strange at all. Pity was, he'd miss it.

"Different, isn't she?" he said. "She was heckuva lot different this morning."

"You're coming, cos I can invite who I want," went on Kenny breathlessly. "An' there's Sam an' Nick an' Aiden an' Alex an' Dob. An' Chris an' Andy an' Kelly, an' Si an' Martyn. And Stew. But not Gavin, I'm not havin' Gavin no way. An' David Chubb an' David Blanchard. And old Bandy. And you."

"It's really good," said MapHead sadly. "Really, really good."

"An' Nan's havin' everyone she's booked. Ever. Last night she goes, 'Where's my little book?' And she goes through all the parking tickets she gave the past like, year or something – and she's doin' the old invites on the kitchen table, you shoulda seen her."

MapHead got up. He couldn't stand much more. He

lifted Nemo's cage carefully onto the windowsill. Nemo had wrapped himself asleep in a corner, warm in a sawdust ball. He was safe in his own world, whatever happened outside. No one would tell him to get up and go. Nothing would bother him. He was beyond botheration. Good old Nemo, thought MapHead. Old Nemo had the right idea.

He put his chin on the windowsill, eye-level to Nemo's world. Then he made himself smaller and colder inside. It wasn't hard – he was pretty much that way to start. He slowed circulation to his ears and his fingers and his toes. Then he hyperventilated a few deep breaths.

Old Nemo, he thought, slowing his pulse by degrees, old Nemo's got the right idea, old Nemo got the right, old Nemo got, old Nemo – oh. Then he fell down.

"Blimmin' heck," gaped Kenny. "Blimmin', blimmin' *heck!*"

Kenny looked round once before he legged it to the staff room. Unhurriedly, head between knees, MapHead assumed his final position. He would not be fully dormant for a couple of hours, in all.

Beyond MapHead, beyond the pot plants, beyond Nemo and his cage and the window, the playground wailed and shrieked. But all the way along the corridor, echoing away to the staff room and in the hollow halls behind, came Kenny's banshee call:

"Mr Bandy, come quick! Mr Bandee – Mr *Bandeeee!*"

# ...and Raptor's World

He was lost. Deeply and endlessly, in an ocean of lights. Gradually the lights grew smaller, rounder. A hundred thousand faces, three hundred thousand faces – roaring, laughing, flirting, aping their neighbours, shouting the odds, screaming, signalling, swearing, sneering, spitting.

He looked up. There were no maps to guide him. In the long mean pit of the amphitheatre, he was entirely on his own.

He wore the Green Mantle proud across his chest. On his brow he wore the charioteer's band of hammered bronze, ribboned gold and emerald down his back. His spiteful lash stood sheathed beside him. With his fitted gauntlets of oxhide he bound the reins tight to his arm in the death-grip. He would not lose his team. Alive or dead, he would pass the painted post. The bareback riders made their final circuit.

The crowd was growing impatient. Coloured

favours streamed everywhere on the wind – crimson and purple, blue and green and white. The acrobats flipped away by the lowly performers' gate. Not for them the Arch of Heroes by which the chariots had entered.

Scores of dismal slaves rushed out to rake the track. The Time-keeper turned his glass. The Watch at the turn readied the yellow pennant that would signal the final lap. The heralds rose for the fanfare.

"Fortune Awaits!" roared the Overseer. The long horns blared, the crowd rose with glory in its throat. Fortune Awaits! Fortune! Fortune or Death!

His team took the start at a bound, the lead horse making half a length over the Purples along the straight, his open-back chariot skewing wildly behind.

"Raptor!" he screamed. "Over hard! Raptor! To the wall!"

"To the wall!" roared the crowd, "the wall!" Raptor, the lead horse, burst bravely to the inner wall with a rush that broke his wind, cutting the Crimsons dead in a crush of harness behind. They forged on, half-blind and deaf, past the hectic turn.

Greens hold the wall! Greens hold the wall! The crowd boiled madly forward wherever the green favours flew. They had the wall and they held it, all the way down and round, forcing the foaming Purples to hug the wall outside.

Two laps, three laps – four! The Crimsons came on with a crack and a rush and a deathly twist in the harness, throttling the lead horse breathless as he came. The Purples plunged across Raptor's neck for the death-or-glory turn, the Watch's yellow pennant unfurling as they charged. The final lap! The final test! They must hold the wall or go down! And they never would go down, not while Raptor breathed!

Neck and neck out of the turn in a ringing clash of axles, they saw the home straight opening before them, dotted with wheels and men. At last he unsheathed his whip. He had scorned to use it till now. How much could he ask of Raptor? Everything and more! He dashed the whip away.

"Raptor!" he screamed, "to the post! To the post for glory! Raptor!"

The furious Purples matched them stride for stride, the painted poles looked down. A hundred metres, seventy – what was it, up ahead? Idiots in the way! Boiling arms and legs, where nothing but victory should be! The barriers, overwhelmed, had spilled the crowd on the track. The choice was clear. He must ride them down or lose.

But he *would* not win that way. He would go down first, and die. Just before he threw Raptor down with a fatal twist of his arm, he glimpsed a face he knew. A face he knew like his hand, a face that willed him on, though he rode it down to win.

"You can do it!" urged the face. "You can!"

The face loomed closer, paler now, and thicker. "Come on. I *know* you can."

And suddenly it was Powers. "You can do it. My MapHead. You *can* wake up."

MapHead lifted his head. He was back in his nest in the rock wool, with the glasshouse humming round.

"I'm dead," he said. "I crashed."

Powers flashed all his fillings in a warming welcome-back smile. "Idiot," he said. "Drink this."

MapHead drank it. Then he screwed up his face. It tasted like nothing he'd ever tasted before. If he had tasted it before, he'd never've drunk it again. A thick and viscous brew which smelled like the inner workings of the rubbish tip outside, with a hint of rotten fish.

He lay back. "I'm dead *now*. What *was* that? No – " He held up his hand. It felt like someone else's hand. "Don't tell me. I don't want to know."

"A simple restorative," said Powers. "I've tried a few ideas, all week. Got it right at last." MapHead sat up weakly. "All week? How long've I been out?"

Powers thought a bit. "Two weeks, less one day."

"You're kidding."

"Wish I was. You had me worried for a while. Who is Raptor, anyway?"

MapHead shivered. "I don't want to think about it."

"'Fortune awaits,' you were shouting. 'Fortune awaits.' But I knew you'd come out of it in time."

Then MapHead remembered Nemo. He remembered shutting all systems down, in the classroom with Kenny, at school, while the playground wailed.

"What happened at school?" he asked.

"I sensed you'd shut down. I went up to school to get you."

"And? What did you say?"

Powers shrugged. "I said, 'He's subject to fits. It happens.'"

Powers got up. He shuffled some papers from a box behind the pipes. "There's cards here. One from Mr Bandy."

It was a funny card. Inside, in Mr Bandy's sprawling writing, it said: "Get well soon, hope to see you back before you go, very best wishes, Geoff Bandy."

"You want to stay a bit, don't you?" asked Powers. "That's what it's all about."

"Can we?" asked MapHead.

"*If* you don't see your mother."

"Why can't I?"

"Because," said Powers, "we can't deal with this in real time. I thought you knew that by now. I made her forget so she wouldn't get hurt. What's going to happen if you tell her who you are and she doesn't remember at all?"

MapHead thought. "She'll think I'm loopy, that's all."

"No," said Powers, gravely, "not entirely. You'll muddle her up. She'll lie awake nights, thinking. And *then* how can we call her when we want to?"

MapHead closed his eyes. He mustered the atmosphere of his dream, the feeling at the post, the feeling he'd had when he threw Raptor down rather than trample the crowd and win. He had had a choice, and he'd chosen. Rather than win the race, he had chosen to win himself.

"Let's," he started bravely, trampling his heart's desire, "let's not call her at all. I don't mind not having a mother. If it's going to upset her to know."

"But it won't," said Powers. "If you play by the rules."

MapHead said nothing. He knew what he felt. It was a feeling as big as Circus Maximus itself.

"You've changed," his father said softly. "You've grown. Can't you feel the power?"

MapHead swallowed. Powers was right. He was subtly changed, and he knew it. He was greater, in some way, altogether. Gain by loss, thought MapHead. Somehow, by losing he'd won. But right now, it didn't help at all. Suddenly he was remembering his maths book. The letter to Mr Bandy. The letter which said, "My mum is the same mum as Kenny's." Had he put it away? Or had he left it open on his desk? He strained to remember what had happened.

"Anyway." Powers jumped up. "I'm off to town now. What can I get you to eat? Nice bit of liver? Quarter of coconut mushrooms? How about some kidneys, or pear-drops? Oxtail, liquorice – anything at all."

"No kidneys," said MapHead faintly. "I don't eat animals, remember?"

What would he like to eat? All he could think of was

grapes. He'd had a lot of grapes in his dream, when he was Roman.

"Just grapes, thanks, I think," he said. Powers threw on his donkey jacket. He'd found it drying on the pipes and adopted it the very first day they'd arrived, and no one had missed it yet. It wasn't the most desirable item, but Powers had taken to it from the first.

"I might just look in at the Café. That warden – remember the traffic warden? – that warden's the talk of the town. They say she might lose her job."

"Mrs Wellbeloved? Why?"

Powers shrugged. "Not being nasty enough. Everyone parks where they want. It's hell up on Fore Street, they say."

MapHead laughed soundlessly. His ribs hurt a lot when he did, especially his right side and forearm. Perhaps it was Charioteer's Arm.

"Be all right for a bit?" Powers looked anxious. "No pickers today, it's Wednesday."

"I'll be fine," signalled MapHead, still laughing.

"Well then, I'll see you later. Don't get up, you're not strong."

MapHead lay quiet a long time after Powers had gone. The garish colours of his dream flashed back, the greedy roar of the crowd swelled once more in his ears. He sat up and shook his head.

He looked around for his kitten, but its nest was empty and cold. The day was chilly outside. He shivered his way to the pipes and sat down, enjoying the feeling as they warmed him. He fished out the box behind them, Powers' box of papers.

Mostly it was shopping lists, receipts for crazy things like hats and string, a battered advertising hand-out, a mail-order catalogue that Powers was keen on browsing. Right at the bottom, under everything else, was a card that Powers had missed. A card from Kenny, it was.

"Get Better Or Else," it said. "To Maps from Kenny." Inside it was tucked another card. This one was got up to look a bit like a parking ticket, the ones Mrs Wellbeloved wrote. Or used to. The only difference was gold edges. And the things it said.

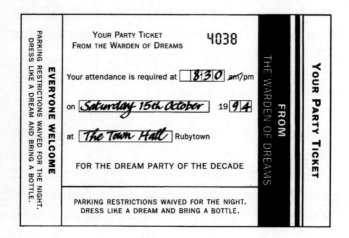

Wow! thought MapHead. Old Mrs Wellbeloved's party. What would it be like? Pretty weird, if it was anything like the invitation. Why had Powers hidden it? Because his mother would be there, of course. Because Powers wouldn't want him to go. But he *would* go, just the same. The fifteenth was – Saturday coming. He would go, and dress like a dream.

But first he'd visit Kenny. There was something he had to ask.

# What Kenny Did
# in the Cupboard

"What *kind* of bottle," persisted MapHead. "A milk bottle?"

Kenny looked up crossly. "Hold that end down, will you? What are you on about, bottles?"

"It says 'Bring a bottle' on the invitation. And I wondered what *kind—*"

"A bottle of booze, you der-brain. What did you think?"

"I don't know," said MapHead humbly. "I've never been to a party before."

Kenny sat back. "You're something, you know that?" He shook his head. "You're really something."

It was Friday night. The night before the party. Kenny and MapHead had banners every which way on the lawn. Silver banners with fringed edges, spelling PARTY TIME! over and over down their length, with red stars in between.

"What about 'Dress like a dream'?"

Kenny shrugged. "Wear anything, I am. Give us that end, will you?"

He concertinaed the banner neatly in its box, along with the other bunting. The Town Hall would take a bit of decorating, that was for sure. Good job Nan Wellbeloved had visited Tarmouth Party Hire. How else would they get the costumes? The banners, masks and hats? "Hey, Kenny. Know where I've been?"

"Nowhere. You been ill."

"Give you a clue, all right?" MapHead flashed up a topographical map of middle Italy. Then he zeroed in. The Seven Hills of Rome, the river Tiber running blue across his nose.

But Kenny wasn't watching. He rummaged crossly for the scissors through a mess of coloured crêpe. Blimmin' things. Where *were* they?

"Don't never," he complained, finding them at last, "don't never pack up on me like that again. You jus' about scared me half to death, you did."

"Watch up," said MapHead. "You're not watching."

He phased a ground plan of Circus Maximus carefully over his face. He ran it past again. And one more time, for effect.

This time Kenny was watching. He flexed the scissors thoughtfully. "OK. It's your Romans model. So?"

"So I've been there. I've *really been*."

"You never. How could you?"

'I did the chariot races, I *did* and I did the Green Mantles and I had a team and a whip and everything.

And what happened was, I was jus' about going to win when—"

"How's it going, boys?" Kay clinked a tray of iced Cokes between them. "Got it sorted yet?"

MapHead blinked his face blank quick as thought. He hadn't seen her coming. He hadn't even heard her. Powers was right. One of these days he'd blow it. And if he didn't, Kenny soon would. Keeping Kenny's mouth zipped was pain enough already.

Kenny'd say: He does maps on his face, did you know? soon as breathe, if he, MapHead, hadn't spelled out in colourful terms what would be bound to happen if he did. He, MapHead, would be gone like a shot for ever, that was what. Then where was the sense in telling? But Kenny didn't think. He'd let it slip in time. He wouldn't be able to help himself.

MapHead cooled his face with his icy glass of Coke. He looked up sadly at his mother. Kay smiled back. She raised her glass in a toast. "Here's to tomorrow – warts 'n' all!" He chimed his glass with hers and turned away. He never felt less like a party. Any way he looked at it, time was running out.

"Where's Nan?" asked Kenny.

"Gone for a facial. Nail extensions, wig-styling – the works."

Kenny groaned. "What's she going to look like?"

"Like Nan, that's what. Uncle Barry'll take the decorations if you've sorted out the stuff. Stick it on the tables in the garage. Coming down the Hall tomorrow,

112

Boothe? Help us put them up?"

MapHead shook his head. "Can't really."

"Well. We'll see you eight-thirty for the kickoff. Dad coming too?"

He shook his head again. "No, he's – got something on, on Saturday."

"That's a shame. Kenny, there's a folding chair your nan wants, under the stairs."

"What for? There's chairs there."

"Yes, but she wants something comfy for Mrs Cousins' mother. Stick it out for Barry in the garage? And the extension lead? Thanks."

She clinked up the glasses and left them to it. MapHead watched her slip in through the patio doors. She was bright and focused always, like a torch that lit the dark.

"You're lucky. She's brilliant, your mum."

"Yeh," said Kenny, "not bad. Take the other end, will you?"

Taking an end each, they lumped the box into the garage. On the tables. For Uncle Barry. Then they went under the stairs. It was while they were deep in the cupboard that MapHead remembered, quite suddenly, the thing he'd wanted to ask.

"You know when I got ill at school? When I packed up on the floor?"

"What?" said Kenny crossly. He forced his way into the cramped-up toe of the cupboard. "Shoe-cleaning stuff, cool box, windbreak, picnic rug. What's this?

Christmas stuff, looks like. Stupid chairs are right in the back. Hold this."

He passed the extension lead back. MapHead tried again. "You know when I packed up? On the floor at school?"

He paused. He would have to come right out with it. "Well, did you see my maths book after?"

Kenny thunked himself on the underside of the stairs. He doubled up, holding his head. "After what?"

"After I fell down."

Kenny tried to stand up and couldn't. He broke wind noisily.

"I should get out quick if I was you." He reeled a bit, himself. "I've jus' about had enough of this cupboard. And I'm sick to death of this—"

He threw out an old umbrella. MapHead picked it up. He backed it slowly out under the hall light.

It was a crazy old umbrella, scorched to hellfire and back – the blasted tip fused solid with the ribs, the fabric, the handle. But, thought MapHead, flashing miles away back to a wild grey day on a storm-struck hill – it was, or had been, red. The fabric nearest the handle. Definitely red.

"What's this?" he asked. "Your mum's?"

Kenny forced his way out of the cupboard, dragging a chair with one hand, holding his nose with the other.

"Used to be," said Kenny, throwing down the chair. "My mum'd like to get rid of it, but Nan won't let her throw it away. It's the only thing she had, after my mum went missing. That an' a dirty great scorch mark, up on Parkway Knoll."

He peeled back the fabric, exposing the blasted handle.

"See that? The lightning hit the end here – see? Ran all the way down the handle, through Mum an' into the ground. Nan said, miracle she wasn't killed. No wonder she couldn't remember."

MapHead hugged the umbrella, wishing it were Powers. Powers could do frightful things, but he couldn't melt umbrellas. Powers had taken the lightning charge, he saw now, through himself. Powers had saved her life, when he might have lost his own. But he wished with all his heart he hadn't had to see the red umbrella to know what he'd known all along.

Kenny snatched it back. He stuffed it in the cupboard.

"Mum gets upset when she sees it. She goes, 'Where was I, all that time I can't remember?' That's why it's under the stairs. Come on. Let's dump this chair an' finish."

They dumped the chair and finished. There was nothing more to do. The garage light pooled out under the half-open door on the chilly autumn evening.

"Want Mum to run you home?" asked Kenny. "She will."

"No worries," said MapHead. "I'll jog."

He started out down chilly Ruggy Lane. The autumn

moon lit the puddles bright as he went.

"See you at the party!" called Kenny. "Meet you eight-thirty by the door!"

He jogged on, past the neighbours. The cottage windows glowed.

"Maps! Hey, Maps!" yelled Kenny.

MapHead turned. Kenny stood waving in the pool of light from the garage. He cupped his hands round his mouth:

"You know that maths you wanted? Mr Bandy took it."

MapHead turned on his way. The darkness thickened behind and before, but one thing was clear as bells. Mr Bandy had the maths book. Mr Bandy had the letter. Mr Bandy Knew.

# Warden of Dreams

"*Lovely Rita, meter maid, nothing can come between us,*" sang Mr Bandy. "*When it gets dark I tow your heart away…*"

"*Wah-wah, wah-wah…*" hammed the chorus behind him, their orange satin shirts throwing back the party lights over the gleeful crowd.

Mrs Frida Wellbeloved, Warden of Dreams, threw a smile like gold from her throne on the Town Hall stage. She'd never cared much for "Frida". Tonight of all nights she was Lovely Rita. Mr Bandy sank to his knees. He really had quite a good voice.

> "*Standing by a parking meter*
> *When I caught a glimpse of Rita*
> *filling in a ticket in a little white book.*"

MapHead laughed till he cried. Then he laughed some more. Mr Bandy, in a frilly satin shirt. Mr Bandy, serenading Mrs Wellbeloved. It was almost too much.

*"In her cap, she looked much older,*
*And the bag across her shoulder*
*made her look a little like a military man."*

*"Oooh-oooh, oooh-oooh,"* chorused the three satin shirts, stepping up round Mrs Wellbeloved in unison.

MapHead and Kenny exchanged a splitting grin. The party crowd pressed thickly around them, dappled red with spotlights, faces turning, flashing, disappearing – all with grins as wide.

"Look," hissed MapHead. "That woman. With the baby."

He looked again. It *was*. The young woman Mrs Wellbeloved had booked outside the bank, the pregnant lady, the lady who'd cried and bitterly slammed away. She wore a shifting dress of blue and a smile a mile wide. She held her tiny baby higher, showing it the band. She looked, thought MapHead, more like a dream than any *he'd* dreamed lately.

"What about her?" asked Kenny.

"Oh, nothing. I know her a bit, that's all."

Mr Bandy was putting everything he'd got into a grand finale. The four satin shirts froze on the last tremendous note, arms raised in salute to Mrs Wellbeloved. Applause crashed down around them as they took their bow, flashing their shirts and posing madly before waving the crowd goodbye. MapHead

118

clapped his hands together as hard as he possibly could, stamping his feet for more. Mr Bandy had surprised him very much indeed.

At last the hoots and whistles died away. Mrs Wellbeloved rose majestically.

She wore a warden's uniform in boggling shades of puce and green, orange, silver and yellow – the swirling patterns echoed on her psychedelic hat of gorgeous wired flowers. Her wig flashed with glitter. She'd really gone to town.

She tapped the microphone and began. "First, I'd like to thank Geoff Bandy and the Trillionaires…"

More applause, hoots and whistles. Mrs Wellbeloved raised her arm for silence.

"…for that astonishing rendition. There's plenty of Geoff Bandy's pupils in the crowd, I know, so he won't live it down in a hurry! But seriously, I'd like to thank you all for coming, and for making this party a dream come true. There's been times, plenty of times, when I haven't been proud to be a traffic warden. There have been times in the past, when I've overstepped the mark. But I'd like to put all that behind us tonight, in a spirit of togetherness." She paused. The crowd grew sombre. Mrs Cousins' mother nodded vaguely in her chair. MapHead watched proudly. His nan was magnificent. Something in what she had to say touched everyone, right through the hall.

"You needn't think, however – " here she smiled broadly – "that in announcing my resignation as

Warden you're going to get rid of me entirely. As a candidate for Mayor, I hope to bring a lot more to Rubytown than my little book of tickets. I hope I can count on your support – " she glared around, mock-fiercely – "or else! Enjoy yourselves! Good night and goodbye!"

She stood down in a storm of cheering. MapHead felt proud enough to burst his buttons off, except he didn't have any. Mayor Wellbeloved. It had a ring to it, like something that was meant to be.

Later: "I thought you might like this," said Mrs Wellbeloved to MapHead through the crush.

It was a ship in a bottle. A small, dimpled bottle with a fully-rigged clipper ship, storm-tossed on enamel waves inside. MapHead could make out every pin, every porthole, every twist in its fine cotton rigging. It was perfect.

"*Would I!*" said MapHead. "Thanks!"

"My father made it," said Mrs Wellbeloved. "It was his hobby."

MapHead examined the little ship; his own great-grandfather's ship. One thing puzzled him. "How did he get the ship through this bit?" He fingered the neck of the bottle. "It's too narrow. Look how tall the ship is."

Mrs Wellbeloved tapped the side of her nose knowingly. "Magic," she said.

"Oh," said MapHead, "right."

"I'm sorry I stepped on your model, Boothe."

"Forget it," said MapHead. "I have."

Then there was dancing! And flashing lights and cider, sweet as any tomato! And hot dogs, crisps and Coke! And Andy Steed's belching contest in the toilets with marvellously enhanced echo, and – yes – the man in the black shell-suit who'd asked his nan if she'd died yet, matching her step for step, under the lights on the dance floor. And Kay, with her white dress floating round her in a space that was all her own, beckoning MapHead to join her, to make the dream complete.

Mrs Wellbeloved's official traffic warden's hat travelled from head to head through the crowd and stopped at MapHead. He wore it at a rakish angle as he danced. And as he danced, the maps flowed rhythmically over his face and phased and melted with the music, and under the pulsing disco lights no one knew or cared; and the spirit of togetherness rushed through him. It was unlike anything he'd ever felt before.

Later, much later, MapHead stood cooling by the door. The party crowd had quartered, back inside. Mrs Cousins' mother had been spooned into a taxi. Andy Steed had gone home covered in Silly String an hour since.

For the first time he considered the long walk home. A very long walk, in fact. But Kay would take him, he knew. He only had to ask.

He wandered over to the main double doors. Nasty

orange streetlights lit the night outside. All along Fore Street the partygoers' cars waited rudely on double yellow lines. MapHead grinned. Hadn't the Warden resigned? There were no rules, tonight.

The chip shop opposite had locked its doors already. Already the deep dark chip fat was finger-cool in its fryers. The windows above the shops looked stonily down on the end of the Dream Party. MapHead watched the chip papers bowling down the road. He could even hear the little scraping sound they made. For some reason, it was a sad sound. His first and last party was very nearly over. He would remember it always.

There were voices round the corner. MapHead listened. After a minute or two, he listened a lot closer.

"Couldn't you stay a bit longer? The lad seems a little unstable."

Mr Bandy, surely.

"We'll be moving on soon, I'm afraid."

And Powers! Powers and Mr Bandy, outside the hall back door! MapHead crept to the corner's nose. It was a horrible combination.

"Forgive me if I'm speaking out of turn. But this business with his mother. It seems to be distressing him."

"His mother?"

"Kay Cooper. He says she's his mother, I think."

A long pause.

"It's none of my business, I know – " Mr Bandy,

softly this time – "but I was hoping to catch you tonight. You might want to take a look at this."

MapHead bobbed once round the corner. He bobbed back, his heart coursing wildly. He shut his eyes tight. Let the piece of paper not be what he knew it was.

"I want you to know," read Powers, "how much it hurts to leave…" He scanned the rest in silence. "Can I ask you where you got this?"

"He wrote it in his maths book. The day he – had the fit. I can only assume he intended me to read it. Perhaps to – say something for him."

A long silence. The bass-beat from the hall boomed dimly on the air. MapHead recalled his letter. "My mum is the same mum as Kenny's." What would Powers say next?

"Thank you for bringing it to my attention," said Powers stiffly. "I'm aware he wants to stay."

"I hope you'll consider it. In my experience, one thing children don't like is uncertainty."

"May I keep this letter?"

"Of course. You know, he's coming on famously at school. Particularly his history project. A natural historian."

"Yes. Very natural," said Powers.

"Well. I must get Mrs Bandy home. I'm glad we had this chat."

"So," said Powers, "am I."

MapHead froze. But Mr Bandy had dodged round

the back of the hall. MapHead watched him cross the car-park, his satin shirt tearing in the wind. Before he could make a move, Powers loomed in his face.

"Dad!"

"I came to collect you. I guessed where you were."

"I was just – cooling off. Brilliant party. You should've come too."

"I wish I had," said Powers.

"I'll just say cheerio."

MapHead said his goodbyes. Then they walked the length of Fore Street, past the sleeping shops. The party boom grew fainter as they went.

"Did you see Mr Bandy?" asked Powers.

MapHead swallowed. "He sang this song. You should've seen him, Dad."

"You heard him show me this letter." Powers brought it out. "Didn't you? MapHead. What have you done?"

"I thought we were going. I wouldn't've written it, else."

"You shouldn't have written it anyway." Powers looked grim. "On your own head be it."

MapHead thought about Mr Bandy. Then he thought about Kay. What might Mr Bandy say? What might she think when he had? He felt his head all over. There was plenty on it, all right. They walked on slowly together. They took the Stonewalls turn.

MapHead broke the silence. "You're all wet. Where've you been?"

"Radleigh Falls cascade. I had some thinking to do."

"Did you do it?"

"The thinking? I did."

MapHead crept his hand into Powers' own.

"Dad. You know I wouldn't leave you, don't you?"

"You wouldn't stay, if you could?"

MapHead shook his head. "It's just, I feel a bit lost sometimes."

Powers squeezed his hand. His son was Powers' only real connection to anything at all. A short while ago distrust had come between them. Now it had gone, he wasn't sure why. Powers struggled to express something he hardly understood himself.

"MapHead," he said. "Remember. There is no map of the heart."

# End of the Season

It wasn't any old glorious Sunday morning. It was the Sunday morning MapHead rubbed off all his hair. He was finished with hair. He was finished with school. Finished with just about everything. There was no uncertainty, now. Only the long bright future, drawing them on as always, somewhere the grass grew greener.

The tomatoes were finished with too. Down all the thundering great glasshouse the long plants lay in heaps. It was the end-of-season clear-out. The wires were down, the strings severed, the green tomatoes stripped. For the first time, the hot pipes were cold. Across the empty house the radio talked up Sunday, while the Sunday workers slogged.

The bags were packed, all two. Travel light, said Powers. That way you don't get stuck. To show he meant it, he set his old donkey jacket back on the pipes in the place he'd found it to begin with. They didn't need baggage and they didn't need favours.

What they did need was some kind of destination. Going anywhere was easy. The trick was, going somewhere you wanted. No guarantees, said Powers. They could fall anywhere at all. But he liked to have something to tilt at.

"Run me Dorset, will you?"

"Hang on," said MapHead, rubbing.

His hair fluffed off quite easily. Powers had zapped it a bit. It had never been proper hair, anyway. He piled it on a newspaper in front of him. He put his school shoes on top and folded the paper smartly. Then he looked around. The tip. The rubbish tip was good.

"What area?" he asked.

"Central southern," said Powers. "Dorchester over to Wimborne."

MapHead flashed up a standard Ordnance Survey, the breadth of his gleaming scalp. It felt good to be free in the air. Facemaps were half a job.

He phased around Maiden Castle. He brought up Badbury Rings; the ancient Cerne Abbas giant, its rude bits smack on his forehead. But Powers shook his head.

"Give me Wiltshire, will you?"

Mo rolled a wheelbarrow by. MapHead drew in his legs. They were high in the corner rock wool, but the work had a way of encroaching. Jan trawled the aisles nearby with a mighty brush and a shovel, collecting slime as she went. She heaped the rotting plants in horrendous fish-smelling piles that Mo would wheel to the tip.

Without warning her brush snapped. She considered the shaft, disgusted.

"Look at the point on that. Might've skewered myself."

"Nasty," said Mo, a bit green round the gills. "Brush in't up to it, really."

"I'm not up to it, either. I'm sickened with all this muck."

"Someone got to do it," said Mo. "Best get it over an' done."

Leaving her half-filled barrow, Mo met Jan in the aisle. Together they forced the muck into empty fertilizer sacks. The radio sang them "Wonderful World" as they did it.

MapHead nipped swiftly down. He tucked his newspaper bundle deep in the stuff in the barrow. Then he nipped back onto the rock wool. He flashed up central Wiltshire. He tracked across it, slowly. Stonehenge, Avebury – Warminster.

"Stop," said Powers. "I like it. Give me a larger scale."

They settled on Avebury stone circles. They would aim wide and hope for the best. Powers made his calculations. The ley lines would pull them west. He would compensate for the drag with a fix on the stones themselves. Plenty of Subtle World pull on those frowsy old pagan stumps. MapHead sorted his school books. His jotter would fit in his bag, along with his ship in a bottle. Pity about the Romans Timeline. No way would that go in. He would cut out the drawings, at least.

Mo tracked out with the rubbish. After a while she tracked back. She biffed the wheelbarrow down.

"What d'you make of these?" She held up MapHead's school shoes.

Jan looked up. "Good pair of shoes, they are."

"I found 'em in the barrow. Just now, when I tipped it out. I never put 'em in."

Jan pipe-hopped down the aisle. She took the shoes from Mo.

"They must've been in the tip. Not bad though, are they, for that?"

"They weren't in the rubbish tip. They were in newspaper in the stuff I emptied out. You put anything in newspaper in the wheelbarrow?"

"No," said Jan. "I didn't."

They looked at the shoes. They looked at each other. Then Mo peeled off her gloves.

"That does it," she said. "I'm off. This greenhouse gives me the creeps."

"Almost five to, anyway. We could just finish up."

Mo jammed her flask into her bag. She unhitched her coat from its post. "Finish up tomorrow. There's somethin' about this house."

"I know what you mean," said Jan, looking around nervously. "Times I've been here on my own – I've felt like a presence or something. Like, you're not on your own at all."

Mo shuddered. She flipped the radio off at the plug. "It dun't do to think about it too much. Got your stuff? Come on."

They left the tools awry and boomed the doors behind them. MapHead watched them wonderingly up the track through the glass. He'd had no idea his school shoes could have such a startling effect.

Powers produced two Danish pastries. They ate them slowly. Then they split a bottle of French dressing between them. The acids would have, said Powers, a unique effect on the gut.

That afternoon, the last afternoon, they strolled up on Parkway Knoll. Then MapHead saw the place – the very, very place – where lightning had struck his parents, almost thirteen years before. He lay on the spot and absorbed it. When he was good and finished, they toiled to the top together. Small children in winter-red hats screamed around the slopes. Denim couples walked their floppy dogs. Older, greyer couples strolled off their Sunday lunch. Grandparents watched at the viewpoint, snug in their cars, their Prazey Savers tartan-effect car rugs not quite as warm as they'd thought.

Powers looked down on the clustered town below. All the pity he felt welled in his heart and his throat. They struggled their best down below, and they worked and they worked and they worked. And all for such a small, hard-tried-for bit of joy, it would hardly fill the cracks in his teeth. Not for them, the tearing thrill of the travelling life. Not for them, the brilliant field of joy that lit its sudden reaches. Not for them, uncertainty, bitter-cold nights, and the bitterer bile of leaving – not for the people below. But for us, thought Powers. For us.

# A Family Again

"Now?" asked MapHead.

"Now," said Powers. "If not now, then never."

It was Sunday midnight at Ruggy Lane. Round the side of the cottage a fox tugged the dustbins. Next door's demented black rabbit jumped and thumped in its hutch. A young hedgehog snaffled bread beneath the bird table. Fieldmice squeaked in the hedge. Powers and MapHead took stock of the patio doors. Everywhere, mischief was afoot.

The rotary washing line dripped quietly onto its peg bag. The lawn around it, the privet hedge, the conifer trees in a heap in the corner, shone ghostly under the stars – under Ursa Minor with its Pole Star and the question-mark Plough; under Pisces and Cassiopeia; under Sirius, brightest of all. The whole great family of winter constellations shone down on MapHead's head.

Powers narrowed his eyes. "That's it, I think," he said.

132

MapHead tried the patio doors. That was it, right enough. Powers had agitated the molecules enough to turn ten patio door locks to putty.

MapHead loomed in the night kitchen. The silent hob would challenge him if it could, the kettle and teapot cry, Stop! Who goes there? Friend or foe? Only me, thought MapHead, as he passed by the cupboard where the red umbrella lay. Friend, or didn't you know?

He took the dark stairs brashly two at a time. His long-neglected night vision was sharpening by the moment. He reached the top. He hesitated. Left or right for Kay? The door on the left, of course. But first, he'd try the others.

Powers composed himself outside. He straightened his suit of silver, fantastic under the starlight. Of course he would wear it for the meeting. Why ever, he wondered, had MapHead begged him not to? What had he meant: Please, Dad, don't wear it, it makes you look like an alien? He simply looked the way he'd looked some thirteen years ago, when he'd first met MapHead's mother. That was the whole point. What could be alien about that?

Inside the sleeping house MapHead entered the bedroom. A tiny bedroom, filled with shattering snores. A glittering orange wig surprised him on its stand by the mirror. MapHead grinned. He crept to the bed and kissed his nan on the top of her stubbly head. He wouldn't be seeing her again. Her snores rumbled on. Already her hair was growing. With luck, it would be back how it was by the time she got to be mayor.

He opened the next door along. This time the bedroom was larger, and filled with twice as much stuff. Piles of Kenny-type stuff, one thing on top of another.

He crossed the debris-strewn floor. A mobile tickled his head. Kenny was sleeping half in, half out of his duvet, his arms flung extravagantly wide. MapHead brought out the note he'd written earlier and searched for a place to put it. There were plenty of places all right, but none that Kenny might notice. It was very important he noticed. "Meet me up the tomato farm eight-thirty this morning," said the note. "Be there or be sorry. Maps."

It was half-term holiday tomorrow. Kenny could meet him, he knew. In the end he drank the water in the glass by Kenny's bed. Then he popped the note inside the empty glass. Kenny'd have to be thick not to see.

MapHead crept away across the landing. There was only one bedroom to go. His mother's room was cool and vaguely scented. He paused awhile at the door. He called up everything he had. Then he sent it out.

One minute, two minutes – three. Suddenly she stirred. MapHead took four measured steps. Kay sat straight up in bed.

"Kenny? Is that you?"

MapHead said nothing at all. That wasn't the way it worked. Come on, Mum, he beckoned. Come on, come on, come on.

She rose like a dreamer and followed. It was just as simple as that. Simple to guide her down the stairs tagging hold of her funny pyjamas, simple to ghost her down the hall past the clock telling twenty past twelve, simple to bring her, dreamily, out under all the bright stars. And not so simple after that.

"Ran," said Kay, using the name she remembered. "Is it you?"

Powers rose. "Kay. It's been a long time."

The mad black rabbit grew quiet in its hutch next door. The fox in the dustbins fled. No one said anything at all. You could, thought MapHead, have heard a whisker drop.

MapHead took his mother's hand. Then he took his father's. He looked up at both of them, and knew, at last, where he came from.

Powers stirred. "This," he said, "is MapHead."

Kay smiled. "MapHead isn't a name."

"Kay," said Powers. "Recollect." And he used his eyes a little.

Kay drew MapHead close. She held his face in her hands. "It isn't – is it?" she whispered. "It is. It really is."

But MapHead pulled away. "Why did you leave me?" he asked. "You didn't have to go." Her dreaming face looked troubled. "It was better I went before you knew."

"But why?" persisted MapHead. "How *could* you go and leave?"

"How could I, Ran?" she asked.

"Because," said Powers firmly, "you wanted the old life back."

"You could've taken me with you," MapHead accused her. "I could've come back and been here."

Powers shook his head. "Then you'd have asked *me* why I left you."

"But why can't we all be together?"

Powers smiled. "We are."

Kay smoothed Powers' head. MapHead boggled. How did she dare? Then she smoothed his own. She wrapped her arms warm around him. This time he didn't draw back. Her pyjamas smelled so good.

"Let's all go travelling like we used to," she said. "Take us travelling, Ran."

"I've made no calculations." It was Powers' turn to look troubled. "Anything could happen."

"*I'll* take us travelling," said MapHead. "Hold hands together. I *can*."

His parents watched him proudly. MapHead leaned on everything he'd learned; Nemo's World, and Raptor's – the sacrifice he'd made. He drew deep on the power he'd won at the chariot races, and deeper still on the melting feeling when his mother held him close. Then he lit up like a comet, engulfing them all in light.

# Into the Emerald Forest

They walked together in a deep and greenish place. The rotting trunks of fallen trees covered the ground, thick with ferns and palms, trailing plants and fungi. There were no flowers on the gloomy forest floor. Only the sunny upper layers showed brilliant forest blooms.

A family party of colobus monkeys leapt screaming through the trees. MapHead looked up. Where the monkeys beat their chest… I know this place, thought MapHead. This deeply greenish place with its hot moist breath of trees. Powers and Kay trod softly on through the gloom. They were deep in the emerald forest.

Powers scrolled rapidly through what he knew. It wasn't much. "In equatorial forests the sun rises quickly and is high in the heavens during most of the twelve hours of daylight.

"Rainfall may be as much as a hundred inches in a year."

"Look," said Kay. "What's that?"

Something with a little pinched face and bright eyes startled away in the leaf-mould.

"The royal antelope," recited Powers, "a deer-like creature with a body only a foot long, is among the smaller forest beasts."

The forest was surprisingly silent. Only the calls of vivid macaws shattered the cathedral quiet. The deep gloom lightened as they entered a clearing. MapHead sized it up.

"It's perfect. We could build a hut here an' plant stuff an' all live together, couldn't we, Dad?"

Powers looked dubious. "It'd take a bit of doing."

"We could search for fruit like the monkeys," said Kay vaguely. "And hunt things, I suppose."

Powers considered the clearing. All around loomed buttressed cottonwoods and mahoganies, throwing their canopies over a hundred metres to the sky. Already the clearing was latticed with small banana plants and treeferns, fighting each other for sunlight.

Powers held up his hand. "There's a river. Hear it?"

They walked on, following the sound. The cottonwoods gave way to raffia palms, the raffia palms to mangroves. The forest floor grew spongy. The river surprised them when they found it. A tributary, said Powers, of something mightier still. They didn't mind the black mud. They didn't mind the tangled mass of twisted mangrove stems. What they did mind was crocodiles.

138

The deep pool they bathed in had none. Powers had seen to that. He'd zapped its banks until the water steamed. Even so, MapHead must stay in plain view. He must not lie on the bottom out of sight on any account, was he listening?

"Do as your father says," said Kay primly – so MapHead splashed her all over. Kay splashed him back. Then they both splashed Powers.

They lay on the rocks a long while, drying off. Then they wandered slowly back to the clearing. Time seemed to stretch endlessly behind and before them.

Kay knelt beside a huddle of banana plants. They were hopelessly congested in their fight for the sun; only one would survive. With a struggle, she tore one up. She looked around thoughtfully.

"Over here, I think. Want to give me a hand?"

MapHead did. He found a stick, and together they lifted the rest. Kay laid them out in rows. "This can be the garden," enthused MapHead. "Then there's room for the hut over there."

Powers watched disapprovingly. "It's not a suitable environment. Malaria, yellow fever – tsetse fly. You've no idea."

After a while he wandered off and left them to it. Angry clouds began to gather with astonishing speed overhead. MapHead and Kay worked quickly. Already twelve small bananas made an orderly row.

"Pass me that one, Kenny," said Kay, absorbed in what she was doing.

MapHead passed her a plant. He overlooked her mistake, though it cut him deep as a knife. He scraped out a hole for the next plant, unearthing all kinds of blind and nameless creatures as he dug. Something white and worm-like wriggled on his wrist. He flicked it off and wiped his forehead with his arm. Sticky heat smothered him like a mask.

"Well," said Kay, surveying the little garden, "it's a start."

"I like gardening, do you like gardening?" asked MapHead.

"Sometimes," said Kay, "but I'm lazy."

"Mothers aren't lazy," said MapHead, surprised. "Mothers do everything."

"I've not been a mother to you."

"No," said MapHead hollowly. "I missed you."

She covered his hand with hers. "Can't we be friends instead?"

"I've got a friend," said MapHead.

Kay smiled. "Perhaps you could use more than one."

MapHead looked at his mother's hand on his. There were no rings upon it at all. It was a hand to be proud of, all the same; a hard-work hand roughened with use, with short, no-nonsense nails. It was a hand that had washed up and cooked and cleaned and ironed tirelessly in its time. But not for him. Coldly, he withdrew his own.

"Anyway," he said, "I don't even know who you are."

"No," said Kay. "I suppose you don't." She sat back and looked at him. "Well, let's see ... my favourite meal's a good curry, my favourite drink is ... coffee, lashings of it. I play netball once a week. Wing Defence, in the mothers' team at school. I like summer evenings – that golden light you get? – and dogs, I like dogs a lot, especially boxers. I like swimming. I like having the house to myself when everyone's gone out. I like Black Forest Gateau when I can get it, sleeping in, clothes that make you look slim – and I hate coat hangers. I've only to touch something in a shop and it falls on the floor." She paused, breathless. "And I like travelling. And reading."

MapHead quickened. "So do I. You know *The Snow Queen*? Where Gerda rescues Kay?"

"I do, but I can't really remember what happens."

"He's forgotten everything, see, and she rescues him. When they meet he cries out the old ice splinter that's made him forget. An' they go home together after years an' years away, and everything's all right."

Kay looked steadily at MapHead. What a strange boy he was – she hadn't realized how strange.

"'Only one alteration could they find,'" recited MapHead softly, "'and that was in themselves, for they saw that they were now full-grown persons.'"

"And you're – how old now? Twelve?" asked Kay, after a pause.

"Almost twelve and a quarter."

There was a long silence. MapHead looked into the

hole he'd just dug. He wished he could lose himself in it.

"I'm dreaming," said Kay. "I dreamed I had you. Now I'm dreaming you've come back."

"No," said MapHead. "I *have*."

"How can we make this right?" asked Kay brokenly.

MapHead shrugged. "We can't. I shouldn't have happened, that's all."

"Don't say that," said Kay. "It's important you happened, like – like a bridge or something."

"A bridge?"

"You know." Kay looked around. The dreaming trees hung heavy behind her.

"Between all this – and everyday stuff."

MapHead followed her eyes. "This *is* everyday stuff."

"Not for me," said Kay. "That's the whole point."

MapHead digested what she'd said. It seemed to make a kind of sense. Suddenly he saw how he fitted in more naturally than Powers ever would.

"Hey," he grinned, "I'm a bridge."

Kay watched his thoughts chasing one another over his open face. What a simple soul he was. She wished she could fix everything as easily.

"I wish," she said, "I wish…"

"Wish what?"

"I wish we could go home together like the people in the story."

"I don't mind that," said MapHead. "I know we can't, but…"

"What?"

MapHead searched her eyes. "Oh, you know," he said.

Kay stroked his cheek tenderly. It was a motherly gesture not lost on MapHead. "Yes," she said. "I know."

A sudden crash behind them brought them both to their feet. MapHead dropped the stick he'd been digging with. Kay took a grip on hers. It was incredible, but – she measured the distance between it and them in the time it took to register the leopard eyeing them steadily from a distance of several metres.

"Is it real?" whispered Kay.

"You better believe it," hissed MapHead. It's a big 'un, all right, he thought stupidly. Sixty or seventy kilograms, at least. Were he and Kay larger than the sort of thing it usually ate? Or were they just about the right size? He had a feeling he might find out at any moment.

"Keep still," said Kay. "Don't move."

The leopard flattened itself in a sinister way. Its skin rippled. It was a gorgeous velvet of golden browns and umbers charged with intricate black spots. The tip of its tail twitched, ever so slightly. It bared its teeth soundlessly. Then it cussed them deep in its chest with a horrible hiss like a dozen bus doors opening.

Trees were the thing, thought MapHead vacantly. Except that leopards were excellent climbers, trees were favourite. The leopard's eyes flashed red in the gloom. It approached with infinite stealth.

Suddenly the rain broke. Droplets the size of grapes plashed heavily everywhere at once. The leopard batted an ear, but its stare was unwavering. The rainstorm rushed through the forest behind it, reaching the clearing, smashing the banana plants flat. The leopard gathered itself and sprang.

There was something, thought MapHead disinterestedly, not quite right in the way it leapt. Something not altogether leopard-like in the way it flopped at their feet and wrestled with itself. Something strangely familiar in the way its skin seemed to boil and grow silver as the rain smashed down on it and them alike. Wake up, he told himself. Do something. A boiling leopard. Some kind of nightmarish thingummyniggle. Whatever it is, wake up!

"Come on!" cried MapHead. "Run!"

Pulling Kay after him, he made for the edge of the clearing. They plunged and tore through the trees in a horrible panic, taking any and every direction, any place a nightmare wasn't. When at last they stopped for breath under the shelter of the canopy, Powers was close behind them. He was even more breathless than they were. He looked, thought MapHead, strangely ruffled. At least there was no sign of the leopard. He crouched to check through the undergrowth. Nope. Not a whisker. Nothing but the sound of the howling rain in the treetops. It was funny how he hadn't been afraid at the time. Not really. For some reason.

"It can't work," Powers was saying. "Can't you see?"

"It could," said Kay, "if you wanted. It could work."

"You'd want Kenny here as well."

"I could get him."

"How would he take to all this?" asked Powers. "You know it's too strange for Kenny. And anyway, where would we live?"

"The leaf stalks of the raffia palm are used for hut-building and its leaves for thatch," MapHead piped up helpfully.

"Can't you see how dangerous it is here?" continued Powers. "What about that leopard?"

"Leopards don't let you know they're coming." Kay folded her arms. "Leopards are sneaky."

"Get off it, Dad," said MapHead. "That leopard stuff was over the top."

Powers stood on his dignity. He brushed a bit of forest floor off his crumpled silver suit. "I'm taking us back," he said. "And that's the way it is."

"It's not that simple," said Kay.

"Yes," said Powers, "it is. You've got your son. I've got mine."

"No, you haven't," said MapHead. "No one's got me. I've got myself."

Powers turned. "You've got yourself?"

MapHead drew himself up. "Don't you *know*? Can't you *see*? I'm not a little kid any more. No one's got me, because *I've got myself*."

Kay looked at MapHead and understood. "Yes," she nodded. "I do believe you have."

Powers searched his son's face. It was true. It had happened just as he'd hoped. MapHead had found his way, just as he himself had at twelve. Soon he would find where it led. Powers could only hope it lay along with his own. If it didn't, he would soon lose a son to the travelling life. But in any case, his, Powers', job was almost done.

"Thanks, Kay." Powers allowed himself the widest of smiles. "He's grown up a lot since he's met you."

"What did I do?" said Kay. "It wasn't me who did it."

"You," said Powers, kissing her hand. "All you."

"My strange navigator," said Kay softly.

"You two," said MapHead, "break it up." For some reason, they weren't listening. He tried again.

"What's your favourite film, then?" he asked Kay abruptly.

Kay thought. It was a test. She had to get it right. She looked to Powers for help. Powers looked steadily back. Then he winked. Something flickered through Kay's mind. A fleeting inspiration. For some reason, she was thinking about...

"Romans," said Kay. "My favourite film is – *Ben Hur*."

"Outstanding," grinned MapHead. That was the clincher, all right.

They made a tight triangle, the three of them. They fitted together like a jigsaw. From this moment on they would be entire, no matter where the pieces fell.

"Perhaps," said Kay, "you'd better take us home."

Powers nodded to MapHead. "Whenever you're ready."

"Not home," corrected MapHead, "just back."

"Don't you mind not having a proper home?"

"No," said MapHead firmly. "I like travelling. And I'm going to do a lot more. I'm going to go everywhere and see everything. And then I'm going to think about it all."

"All in good time," said Powers.

"And when are you going to start on this great expedition?" laughed Kay.

MapHead spread his arms. "Hey," he said, "I've started."

At last they all joined hands. MapHead centred himself for travelling. It was funny, he knew how to do it. Perhaps he'd known all along. There was nothing at all he couldn't do. For the first time, he saw what it was to be as limitless as Powers.

*Will I see you again?* Kay asked, at the last, with her eyes.

*In your dreams*, answered MapHead, with his.

He watched her steadily until the moment they left. He wanted to keep the moment, always. The emerald forest behind her with its shimmering rain-drenched trees, the collar of her funny blue pyjamas and the way it poked up in her hair – these were things he would never forget if he sat in a thousand rainstorms.

"Hold on to your hat!" cried Powers.

"I love you, Mum!" cried MapHead.

"Love you too!" sang the air as he closed his eyes.

He gripped her hand. He turned up the heat. The emerald forest was history.

# Breakfast With
# Mr Bandy

Monday morning dawned bright as a brass button. At seven-thirty precisely, MapHead turned in at the drive.

Mr Bandy's house was an old Victorian red brick job, mock-Tudor gable ends and all. A large hydrangea wilted in a pot at the front door. Already the first winter frost had nipped its acid-blue flowers.

MapHead collected himself. He would say goodbye, of course. Then he would tidy up. No loose ends, said Powers. Powers had looked at him sternly. Haven't you got some tidying up to do before we go? Oh, right, said MapHead. Mr Bandy. Mr Bandy was a loose end, all right.

MapHead lifted the brass knocker. He rapped smartly three times. He waited. He knocked again. And again, four times together. At last there was movement inside. Someone bumped down the stairs, approached the door – and opened it.

"Yes?" blinked Mr Bandy.

"It's Boothe," said MapHead. "We're leaving at nine o'clock this morning. I came to say goodbye."

Mr Bandy wrapped his striped towelling dressing-gown tighter. He ran his hand through his hair. He looked a bit like a soft toy discovered behind the cupboard after years of fluff and neglect.

"You're an early bird." Mr Bandy peered at MapHead dimly. "What's happened to your hair?"

"Oh, that. I rubbed it off."

"You rubbed it off? But why?"

MapHead shrugged. "Don't need it where I'm going."

"Where *are* you going, Boothe?"

MapHead shrugged again. "Somewhere I don't need hair."

Mr Bandy wiped his eyes. It was one of those perplexing exchanges. This child, he thought – what *is* it about this child?

"So. Would you like to come in and have a cup of tea? Mrs Bandy's asleep, I'm afraid." MapHead followed Mr Bandy into his kitchen. It was a small, old-fashioned kitchen covered in unfriendly-looking white tiles. MapHead sat at the table. It held a salt and pepper set, a Sunday paper from the day before, a few fraying raffia place mats and not a lot else. Mr Bandy yawned shatteringly. He filled the kettle and clicked it on. He brought out cups and plates. He seemed to have forgotten about MapHead altogether.

"You were brilliant at the party," said MapHead,

toying with the salt and pepper. "I didn't know you could sing."

Mr Bandy winked. "Neither did I. Fancy a boiled egg?"

"Yeh, please," said MapHead, willing to try anything once. "Thanks."

Mr Bandy clapped a pan on the work surface. He shushed himself with his finger. "Mustn't wake Eileen. Five-minute egg all right?"

"Fine," said MapHead, mystified.

Mr Bandy filled the pan from the kettle. He popped in the eggs and set the heat. "I'll just dash some water in my face," he said. "Won't be a tick. Mind the eggs?"

MapHead watched them knocking together in the pan. He hoped he'd like bald eggs. He wasn't sure he would. He hoped he was minding them right.

Mr Bandy reappeared. He'd pulled on a lumpy tracksuit. He glanced at the clock. "Just in time," he said.

He spooned out the eggs and they sat down together at the table. MapHead looked at his egg. He watched Mr Bandy decapitate his. He took up his knife. Sitting in its little blue cup, the egg looked so exactly like the top of his own head, it made him feel rather strange. He set down his knife and coughed.

"What?" asked Mr Bandy, through a mouthful of egg-top.

"I don't think I like bald eggs."

"Here," said Mr Bandy. He leaned over and

whipped the top off MapHead's egg, quick as a wink. The inside looked quite appealing.

"Soldiers?" asked Mr Bandy.

MapHead looked blank. Mr Bandy showed him. "You dip 'em in your egg. Like this." MapHead dipped and ate. It was really rather good.

"Don't you – " asked Mr Bandy – "don't you have boiled eggs at home?"

MapHead shook his head. "We just crack 'em and drink 'em down."

"You just," repeated Mr Bandy, "drink them down." He wiped his mouth. "You have tea, I suppose?"

"Course we do," said MapHead. "When the boiler's up."

Mr Bandy changed the subject. He couldn't face the boiler.

"So. How do you feel about leaving?"

"OK," said MapHead. "Thanks."

"But I thought you wanted to stay."

"I did, but now I don't. Now I want to travel everywhere and see everything."

Mr Bandy smiled over his teacup. "Perhaps you'll visit Rome one day."

"Rome for starters," said MapHead happily. "Then the rest."

MapHead washed his soldiers down with tea. He hadn't realized how hungry he was. He hadn't had anything much to eat since the Danish pastry and French dressing yesterday lunchtime. Anyway. Bald eggs were a lot nicer than ordinary ones. He took another slice of bread.

Mr Bandy joined his fingertips. "I'll be giving Little John to Andy Steed, as you suggested in your letter. I think he'll make a decent stab at it."

"Yes," said MapHead. "My letter."

"You know, Boothe," said Mr Bandy, looking sky-wards, "I was really very flattered you wrote me that…" A blank look came over his face. "What are we talking about?"

"The weather," said MapHead. "Nice day."

"Oh, right," said Mr Bandy. "I hope it is. Let's take a look, shall we?"

He got up, rubbing his head. On his way over to the window he bumped into a chair and knocked himself on the edge of the drawer. He looked, thought MapHead, more than a little forgetful. Now all the loose ends were tied. Mr Bandy would remember nothing about his letter, nor what it had said about who his mother was. He was nicely tidied all right.

Mr Bandy drew back the kitchen curtains. The eight o'clock day flooded in.

"Oh," said MapHead, jumping up. "There's some-one I've got to meet."

"Well," said Mr Bandy. "I'd better show you out."

MapHead followed Mr Bandy to the front door. He was going a bit bald himself, noticed MapHead. A lit-tle, on the top of his head. How old was Mr Bandy, anyway?

"Take care of yourself now, won't you?" said Mr Bandy on the doorstep. "Come back and see us one day."

"No way to stop me," grinned MapHead. "Thanks for breakfast."

Then he kissed Mr Bandy on the ear. He'd meant to kiss him on the cheek, but for some reason Mr Bandy had flinched at the vital moment.

Halfway down the drive, MapHead turned. Mr Bandy was still at the door, rubbing his ear thoughtfully. With his other hand, he waved. "Goodbye, Boothe."

"Are you seventy or something?" called MapHead.

"No, Boothe, I'm not seventy or something. I'm forty-two at Christmas."

"I hope I know as much as you do when I'm forty-two," called MapHead.

Mr Bandy smiled. "I hope you know more," he said.

# MapHead and Kenny Together

MapHead hurried back. All the way up through the woods he wondered if Kenny'd be there. Would he've seen the note by his bed? Would he've even woken up in time? Half-term was, after all, half-term.

No worries, thought MapHead. Soon as he crested the rise he spotted Kenny on the bottom hedge. Good old Kenny. Not for the first time, MapHead felt good-bye sitting heavy on his heart. The rusty clock in the packing shed told eight thirty-five exactly. He had twenty-five minutes left. They would leave from the centre of the far field on the stroke of nine. But Powers, he knew, would wait. One day soon he would-n't have to. MapHead had come of age. This journey, they both knew, was simply the first of all the journeys that would come after, not all of them together.

The ducks scattered as he ran down the track. The peacocks flustered two separate ways in their panic to avoid him. He looked round. They came together again as though joined by an invisible rubber band. They watched him run on, incuriously.

"Kenny!" called MapHead. "Hey, Kenny!"

Kenny looked round. He cradled MapHead's black kitten in his arms. He'd been smoothing it a good ten minutes.

"What's with the dome?" boggled Kenny.

MapHead smoothed his head. "Better for maps," he said.

Kenny rolled his eyes. "Radical. So where were you? I got here twenty-five past."

"Saying goodbye," huffed MapHead, hauling up beside him. "We're leaving nine o'clock sharp. That's why I left you the note."

"Did you give it my mum to give me?"

MapHead nodded. "Hey, Shakey. Let's have 'im a bit now, can I?"

MapHead took the kitten. It was reluctant to leave Kenny's lap, but he smoothed it content with long and knowing strokes. Something else, thought MapHead, to miss in the cold of the night. Along with everything else.

"So why've you got to go?"

MapHead shrugged. "My dad's got things to do. We always move on somewhere else."

Kenny fell silent.

"Hey, I'll be back," said MapHead.

"Yeh?"

"One day, for sure. Wait up."

Kenny brightened a little. "Should've seen my place this morning."

"Oh," said MapHead. "Why's that?"

"My mum wakes up like, soakin' wet and muddy, says she had this dream she was plantin' stuff in the jungle. My nan goes, Kay, look outside! An' guess what?"

"What?"

"You know them conifer trees in the corner? My mum's been goin' to do a hedge with? They're all like, planted all over the grass in rows an' stuff – all over the middle of the lawn, an' the lawn's dug up – some mess! My nan goes, look at the state of your hands. Look at the state of the garden. You mean to say you got up an' did all this in your sleep?"

MapHead started laughing. It was all so near the knuckle. So shallow, yet so deep. So funny, so not-funny. So very, very Powers.

"Then," said Kenny, cracking up himself, "my mum goes, I think I must've. My nan goes, you want to see a psychiatrist, you do. My mum's laughin' – she can't stop. She looks out the window, she goes, it's not bad, I rather like it. And she's laughin' an' stuff, an' my nan starts up, an' we're all laughin' like mad—"

Kenny was killing himself. He could hardly get the words out.

"Anyway," he finished, catching breath. "Then Mum goes, it's funny, I'm really like, peaceful inside. I haven't felt so good in a long while. I'll have to do

157

more of my gardening at night. You do, says Nan, an' I'll send you up the funny farm." Kenny shook his head. "Some crack it was, I'm tellin' you."

MapHead wiped his eyes. Had he been laughing or crying? It was funny and painful in equal parts – like all the best things, he guessed. But funny, sad or indifferent, time was ticking away.

"What time is it now?" he asked.

Kenny checked his watch. "Twenty to, just gone."

MapHead cleared his throat. "Want to see the Green Mantles? The real Circus Maximus? I can take you there if you want."

"How'd you mean – take me?"

"I've got twenty minutes. I'll take you to the chariot races if you like, I can."

"Yeh," said Kenny, "but how?"

"The thing is," said MapHead carefully, "the thing is, you can do anything you want to, *if* you want to enough. But it's cruel and bloody," he warned.

"I don't care, I want it," said Kenny. "Anything?"

MapHead nodded. "Anything at all. But you've got to close your eyes."

Already it seemed to Kenny he heard the drumming of hoofs; the clash at the turn, the thunderous surge of the crowd.

"Hear it?" said MapHead.

"*Do* I!" said Kenny.

They joined hands. Kenny took a deep breath. Then he closed his eyes.

# MAPHEAD 2

"Our deepest fear is not that we are inadequate.
Our deepest fear is that we are powerful
beyond measure."

*~ Nelson Mandela*

# Up the Multi

MapHead stepped out of a ball of light and removed a tadpole thoughtfully from his mouth. He looked around as the glow settled slowly around him. At least he'd landed the right way up. The sign overhead told him that much.

LEVEL A, said the sign. MAXIMUM HEADROOM 2M(6FT) MULTI-STOREY CAR PARK – CARE WHEN ENTERING.

There wasn't a lot else to see. Gloom. Concrete pillars stretching away into darkness. Orange box-lights overhead. And cars. Lots and lots of cars. One car had voices inside it. MapHead pricked up his ears.

"What *is* it? An' I want to *know*!" The little boy in the blue car was pointing right at him. "Looka that thing over there!"

"Maxie, belt up." The boy's mother started the engine. The blue car grunted and roared.

"It's a *big* light, glowin' or something. An' I'm goin' to *zap* it, I am."

163

"Got your seat-belt done up? I'm not sure you've done it properly." Maximillian's mother fiddled with Maximillian's seat-belt. Then she looked up and saw the light. *"What in the world—?"*

A boy in wet trousers in a bursting ball of brilliance. That was what it was. A bright – a *very* bright – light. A boy bursting out of it, glowing gently, and – waving. At Maxie. In the multi-storey car park. Over SuperFare. On a Tuesday. The strange boy waved again. The grim-looking orange box-lights lit up the top of his head. A bald head, swimming with lines.

"I'm waving at him, I am." Maxie waved back. "An' he's *funny*, he is. Why is that boy funny?"

"Beats me. I expect it's a trick, don't you?" Maximillian's mother whitened, straightened, and suddenly pulled away. The Volvo jumped across E deck and nosed down the exit ramp. She eyed her mirror anxiously. The apparition – whatever it was – waved to them all the way. Maxie waved back as they took the ramp, craning out of his seat-belt to the last.

"An' I want to come back an' see him! An' he'll be here *next* time we come."

"We can hope."

She was brushing him off, Maxie knew. He watched her face in the mirror. When the sunshine flooded in at the exit where the money slotted into the ticket machine, his mother's face relaxed.

"I don't like these multi-storeys much, do you?" She put on a smile that said *Phew*. "Let's have some lunch.

164

Like to stop at Pizza King?"

When the exit ramp had finally swallowed the waving boy in the car, MapHead dropped his hand and grinned. How nice people were. How friendly. It was only a shame they had had to hurry away. There were one or two things he wouldn't have minded asking the friendly looking boy in the car. Now he would have to find out for himself how things had changed.

The dimpled concrete ceiling of the multi-storey car park stretched away in the gloom. LEVEL E, said a bunch of big black letters. MapHead shook some pond-gravel out of his trousers. He should've known better than to kick off out of a pond. There were always going to be problems with gravel and tadpoles. It was just that it had come upon him so *suddenly*. One minute he was taking time out at the bottom of a deep and secret pool in southern Greece, the next he was thinking, *Rubytown*. No sooner thought than done. Not like before. Before he'd learned travelling properly, anything might have happened.

MapHead licked his pond-tasting lips. A drink would go down well. Olive oil, French dressing, anything. Where to get one? MapHead sighed. Things had changed a lot since he'd last visited Rubytown. *He'd* changed a lot since he'd last visited Rubytown. No Dad, no Mum, no traffic warden, instead a hulking great-big sandwich of a car park like nothing you ever saw *in* space or out of it. Glowing orange box-lights. Petrol smells and shoppers. Strange marching letters ballooning over the walls. Someone had been busy with a spray can. MapHead frowned. Someone who couldn't – didn't – spell very well at all.

BUZ N'AG - bAck by yooR demand

biG shout 2 - niK * Biz * CJ * mArkey * pEtE

SEE ya! wouLdn't like 2 B U wHen the trifs BeAt yA! revenge is sweet - BS.

What did it all mean? MapHead read the messages over and over. After a while his thoughts wandered. He'd been away. It was natural to find things confusing when he came back. MapHead travelled in bursts of light from one place to another, mostly in the spaces in between places and things, a subtle world where ghosts milled and slack dimensions shifted. The obvious world of people, places and things made up everything you could touch and see and taste. The Subtle World made up all the things you couldn't.

MapHead sat on a car and thought it over. How long had he been away? In subtle time, a lifetime. In real time a year, maybe two. The car park was a funny place to pop up in. But it could have been a whole lot worse. He might have turned up anywhere. Better, by far, in a dim concrete sandwich filled with cars than in the middle of a field with either foot in a cow-pat – or worse, the sewage farm. Even the *best* fix on Rubytown might have left him upside down in the cake shop, or wearing a hanging basket for a hat. He might have ended up in the dentist's chair just as he brought down his drill. In a maths exam. Under a bus. On top of a bus. Inside a cow. Up a chimney. Down the pub. Half undressed in Woollie's Pik 'n' Mix. MapHead thought about all the awkward and unpleasant places he might have materialized in and then felt glad he hadn't. Luck, of course, came into it. But he was getting better, he knew.

aeROSOL DEMOnS – THE
Stoned Triffidz say Chill

bIG ShoUt 2 – ALL thAt Know mE.
aRt not vANdalism – ReSPeKt

Who *were* the Stoned Triffidz, wondered MapHead. He hadn't known they existed before he read their name on the multi wall. He might never hear of them again in his life. Or there again, he might. That was the joy of travelling. Anything could happen.

Greece had been good. Especially the journey out. MapHead grinned, remembering the round O mouths of the aeroplane passengers when he'd waved to them from the wing of the 747. He hadn't been able to materialize too well, on account of they were tearing along at about five hundred miles an hour. Probably he looked pretty faint – it might have been just his smile, a bit like the cat from Cheshire in an Alice book he'd read. It would've been a whole lot easier *not* to have popped out of a sunburst of light on the wing of a jet plane to goosebump everyone in it, but MapHead couldn't resist it. Neither could most of the passengers. They goggled and pointed and steamed up the aeroplane windows. MapHead had grinned and waved. He guessed he beat the in-flight movie hands down for watchability.

Yet his father had warned him sternly not to do it. Things like boggling aeroplanes were strictly out of bounds. Powers had warned him about a lot of things before he'd left, mysteriously and finally, for a space of seven years. Not one day more, nor less. Seven years would pass, whether they wanted to or not. Then MapHead would see his father again. The meeting-place would be sent to him in a dream. A magic dream of his father. MapHead had better be ready. He'd better, warned Powers, be able to account for *anything and everything he'd done in this world or any other.* Powers' eyes had flashed dangerously. Power was responsibility. No taking advantage. Plus his task had better be done. Or MapHead would know all about it.

"All about what?" MapHead teased. He knew about joking now.

"All about the back of my hand."

"Yours and who else's?"

"The hand," said Powers fondly, "of the one who loves you best."

*The one who loves you best.* The sorry time of parting had come round more smartly than they knew. Now that the meaning of parting stood over them, deepening like a well, they had to go hollowly through it, MapHead knew, and come out again and go on. There had to be partings, as well as meetings. Without partings there could *be* no meetings. MapHead visualized his happy reunion with Powers in seven years' time. Then he blinked and said, "You know my task?"

"What about it?"

"I'll know when I find it, right?"

"Right."

"But why do I have to do it?"

"Because you're my MapHead, of course."

"But why?" MapHead persisted.

"You're thirteen. You've come of age." Powers gripped his son's mind with his. *"Power to move mountains is yours to do as you please with. What,"* Powers asked, *"will you do with it?"*

"Anything I like," MapHead returned happily.

"No," said Powers, "you won't. You don't understand. That's the point."

"The point of what?"

"Standing on your own two feet. I had a task once, too."

"You did?" MapHead swallowed. "What was it?"

"Something I never thought would happen to me. Something that made me what I am."

"What are you?"

"A space the winds howl in. A thing that flashes from place to place. An awful thing. A lonely thing. Until I met your mother."

"No need to be lonely."

"Yes," said Powers, "*there is*. I told you. You don't understand."

"My task." MapHead thought. "How will I know when I've done it?"

Powers smiled. His teeth gleamed. "Oh," he said, "you'll know."

MapHead flashed his feelings around his scalp with all the sorrowful-sounding placenames that he knew. Usually he displayed cheery, multicoloured maps over his bald and uneven head. That was being MapHead. Maps of Rome had been favourite – Rome had been home for a while before Greece – but maps of any place MapHead had ever seen or read about could suddenly light up his head with wiggly fjord coastlines or brimming inland seas, mainly whenever he was happy, and he almost always *was* happy. But now the mood was dreary. MapHead flashed up Sorrytown, God's Tears, Heartbreak Point, Port Regret, Meet-No-More and Cape Farewell. Placenames were poetry to MapHead. It was all the goodbye that he knew. Maps were so much easier than words. Words had a way of getting muddled, or meaning two things at once. MapHead sometimes got muddled with words. But not as much as he used to.

Love. Trust. My son. Powers covered MapHead's face

170

with his hand. Then he glowed and thrilled. The air grew thick and heavy and burst into silver light. MapHead opened his eyes at last. His father had gone, travelling in lightning time to some place in the Subtle World, that non-place of dreams and ghosts and visions that fitted like shrink-wrap round the world of *here* and *now*. For the first time since for ever, MapHead was alone. Seven years to prove himself, seven years to *be* as much as he could be. Seven years to find a task, a task that was MapHead's alone and might just prove as much as one lonely slaphead might have it in his empty heart to do. My funny heart, thought MapHead. My funny, empty heart.

MapHead stopped thinking when the car he was sitting on moved. The electric orange box-lights glowed, the car-deck stretched away. The woman with the trolleyload of shopping was busily transferring it to the car. That was the reason the car had moved. He hadn't seen her coming.

MapHead watched the woman incuriously as she filled up the boot with carrier bags. He watched her fish her baby out of the shopping trolley and strap it into the car. She didn't notice MapHead at all, because he didn't want her to. MapHead had a way of being invisible if he wanted. It was a *subtle* thing he'd learned.

The baby crowed in its seat as the woman finished up. MapHead felt sorry for the baby. For some reason its mother had strapped it into a seat facing the back of the car, so the baby couldn't see where it was going. It was a nice baby. Ruddy, with brilliant dark eyes and a fetching vermilion suit.

MapHead watched as the baby's mother delved finally into the boot. Then she clipped off with the trolley. He watched her park the trolley in the trolley park some little distance away where level E met the sun.

The baby crowed and pulled off a sock. It looked at MapHead, and MapHead let it see him. The baby stared, then chirruped, stuffing the sock in its mouth. *Bang – crash – clip – clip – clip –* it hadn't taken her long. Mrs Shoppingtrip had parked her trolley. She was heading back to the car. She would jump in and drive away with her baby and that would be just about that. *My funny, empty heart.* MapHead watched the baby suck its sock. The baby crooned to itself. Its mother approached at a fast rate of knots. The baby crooned and kicked. Something about the way the baby flailed its red-suited legs for joy tipped the balance in MapHead. He watched Mrs Shoppingtrip rooting in her pocket for her car keys. Then he ran a tape-loop in and over his head, considering the likely echoes, past and future, of the move he was about to make.

Mrs Shoppingtrip ducked into her car and started it up. At almost the same moment MapHead slipped softly into the seat beside the baby.

EXIT RAMP AHEAD said the sign, as they spiralled down

172

a solid flume of concrete into the fusty petrol air. PLEASE HAVE PARKING FEE READY.

Mrs Shoppingtrip had. She really was – noticed MapHead as he scanned the baby's brain and found it filled with juicy shapes and a large and nameless pinkness – she really was quite a good driver.

# A Number of Things

The baby's name was Holly. MapHead scanned rapidly through anything and everything he knew about Holly and hollies everywhere, covering *Buddy Holly's Greatest Hits*, a history of Hollywood, the ad for Holly Homebaker's Instant Cheesecake Mix, plus the entire register of names at the school he'd once briefly attended – which introduced two more Hollys – in less time than most people could list them. But nothing much helpful came up, except lots of stuff about plants. *Ilex ilex (Holly) – a berry-bearing evergreen mainly colonizing domestic woodland, tenacious in most deciduous habitats. Ilex aurora – golden holly (sterile). Ilex varigata – variegated leaves, low habit.* MapHead scratched his head. The things he knew about holly didn't seem to help much at all, not even the song. *The Holly and the Ivy, when they are both full-grown, Of all the trees that are in the wood, the Holly bears the crown.* Trees bearing crowns seemed less than helpful. The baby didn't look

174

spiky and green. Why name it after a plant?

The baby Holly lived in a room stuck around with perplexing pastel shapes. Soon after they got in from shopping, she had had to be unpeeled. A large dog watched closely as Mrs Shoppingtrip laid her baby on a padded plastic mat covered in pictures of yellow and orange ducks. MapHead had – invisibly – sat down beside the large honey-coloured dog, but the dog had moved away anyway. Probably it saw him, MapHead realized. Invisibility was a tricky thing to get right. It had to do with blocking the way people saw you – with absorbing light instead of reflecting it. Dogs didn't go for it much.

On the baby's chest of drawers were stickers showing a world of many things. MapHead lay on his side and hopped in his mind from one to another, finally losing himself in all of them. The chest of drawers was white and unpleasantly shiny with flat white knobs and a built-in mirror on top. From his position on the floor, MapHead could just see the top of his head in it if he sat up as straight as he could. The picture stickers covered two of the drawers. They had on them: a pig eating a chocolate eclair, a Father Christmas, a toothy snake, a one-eyed monster in a spaceship, a strawberry ice-cream cone, a surprised octopus, a dog with a bone, a spaceman, a sun with sunglasses, a juggling clown, a sad-looking ghost, a mouse gorging cheese, a witch and a moon, lips blowing bubblegum, two teddies, a surfing frog, an Easter egg, a pink rabbit doing a handstand, a smiling python, a planet Saturn, a bee, a tarantula, a skeleton, a Hallowe'en pumpkin, a parrot, another spaceship, an electric guitar, a birthday cake, a Christmas tree, two hearts pierced by an arrow, a Concorde and a globe.

Phew. It reminded MapHead of something. *The world is so full of a number of things, I'm sure we should all be as happy as kings.* A poem. That was it. A poem from childhood days, way back in time. From a yellow-bound book in a cave. MapHead had spent a lot of time alone in a cave with a book, when he was very much smaller, while his father was off doing things you couldn't put a name to. Usually Powers had brought back food. And usually MapHead had eaten it. But it was food of another kind entirely that had kept him filled with pictures. Once he'd been old enough to discover the trailer park near the cave, there had been many more pictures, of course. Standing tiptoe against the trailers, MapHead had watched TV through the windows for hours. Mostly, he never got shouted at. Mostly, they never even saw him. MapHead had even seen baby-wipe ads. He knew about babies a bit. But he'd had *no idea at all* they had so many layers.

MapHead and the large honey-coloured dog watched closely from different sides of the duck mat as the baby came unpeeled. It took a lot of doing, MapHead thought. He wasn't at all sure the baby liked it. He wasn't at all sure *he'd* like a wet vest pulled over

176

his ears or his arms wrenched out of a cardigan. Mrs Shoppingtrip tugged and pulled and fiddled. The baby kicked good-humouredly to start with, then several shades of upset crossed her face. Finally she reddened and cried – loud, then louder, as Mrs Shoppingtrip ruthlessly unpopped her clothes. MapHead tuned in, distressed. The baby felt hot and prickly. Its mind filled with irritated shapes. Of course it was tired of lying on its back having its legs bent for it the way they didn't want to go. Couldn't its mother *see*?

Off came the red suit. Off came the plastic wrapping under it. How many layers did a baby *have*, MapHead wondered. Inside its plastic wrapping the baby was all thick wet towelling and milky little legs.

"Weg. Mind out." The dog sneezed and shifted as Mrs Shoppingtrip moved around it. "Weggie," she said, through the pins in her mouth, "get the cream for me, will you?"

The dog Weg crossed the room to a pink-lined wicker basket and clamped its chops round a smooth white pot. It recrossed to Mrs Shoppingtrip, wagging its tail, grinning around the pot. The pot said, "Petroleum Jelly – Best for Baby." Mrs Shoppingtrip applied it vigorously to the baby's nether regions. The baby kicked and weed. MapHead felt quite ill.

The corridor from the baby's room took a plunge down a steep flight of stairs. Beyond a hall with a phone and a calendar and row of puffy-looking coats lay the herb-smelling kitchen, MapHead knew. He wandered downstairs to revisit it, having passed through once already in the rush to unpack the car and unpeel the baby upstairs. It was a lot like he remembered it. The kitchen looked a bit like a grocery shop someone had turned upside down to see what might happen inside it. All of the shopping that had taken up most of the boot of the car had been brought in and dumped willy-nilly over the floor in crackly translucent-white bags that said SuperFare over and over. Out of the tops of the bags poked an astonishing variety of bottles and cans and loaves and blister-packs and three-for-the-price-of-two offers.

MapHead considered the shopping. Perhaps he might put it away. Mrs Shoppingtrip was busy with her baby. He would be doing her a favour. It was a task, wasn't it? Not *the* task, of course. But it would add to the general sum of *helpfulness* in the world, MapHead knew.

First he filled up the dog's bowl with hard-sounding pasta shapes. "Wholewheat Conchiglie," said the packet, maybe because they looked like little conch shells. MapHead tasted a few, rapidly analyzing the contents. Mainly carbohydrate. Some proteins, some sugars, some fats. Quite a bit of fibre, plus sodium present as trace. The dog Weg would be well-fed on *that*, MapHead thought. After he'd crunched his way thoughtfully through all of the hard little conch shells that wouldn't fit into the dog's bowl, MapHead tipped biscuits into the muesli bin with an uneven sort of feeling it might not be *quite* the right – then he put the cocoa pops where they looked as though they wanted to go. Was it *his* fault the tin was so full they cascaded out on the floor? He opened a cupboard over the kettle and a whole load of cookbooks fell out. MapHead turned them over. *Easy Pasta Cooking With Lisa Handslip*. *Cook Family!* by Lottie Reekie. *Pete Burns' Seafood Kitchen* by Pete Burns. *You Can Make Blood Sausage* by Caroline Quickly. He flipped through the pictures and stuffed the books back over the kettle. The people who wrote them had some pretty funny names.

MapHead was feeling quite at home in the kitchen by the time he heard the footfall on the stairs. He'd put away the shopping – finally, just about anywhere he could cram it – and improved culinary storage capacity no end. Plus, the fridge was sorted. MapHead had taken everything out and put back the things that really *needed* to go in, plus everything new that wanted cooling down a bit. Poor Mrs Shoppingtrip hadn't a clue how to organize her fridge. It had needed sorting badly.

The footfall on the stairs reached bottom. MapHead held his breath; the door opened; Mrs Shoppingtrip entered the room. She took in the changed kitchen slowly. A range of different expressions crossed her face, none of them quite equal, MapHead felt, to the scale of the improvements.

"Well, I must be going mad, that's all – who in the world's done *this*?"

Mrs Shoppingtrip opened and closed her mouth. Then she opened and closed all the cupboards. Finally she picked up Weg's bowl of pasta and sniffed it. Then she sat down at the table and stared at her hands. After a long search for the tea bags she made herself a cup of tea. Then she examined her face in the kitchen mirror.

There was quite a lot – reflected MapHead, as he visited the room upstairs labelled JACK'S ROOM, ALL RIGHT? – there was quite a lot he had yet to learn about human behaviour. The expression on Mrs Shoppingtrip's face as she took in the kitchen improvements had been conspicuously lacking in approval. It had been, MapHead thought, an interesting experiment, but not one he was anxious to repeat. Probably it was the biscuits in the tin labelled MEASLEY or MUESLI. He'd known, at the time. That was what had done it.

JACK'S ROOM, ALL RIGHT? was a different kettle of fish altogether. For a start, it had the mark of someone MapHead knew and understood. There were cups and plates and books, apples and shoes and crisps in a comfy-looking muddle over the floor, plus a nest of clothes at the foot of the bed that looked as though someone had slept in it. Posters of men in dark glasses and big trousers with names like Kool Kutz, The Breeze, Prince TJ and Dr Dub looked down over Jack All Right's bed. MapHead guessed they were the same men on the slippery pile of CDs that sat in a corner of Jack's shelves. In pride of place on the floor lay a half-finished poster scattered with felt-tips. MapHead uncapped the purple and set to work. It wasn't until he'd completed colouring in the balloon-shaped letters someone else had started that he saw, with difficulty, what the letters actually said:

## * HOT SOUNDZ *
## * COOL RATES *

DJ BLACKJACK   **PRINCE OF THE MIX**

MapHead capped his felt-tip and looked at the message. It reminded him of the strange marching letters on the wall of the multi. Hot soundz. Cool rates.

DJ BLACKJACK   **PRINCE OF THE MIX**

It might have read BIG SAUSAGE FRITTERS RULE THE WORLD for all the sense it made to MapHead.

After he'd finished off the end of a stale Wagon Wheel he found stuck to a plate beside the telly, MapHead picked up a book and flipped it open. JACK BRADLEY STAMP KEEP OFF shouted childish red crayon inside. MapHead put it down again quickly. Then he switched on Jack's TV. A picture of a spade cutting into a lawn jumped up. Then the screen filled quickly with a woman in a hairband and a green quilted waistcoat telling another woman – rather bossily, MapHead thought – how she could get rid of grass that wasn't really doing anything by covering her garden with cocoa-bean husks. They smothered weeds and filled up awkward corners. They really were low maintenance.

MapHead thought he'd rather have any amount of grass that wasn't doing anything than the bossy-looking woman with her cocoa husks. He switched programmes and sat down, settling happily to his favourite occupation, channel-hopping for anything and everything funny, smart or informative. Soon he was watching penguins huddling grimly at the South Pole, their penguin babies cosily enfolded on their feet. *Polarwatch*, said the screen over chafing icebergs and driving snow – *Long Night of the Penguin*. The programme featured ice floes thick with penguins; penguins firing themselves like bullets into mountainous seas; penguins hunched together in their hundreds, in walls against the wind. MapHead moved closer to the screen, his scalp crazed with polar maps. A million questions jumped up in his mind: *Why did the penguins stay there? How did they walk or eat or sleep, with their babies on their feet? How could they stand around for weeks on end without food? Couldn't they go somewhere warmer?*

BAM! The bedroom door opened suddenly. MapHead jumped up. He hadn't heard anyone coming up the stairs over *Polarwatch – Long Night of the Penguin*.

A boy with startling orange hair burst around the

door. He wore a bright red T-shirt and a flushed smile pickled with freckles and the kind of good-humoured shine that said football practice after school.

MapHead dropped the TV remote and flushed a scale 1:5 map of the St Lawrence Seaway over his head in a guilty panic. He forgot about penguins. He forgot about penguin babies. Most of all he forgot about *blocking*, realizing, too late, that the boy in the red shirt saw him.

MapHead adjusted his face the best way he could. He scrolled through what he knew about the game of football, taking approximately eight seconds to cover Best to Giggs, inclusive. He smiled wide, but not too wide.

Then he said, "Did you play football?"

The redhead stared. Then he nodded.

"That's good," MapHead said simply. Then he said, "Who are you?"

The redhead swallowed gamely. "I live here. *Who are you?*"

# The Family Stamp

"Will there be hornets? In our picnic?"

"You like hornets, don't you?"

"And al – stuff?"

"And alfalfa. Yes." MapHead's father smiled down.

"*And* cactus milk? *And* those fries from the trailer-park?"

MapHead was five. It was the most he'd said in a long while. Usually, he flashed up maps over his head by way of talking. That was being MapHead. So was learning – finally – to read, all on his own, on a rock in a cave with his father. His father hadn't helped much. MapHead had worked it out for himself, in place of anything better, like friends and family to grow up with. These were strange days, MapHead knew. His father Powers had put his travelling life on hold to bring him up in a cave, far from his mother and anyone, ever, remotely like him. Not that there ever was anyone like him, MapHead knew. Wasn't he unique? There was no one to touch him with animals, that much was certain. Any animal alive would bend its neck and surrender, once it got the MapHead touch. MapHead had had a few pets. The only trouble was Powers. Powers had a tendency to melt small animals for dinner. But only the ones with no names.

The day the letters finally dropped into place and made sense, the day MapHead could really say he'd learned to read, was a day his father Powers had sniffed the California air and taken out a very special picnic. MapHead watched him pack it. Then he fetched his book.

Opening *The Snow Queen* proudly at a well-thumbed place, MapHead read, *"Thou art so powerful,"* continued the reindeer, *"that I know thou canst twist all the winds of the world into a thread, and if the pilot loosen one knot of it he will have a –"*

"Favourable."

"*– favourable wind.*" MapHead snapped his book shut. "And I will be, one day, won't I?"

"Won't you what?"

"Be powerful."

Powers smiled. "More powerful than you think."

The picnic day held powdery clouds that grazed the tops of the mountains all around Mesa Rosa National Park. Powers chose a spot on a bluff-shouldered ridge where pines marched up in the folds. First they ate hornets and avocado and biscuits shaped like bones that Powers had pocketed in the pet store, and piles of vivid alfalfa by way of a salad. They washed it all down with cactus milk and root beer. Then they finished off with dog-eared French fries newly grazed from the burger-joint bins as an extra-special treat. After dinner Powers dozed in the shade of a flat rock shaped like a tabletop. MapHead took up rolling down the bluff. First he rolled a little way to see how far he could go. Then he rolled right into the poison ivy and jumped up howling quite a lot. Finally he rolled all the way down the bluff-shouldered ridge so fast he couldn't stop, faster and more and more hurtfully, bringing sand and loose stones after him, till at last he crashed into something knobbly and teatime-sounding and fetched up smack against a man.

A big man with a beefy face. The beefy man looked at MapHead. He looked at his family's smashed-up picnic on its big red florid tablecloth. He looked at the burgers MapHead had rolled on. He didn't look too pleased at all.

"It's fine. 'Cept I hurt my arm." MapHead got up and patted a few things in place. "We had a picnic, too. With hornets and al-stuff and *everything*. On account of because –"

The big man's face darkened. He brushed off MapHead's hand.

"– on account of because I can *read*."

The beefy man got up. He levelled a fork at MapHead. "*Hey, kid. You're a dead man.*"

"You silly." MapHead grinned. "Could a dead man

do *this*?" And he made a map dance on his face. A map of Mesa Rosa National Park, obligingly centred on the ridge. Colours and outlines flushed across MapHead's extraordinary scalp as pigments triggered from cell to cell, faster – as fast as – the thought.

The big man stared. Then he dropped his fork and did a dance of his own. MapHead always thought it was funny, looking back. The reason the man did a dance was, Powers'd heated the fork the man held in his hand with his distant, all-seeing eyes. That big fat man dropped his fork and started dancing around shaking his hand and forgot all about killing MapHead for rolling over his picnic pretty quick, you bet. MapHead smiled, remembering.

The orange-haired boy in the football strip in JACK'S ROOM, ALL RIGHT? smiled as well. He remembered that big fat man as well as MapHead – the whole unfolding scene – plus what Powers had said after. Jack cocked his head and listened to the thoughts inside his mind. *Blue Peter* blared on the telly behind him. He'd come home to find a baldy boy in his room. That was about all he knew. Except for the flood of memories. Someone else's memories, vividly remembered – so vividly, in moments they seemed like Jack's own. He'd forgotten about that picnic, he didn't know why. Forgotten how MapHead crashed into it. Forgotten he even *knew* MapHead. Jack smiled as it all flooded back. That man had jumped up so angrily. It wasn't so brilliant, Jack supposed, to have your picnic squashed.

*All the same, it'd been pretty funny, the way that man had jumped around with a bright red face, so even his family was laughing.* MapHead smiled along with Jack as his – MapHead's – memories unfolded inside Jack's mind. *That big fat man. With the hot fork.*

It had been easy to stop the orange-haired boy in the doorway; easy to empty his mind; easy to fill it up for him again, with whatever MapHead had wanted. What had been hard was being panicked into it in the first place. Interfering in someone's thoughts was decidedly iffy, MapHead knew. He wasn't, he knew, supposed to do it. His father Powers had said. *Don't take advantage. Respect.* But before he knew what was happening, he'd done it all the same. The meeting with Jack had been so sudden. What else could he have done?

Soon as they'd said hello, MapHead had taken a deep breath and dropped every memory he'd ever had straight into the flushed-looking red-headed boy's mind, so that the red-headed boy would know who he – MapHead – was. It was so much easier than explaining. The door to the bedroom had said JACK'S ROOM, ALL RIGHT? Here was Jack himself. *Watch out, Jack. Coming through.*

Jack had stood perfectly still and taken it all in, just as MapHead had posted it all into his brain, red-hot, firsthand, like his life was Jack's and Jack's life nothing but a dream. The day of the I-can-read-picnic; a lonely childhood in a desert cave with story-books; red-shadowed canyons and mountains; the tomato house he'd once lived in; his father; his mother, his brother; waterfalls, jungles, ravines; Rome, Greece, Arizona; his life in school, where he called himself Boothe; the spaces between worlds, where anything was possible – MapHead showed Jack everything, so Jack would *understand*.

"I'm six now … now I'm *ten*…"

MapHead concentrated fiercely. He was good at dropping pictures into people's minds and blending the edges in with what was there already. A pulse beat fast in Jack's neck. His damp hair stiffened and dried. His breath came shallow, then shallower, as MapHead poured impressions into his head, the way he knew he could without trying. When MapHead had no more memories left to send him, he finally let Jack go.

"That's it." MapHead waited.

Jack swallowed. "Wow." A slow smile crossed his face. "Now I know who you are."

"Haven't I just *shown* you?" MapHead watched him anxiously. "Hey, Jimmy-Jack."

"Don't call me that." Jack shuddered, yawned, stretched and peeled off his shirt to wash for tea.

"Jimmy-Jack. It's your name."

"Maybe it used to be. How did you know?"

"I can see it." MapHead looked into his eyes. Jack was OK. He shouldn't – probably – have messed around with Jack's mind. But what was done was done. "I can see lots of things you can't. I can see Jimmy-Jack's your name."

189

"My name when I was a *kid*. It's Jack Bradley Stamp. Call me Jimmy-Jack now, you die."

MapHead paled. "Why would I?"

"It's just a line, don't worry." Jimmy-Jack grinned. "Want to watch me clean up? Smells like chips for tea."

They nudged each other in the bathroom like they'd known each other for *always*. MapHead let Jack see what he was like, more than he'd dared show anyone ever before. In the hollow green chill of the bathroom he showed Jack the prettiest maps he knew; maps with funny or rude place-names; maps within maps; sad maps, happy maps; maps that crept along his neck; maps that began at his temples in an ink spot and burst over his face like an April monsoon.

Jack watched MapHead's head in the bathroom mirror. How could a person make maps on their *head*? It was astonishing; amazing; unreal. Yet Jack felt entirely comfortable with it. He knew how the maps had started. He knew where MapHead came from, his innermost wishes and secrets, as well as he knew the fine crack in the corner of the mirror that his father always told him to mind. He knew that MapHead was odd and well-travelled; unused to talking much; lonely, different, far-flung. It was as if he'd known MapHead for years.

Even so, it was amazing. "Wow. I mean, *wow*. I mean, like – how do you do it?"

MapHead shrugged. "How do you breathe?"

Jack shrugged back. "I just do."

"Same with maps. Except sometimes I do them when I'm angry."

"When you're upset?"

"I suppose."

Jack was solid. He liked MapHead, whatever. MapHead's heart filled. No longer alone as a wet fish at a disco, but one among others, in a bathroom flicking soap with instant nearness to someone he'd only just met, MapHead unfolded like some secret bloom that had waited seven years for the rains. He would OD on the feeling in a minute. This was what it had felt like, the time he knew his half-brother. Jack Bradley Stamp wasn't MapHead's brother-in-blood. But somewhere there was a place they shared, a place where one thought knew the next, so that *which thought it* meant nothing so much as a taste shared, a smell well-remembered, an echo sounding between them. MapHead's memories were Jack's now. It felt great to have someone *understand*.

"MapHead – Boothe, I mean."

"What?"

"Can I feel your head?"

MapHead grinned. "Feel your own head."

Jack Stamp pulled the plug and buried his face in a towel. "So why are you here?" he asked.

"That's something I have to find out. Anyway. Why are you?"

"Why am *I* here?" Jack found his face in the mirror. "Because. I don't know. I just am."

191

"Same here." MapHead squeezed the soap. It felt silky and smooth and green. He smoothed it – like a pet – in his hand. "I'm just here, and I have a task. And when I find it, I'll know. And what I'd like is, a bath."

"A bath?"

"Tonight. Please."

A bath. Jack Stamp grinned. With a gap between his front teeth he could've posted a letter through, he had a grin not easily forgotten. "If *that's* all you want, no problem."

"No," MapHead said seriously, "that's not *all* I want. But it's all I want for tonight, if you mind."

"If you *don't* mind," Jack corrected.

"No," said MapHead, "I don't."

MapHead hovered during tea. He soon got to know the family – Mum, Dad, Lois, Jack, plus the baby, Holly. Elder sister Lois was interrupted by the phone at her second mouthful and spent the rest of the meal in the hall. MapHead sat soundlessly in her place. Jack grinned, enjoying the joke. Having a guest at table no one noticed was a pretty strange experience. It wasn't that MapHead was invisible, so much as *blocked out* in the minds of the family. They simply couldn't see the patch in their field of vision that MapHead took up, on account of he'd fixed it that way. The place where MapHead sat looked exactly like empty space to everyone but Jack. Jack watched his parents talk over and through MapHead, without a clue he was there. If it hadn't been so weird, it would have been funny. As it was, MapHead made faces. Jack threw a few faces back. Jack's mother stared.

Then she said, "Jack. Are you feeling all right?"

Jack shrugged. "I'm fine. Why wouldn't I be?"

"You're not eating much."

"So. I'm not hungry, all right?"

"No need to sound so cross."

"Well. I'd need like, five hundred *hours* without food for serious nutritional depletion."

"What did you say?" Jack's mother looked at Jack.

"Just get on and eat." Jack's father looked up. "I'm not sure I like your tone."

Jack was about to tell his father he wasn't crazy about *his* tone, when suddenly he decided not to. Instead he made a *der* face at MapHead. MapHead felt uncomfortable. Something strange with Jack. He didn't like the vibes.

Jack's father said, "How long has that girl been on the phone? Her meal's going to be stone-cold by the time she gets to it."

"She can mike it. That's her look out."

Mrs Stamp lifted the baby Holly out of her high chair and sluiced off her plastic bib in the sink. MapHead watched as the baby had her hands and face wiped very thoroughly with a flannel. The baby put up with a lot, MapHead decided. He looked at Jack, and knew in a moment that Jack resented the baby. MapHead looked away, chilled by what he saw. He drew closer to the baby. She smelled milky-sour, of talcum and wee, plus another smell all of her own. MapHead warmed to Holly. Eat, don't talk. She had the right idea.

They passed Lois Anne Stamp in the hall. She'd been on the phone forty minutes. The conversation showed no sign of flagging at all.

"*I know, I saw it, it's grim. She wears it like, every time.*"

A pause. MapHead lingered in the hall to know what the call was about.

"*No way. I went with him on Friday. And you know what he said when we got there?*"

Jack motioned to MapHead. "Come on."

"*I know, he's a beast. So why did she go?*"

Lois covered the phone and looked at Jack. "Do you mind?"

"Mind you taking up all the hall and boring the –"

"Jack."

"– back-end off everyone so no one else gets to use the phone unless they book it three days in advance? No, I don't mind. What's new?"

Lois made a face. "Oh. Excuse me." Then she continued where she left off.

"*Sorry. No. Just an earwagger. Who did you think? Only Grimbo.*"

MapHead considered the top of Lois' head as he and Jack climbed the stairs above her. Lois was flame-haired, almond-faced and considerably taller than he was. MapHead's ears burned. He would've given a lot to have been the telephone receiver. For some reason he couldn't quite fathom, he wanted to know what Lois was talking about more than anything else in the world.

"What is she talking *about*?" he asked Jack softly.

"Who cares?" Jack opened the door on his room. "She's always on the phone. She talks a load of—"

"Jack! Where's the *TV Times*?" Jack's dad called up the stairs.

"In the kitchen, last I saw. Dad!"

"*What?*"

"Did you ask Mr Jameson?"

"About fixtures? I will, when I see him."

"*Gruesome. She didn't buy the trousers? Red or white? Oh no!*" Lois crowed under the stairs.

"I'm having a bath now!" Jack shouted.

"I needed to know that!" Jack's dad shouted back. "Let me know what colour soap you use, will you?"

"*Oh, gross! That's totally – so when is she taking it back?*"

"I'll fax you!" Jack shouted.

"Fax you back!" shouted Dad.

"*She's getting the jacket as well? What does she think – he'll notice?*"

The conversational crossfire stumped MapHead completely. Stifling a desire to go and sit in the garden among silent, forceful, growing things that didn't say *anything at all*, MapHead wondered, for the first time, if he could live with the Stamps. They were pretty

195

much like the families he'd seen on TV, only quite a bit noisier. He liked them. 'Specially Lois. And the baby, Holly. Jack, too, of course. Three reasons to stay. Probably there was another reason somewhere. But three was plenty for now.

He watched as Jack Stamp ran the bath. A bath for him, MapHead knew. The water thudded into the tub in a satisfying way. A pulse beat slow in MapHead's neck. He watched his reflection rock gently in the bathwater with Jack Stamp's reflection beside it. For a moment, his feelings blurred. For a moment, in place of Jack Stamp, it seemed to MapHead his half-brother, Kenny, ran the bath beside him. Kenny turned to accuse him. *Why don't you come to visit? Why don't you stay with us instead of them?*

"I said, how hot d'you want it?" Jack Stamp stared. "Didn't you hear what I said?"

MapHead steadied himself. "Not hot. Just cold," he said.

"You want a *cold* bath?"

"Please."

"World of the Strange." Jack Stamp rolled his eyes.

MapHead looked at Jack uncertainly, not sure of anything now. Jack turned off the hot tap. Then tilted his head and said, "You've got a brother somewhere around here, haven't you?"

"A half-brother," MapHead corrected.

"But you don't hardly ever see him, because he lives with your mum and you live with your dad."

"That's right." MapHead smiled, relieved. It seemed so simple when Jack said it. He'd forgotten Jack knew – almost – everything about him now. Somehow it made all the difference. He felt calm and smooth and open, with all his nerve ends extended. He liked the bathroom a lot. It was cool and green and helpful to growth and the window-ledge bulged with plants. MapHead needed cool and green like a lifeline. Water, and then some quiet. He wasn't like Jack. These were the things, the life-sustaining things, he needed.

"Shampoo. Soap. Towels. Plus there's all Holly's bath toys, if you're into plastic ducks. Mum'll bring Holly up in a while, you've got about half an hour," Jack warned. "Go on, then. Get in the bath."

"I will in a minute. Why?"

"Can you do maps anywhere else but your head?"

"I'm not a freak." The pulse in MapHead's neck quickened. "I'm just like you. I thought you *understood*."

"It's funny." A strange expression crossed Jack's face. "I feel kind of different myself."

"How do you feel kind of different?"

"I don't know. It's weird. I don't feel the same since you came."

Whatever the charge between them, it seemed to fill the room. The water in the bath waited coldly. A drip dripped – *plink!* – off the tap. MapHead felt sad and cruel, both at the same time, exactly the same way Jack Stamp did. Jack Stamp had seemed happy to start

197

with. Something had got in the way.

"Why not tell your mum?" MapHead asked after a moment that seemed like ten.

"Tell my mum what?"

"Who I really am."

"You're joking."

"I mean, tell her I'm Boothe and I'm staying. That way I won't have to hide."

"You don't understand. She'll do things."

"What things?"

"Things like check with your parents. Things like call the police."

They both thought deeply for a moment. It would be about as easy to explain how a strange kid with a bald head popped out of nowhere and came to live in the house like the family cat as it would be to get the family cat to make a curry with all the trimmings.

"I suppose we could tell her you're a friend of mine or something," Jack said dubiously.

"Too bothersome," said MapHead. "I know another way."

"Oh," said Jack, "what way's that?"

"I'll get inside their heads. And make them think what I want to."

"You'll get inside my parents' heads?"

MapHead nodded. "Kind of."

"I thought you weren't supposed to interfere with people."

"I'm not," said MapHead. "How did you know?"

"I'm not sure." Jack Stamp closed his eyes. A drip dripped off the bath tap and plinked coldly into the bath. "I know a lot of things I never knew before."

"It's OK just sometimes." MapHead swallowed. *You're not supposed to interfere with people.* What had he done to Jack? "Just sometimes, if I'm careful."

"Hmm," Jack said. "I don't know."

"It's that, or maybe I'll go."

"Don't go." Jack looked stricken. "Don't go, just – be careful."

As MapHead submerged in the bath, alone and fully clothed, and let the water close over him a full twenty comforting minutes so that the baby Holly's bath ducks looked down from the soap rack only very slightly distorted by the still window of water between them, he thought many thoughts which folded into one another. Chief among them was one which surfaced repeatedly and lived in the bath ducks' eyes. It was a watery, helpless kind of a thought for a boy striking out on his own, a boy with a task ahead of him.

The bath ducks looked down through the still, cold water and the thought ran on and on.

*Dad. I'm not as good as I thought on my own. I feel weak and small, not powerful, like I thought. I don't know what's right and what's wrong. I didn't know I'd have to choose all the time. Dad, I'm drowning, help me. I don't know what I'm doing...*

# Don't Worry, Be Happy

After MapHead's bath was over, MapHead and Jack sat on the roof for a while. Jack's room was an attic room with friendly sloping windows that cracked open and swivelled all the way around if you wanted. It was pimps to get out on the roof.

"*Pimps?*" MapHead queried, raising what eyebrows he had. He hadn't actually said it. But still Jack picked it up.

"Easy-peasy." Jack coloured slightly. "From when I was six. Easy-peasy-pimpsy. Pimps. Family joke. Kind of."

"Fine." MapHead smiled in a ghastly way. He wasn't feeling too good. What bothered him most were the feelings swimming around in the night air – feelings that clung to him like his wet clothes, with much less comfort about them. Somewhere beyond the stickle-backed town, his own family slept in their cottage. They would sleep a long time before they saw him. But it didn't make him feel any better.

The nightscape beyond Jack's garden rolled away to a misty moon over country hills far distant. The mysterious garden beneath him reminded MapHead of other gardens, other times, other moonlit meetings. Only this garden had new shapes, shapes MapHead penetrated with his night vision to find out the nature of things. The bulky-looking stuff running along the fence was runner beans glowing with strength. MapHead could see the tips of the plants building cellulose and inching further, higher. The runner beans glowed green with manic energy. The mice in the hedge were tiny sparks of sapphire.

"So where will you live?"

Other gardens, other times, other friends. Mainly his half-brother, Kenny. MapHead sighed. He'd promised, sometime, to return and say hi. Maybe he would, but not now. MapHead smelled the night air. What was his business here?

"Hey, Mappers. You with me?"

MapHead stirred. "What?"

"So where will you live?" Jack repeated.

MapHead thought. The warm light of Jack's bedroom shafted out of the open Velux window in the roof and lit up the side of the chimney. Muddled household noises rose – quite loudly – into the night. MapHead could make out the baby Holly grizzling in her cot, the sound of the telly, the sound of someone on the phone, the growl and grind of the dishwash machine he'd tried – and failed – to neatly stack with groceries.

"I'll prob'ly live here," he said carelessly.

"Where, here?" Jack looked around. "In my room?"

"*Here*, here." MapHead shifted uncomfortably. "Probably I'll sleep up here. Then I can see what's happening."

"You're going to live on the *roof*?"

MapHead got up. He'd been leaning against a smooth black disk beside the chimney. MapHead considered the sculpted-looking disk. He tried to set it straight. Finely meshed and wonderfully smooth, it had the feel of an object of power. These things only cropped up occasionally. You had to *know* when you found one.

"On the roof," he said. "Why not?"

Jack had shuffled down into the gully where the chimney made a *V* with the roof. He lay on his back a while, testing it out. He closed his eyes, imagining living on the roof.

"*Can you shut that door? Thank you. And then you know what she did?*" Lois. On the phone. The sound of her voice wafted clearly up from the hall. "*She only went and put pasta in the dog's bowl and half the shopping in the dishwasher and then – get this – the goldfish in the fridge! Of course, in its bowl. I know. She must've completely wigged out.*"

"You're lucky, having a brother," Jack said suddenly. "I hate having sisters."

"Why?" MapHead asked, knowing Jack "remembered" Kenny, and everything else – or just about everything else – almost as clearly as he did.

"'Specially Holly. I hate her."

"Holly's only a baby."

"So? That makes me *like* it?"

*"And she filled up the muesli bin with biscuits, and all broken biscuits on the floor … and she doesn't remember doing any of it, and Dad says postnatal stress…"*

"Like what?" MapHead asked.

"The fuss. You know. The clucking." Jack put on a treacly voice: "Oh, a late baby, they're always the best. It's just like starting over. You must be so thrilled. How much did she weigh? Oh, you poor thing. She didn't."

"JACK!" Jack's father's voice rose thunderously over everything else. "JACK, ARE YOU UP THERE? WHAT'S UP WITH THAT DISH?"

Jack dropped deftly down through the sloping roof window onto his bed. He bellowed back down the stairs, "I don't know, what about it?"

"Has it fallen over?"

"How do I know?"

"Reception's rubbish! I'm trying to watch the film on TV Gold!"

"Nothing to do with me!"

"Can you see it out of your window? I only realigned that dish recently!"

"Looks OK to me! Maybe the telly's gone wrong!"

Jack waited, poised to slam up the window overhead should his father climb the stairs. Out on the roof was pimps. It was also Certain Death should his parent realize he did it. Instant removal to the spare room downstairs would follow as surely as – well, pretty surely.

Jack breathed easy as the living-room door slammed shut. Outside on the roof, MapHead appeared anxiously above him. Jack pulled the window open again. He looked up at MapHead. "What?"

"Don't come up, it's not worth it," MapHead said, the bedroom light throwing shadows over his face, his uneasy scalp swimming with lines. "Probably you better go to bed."

"You're kidding me. At *nine*?" Jack looked indignant. "You better put that dish back how it was. The round thing next to the chimney? It's messing up Dad's telly."

MapHead ignored him. "See this?" A map of Antarctica sat on his head like a hat with ragged edges. "What do you know about penguins?" he asked Jack sternly.

"Penguins? Why are you so interested in *penguins*?"

"I'm not sure, but I'm going to find out."

Jack looked at MapHead. The Antarctic Peninsula straggled over his face, the Weddell Sea pooled on his head behind it. The map was instantly replaced by another as MapHead's agitated scalp plotted a new scale every few seconds. Jack felt suddenly jumpy. It didn't take a genius to see the mood had changed.

"Hey," Jack said, "it's all right."

"There's something I have to do." MapHead struggled with himself. *What was his business here?* "I have to be alone. Not for long."

"It's cool. I'll see you later."

"Not for long," MapHead repeated.

"Not for long. Right."

"Don't worry, be happy."

Jack grinned. "Trust me, I will."

MapHead withdrew from the window. Jack sat thoughtfully down on his bed. But MapHead reappeared.

"Hey, Jimmy-Jack."

Jack pulled a face. "Hey Jimmy-Jack, what?"

"Will it be all right?"

"Will what be all right?"

"Me. Being here. Will it work?"

*"It's you and me,"* Jack said slowly. *"Just you and me, OK? Who needs anyone else?"*

MapHead thought. Then he said, "You won't watch me, will you?"

"When?"

"Just now. After I go."

Jack watched the Ross Sea pan over MapHead's scalp. "Hey," he said, "why would I?"

But all the same, he did. When he stood up and peeped through the window, when he saw MapHead brighten like a taper, alone on the edge of the roof, and burn with a steady white light, he could hardly believe his eyes.

MapHead knew Jack was there. He knew how Jack felt when he saw him. He knew what would happen next, how Jack would react to it, how everything that *is* and *would be* would be very slightly changed, and still the world would turn. Maybe he shouldn't do it – especially not in Jack's view. Maybe he shouldn't travel in a flash somewhere his heart pulled him. Maybe he shouldn't flash back again. Maybe he shouldn't even think it.

Even as he thought it, MapHead felt the pull. There was nothing he could do. When the travelling life called, he had to *go*. Holding all of this and more in his heart, reaching the very edge of the roof, MapHead took the night air into his arms and launched himself off into space.

# The Huddle at the Bottom of the World

The first emperor penguin MapHead approached shuffled away from him quickly, head down, flippers in, rocking from foot to foot, like a man with his legs tied together. The second took a peck at him. MapHead retired to a respectful distance in the lee of the wind and watched the huddle.

What had looked like a black standing mass as he'd flashed in over the ice shelf had resolved itself into penguins as he'd come closer. Lots and lots of penguins. Standing around in a huddle. In the bitter freezing cold. Now was the time to understand them.

But you couldn't ask a penguin. You couldn't say, Excuse me, but why *do* you stand around in the cold when everything with a brain heads north? North being warmer, south being colder still, MapHead reminded himself. That was the Antarctic for you. Here at the bottom of the world *everything* was upside down. Even night and day had decided to take a rain check and only clock in, turn and turn about, for six months at a time together. Already the six-month-long night was deepening, the bitter wind singing more intensely. It would be a long haul for the emperors, huddling together for warmth; a very long haul till the Antarctic day finally lit the sky with overarching colours.

MapHead watched the penguins for quite a long time. Then he thought he'd join them. He made himself grey and blank all over. Then he approached the huddle. Close up, the penguins seemed larger than the ones he'd seen on TV. As big as a man around the chest, standing over a metre tall, the emperors were on the move even as MapHead slotted himself into the wall. Huddling together – some three thousand or so in one group – to conserve heat, the penguins shuffled constantly in a clockwise direction so that each took his turn on the outside. The wall of penguins on the outside edge of the huddle took the bitter brunt of the wind. MapHead felt it hit him. Inside, the huddle smelled fishy. But no fish had reached them for weeks. Ever since the females had handed over the eggs to the males and left, the ice-locked sea had grown further distant, the thought of food more remote. Not a penguin there remembered fish. MapHead searched their minds. Nothing but grit and instinct. The instinct to sit there with something round, approximately an egg, on their feet. Every emperor penguin's brood-pouch – the flap of skin designed to enfold and protect it – bulged with an emperor penguin egg. MapHead began to feel jealous.

At least he fitted in. If he were to move now the wall would be broken, and the howling winds howl in. And that, MapHead knew, couldn't happen. The eggs must be sheltered at all costs. What the penguins were nursing on their feet was more precious, by far, than their lives, nothing less than the Future Nation of Penguins. It was awesome to join them. Even more awesome to hear the Antarctic night screaming and raging overhead. MapHead began to dream a dream as he shuffled from right to left with the cold, blank press of the penguins. He dreamed he laid a golden egg, an egg so precious he dare not show it to anyone. He nursed it in his brood-pouch and felt a glow when he thought of it. But one day it began to grow bigger. It grew and it grew and it grew. MapHead felt he was bursting. At last he rolled out the egg. Something was tapping inside it, something that wanted to come out. When it hatched and came out, the Something turned and looked at him. *What* – it seemed to say – *what d'you think you're looking at? Aren't I the picture of yourself?*

MapHead opened his eyes. The huddle stood far in the distance. A lordly ice shelf reared above him in spangled shades of green. He felt like Frankenstein's monster. Alone and very lonely, at the bottom of the world.

*Ice mast-high came floating by*
*As green as emerald…*

MapHead sat under the ice shelf a long time while thoughts and dreams and half-remembered poetry rushed by him. *I want to fit in*, ran the pulse in his head. *I want to be one among others*. For the first time, some of the things his father had said came home to him with real conviction. Hadn't he – MapHead – said, You don't have to be lonely? Hadn't Powers said, Yes, you do?

The power to do *anything* was incredible. Incredibly isolating. If all places were the same to him, where did he belong? *I want my dad*, MapHead threw at the uncaring ice shelf. Fathers and sons, like the penguins, stuck together – didn't they? Penguin dads didn't flash away and leave you to fit in – or not – by yourself. They all stuck together in a wall. Penguin dads. Fathers and sons. The best dads in the world.

The wind whistled. The penguins shuffled. The ice shelf reared its lordly head in a million shades of green. MapHead felt a coldness touch him like nothing he'd ever felt before. The penguins would mate and roost every year whether or not anyone saw them, the six-month-strong sun would rise and set like anything, whether it set on him or his shadow. Everything would go on, whether he did or not. That was its beauty and its strength. *His* life, his hopes, his dreams. Nothing cared, so he'd better.

He wouldn't end up lonely like Powers. He had life, and a task, ahead of him. Plus, he was just starting out. He could fit in anywhere, he knew it. Anyone could be extraordinary on an ice floe. The challenge was, to stay with an ordinary family. MapHead rose and jumped a mile in the thinking. On the highest point of the ice shelf, he looked down on the emperor penguins. Then he burned with longing for something warm and real. In the longing was the thought. And in the thought was the travelling.

# BlackJack

MapHead opened his eyes. Shiny pink-toned dolphins revolved gracefully over his head, dipping and flashing coolly in the morning light from the window. MapHead watched them blankly. Then he turned over to face the drawers stuck with stickers of many-splendoured things he'd noticed the day before. At nappy-changing time.

*A pig eating a chocolate eclair, a Father Christmas, a toothy snake, a one-eyed monster in a spaceship...*

Morning in the baby Holly's room had the same smell as the baby Holly, MapHead noted lazily. Kind of smooth and scented and *comforting*. The baby Holly slept on in her cot and above her the dolphin mobile nodded and flashed in the light.

MapHead considered the baby. She was, above all things, pink. Warm and pink and lovely, MapHead thought. He didn't remember exactly when he'd lain down on the floor beside her cot. He'd finally homed in on the only place he felt comfortable sleeping sometime after he'd finished *travelling*. He'd been tired when he'd finally flashed in. When he'd finally lain down in Holly's room, dog-tired, penguin-stiff, he'd slept like – how did babies sleep? He'd slept, at any rate, like something slept that was very tired indeed. With the long night of the penguins fading behind him in subtle time, MapHead sharpened to the real world he had a foot in. Someone, sometime, had called him a bridge. A bridge between two worlds was really, he supposed, what he was. Except they weren't separate to start with.

MapHead ran a health check on himself. Apart from a temporary glitch in the absorption of fluids through his skin, probably as a result of exposure to sub-zero temperatures during the night, he appeared to be ticking over nicely. He felt perky and ripe for business, any business going. One thing he would settle this morning would be Mrs Shoppingtrip. It was high time he and Jack's mother met eye-to-eye.

MapHead wrapped up his health check. Then he ran a health check on the baby. While he was doing it she opened her eyes and gazed up at him and MapHead experienced a falling sensation not easily forgotten. At last he understood. Falling in love. Except you couldn't fall in love with a baby.

Holly chirruped and jerked her arms and legs. She wore a pink zip-up outfit that niffed a bit every time she kicked. The nasty niff had something to do with a stain the colour of toffee around her middle where something that shouldn't have had leaked out. Holly didn't care. She kicked lots of times together, then held her legs out stiffly, clenching and unclenching her fists, watching MapHead, and behind him, her dolphins turning lazily. MapHead grinned. Holly grinned back gummily. MapHead saw, with amazement, she hadn't a tooth in her head. He wondered how she chewed her food. There was a lot he didn't know about babies. Her father should, MapHead thought, have someone to watch over her at night. The baby Holly was precious and should be protected. Anyone – *him* – could come in.

Breakfast was MapHead's first meal in the house as a proper guest of the family. He entered Jack's mother's mind and rearranged a few things as soon as she came into the kitchen. He dropped in a short picture story with friendly feelings to go, and let it simmer. Valerie Stamp's pale blue eyes grew vacant. Nothing happened for a minute or two. The dog Weg stirred in its basket. The clock ticked on the wall. Then Lois and Jack came in.

"Who's this?" Lois eyed MapHead coldly.

Jack did a double-take. "This?" he said. "Who?"

"Your friend, of course. Doesn't he talk?"

"'Course I do," MapHead told her.

Lois made a face. Jack grinned. She really did see MapHead. So, it seemed, did his mother.

"This is Pete Burns. He's staying a while." Jack's

mother took out breakfast things busily. She thought a moment. Then she opened the bread bin and brought out some muesli. "I'm going mad. More cocoa pops, Pete?"

MapHead motioned "no" over a bowl of chocolate milk. He especially liked the way the cocoa pops made the milk brown straight away. He swallowed and smiled at Jack's mother. "Thank you anyway," he said.

Jack shook his head and mouthed, *"How did you do it? How did you fix things with Mum?"*

MapHead grinned back. *Pimps.*

"Why haven't you got any hair?" Lois sat opposite MapHead and looked at him directly.

"'Cos I don't want any."

"Oh."

Mrs Stamp frowned. "Lois. Please. Mind your own business."

"Well. I'm only asking."

"If you must know, Pete lost his hair saving a puppy from a chemical accident many years ago." Val Stamp turned a shattering smile on MapHead. "I hope you don't mind my saying. *Such* a brave thing to do."

Lois' mouth twitched. "What kind of chemical accident?"

"The kind where puppies get caught in it," MapHead said stolidly. "S'long time ago now."

"So will it ever grow back?"

"It would if I wanted, but I don't."

That seemed to clinch it for Lois. She watched

MapHead's every move over breakfast like she was storing up a blow-by-blow account to share with her friends, which, in fact, she was. Breakfast was an irritable business. The clock on the wall, MapHead noticed, seemed to make everyone unhappy. Everyone checked the clock on the wall, then rushed around looking grim. It would be a simple matter to fix it, MapHead thought. No reason not to be happy.

Lois was pretty grim anyway. It was the first time MapHead had seen her without a telephone receiver attached to her face. He waited for – what would be – the sunny warmth of Lois' smile. But Lois never smiled. Everything made her cross. Especially her school bag. She fought with it by the front door, her tightly bunned hair pulling her forehead, the cuffs of her coat interfering as she tried, for the final time, to introduce a thickly bound book entitled *Germany and the Industrial Ruhr* into a bag three sizes too small for it. She tossed back her head and jammed the *Ruhr* under her arm.

"I'm *sick* of this bag and I'm going."

Lois slammed out of the house. Jack's mother gave him a lunch-box. Then she handed one to MapHead.

"I'm out of salad cream for sandwiches, so I've done you pickle instead. Cheese and pickle all right for you, Pete?"

"Pickle," said MapHead tonelessly. "Trouble, to be in difficulty. *In* a pickle. What is pickle?"

Val Stamp smiled. "Pickle's nice. I'm surprised you

don't have it."

"I do," MapHead said quickly, getting the right meaning. "*A solution of brine or vinegar in which food is preserved.* I have tons of it. All the time."

On the way to school Jack seemed preoccupied. At first they followed a growing gaggle of kids all dressed the same as Jack. Then Jack took a sharp left up a street everyone else seemed to be coming down.

"Won't I need blue clothes like you?" MapHead asked.

"What?" Jack seemed lost in thought. His mood had changed since breakfast.

"If I'm going to school. Won't I need blue clothes like you?"

"Yes," Jack said testily. "Probably."

The morning seemed crisp and hopeful. A warm sun swam between terraced houses and flashed on the tops of cars parked endlessly along a main road that stretched away in front of them to a grey-walled garden sombrely flanked with yews. No one walked behind or in front, MapHead noticed. The tide of blue-clothed boys and girls had entirely melted away.

"Why's your dog called Weg?" he asked suddenly.

"The Wegster?" Jack looked up. "He was Walter first. Walter, Watters, Weggie, Weg, Weggie Wegsford. Whatever."

"I see," MapHead said, not seeing at all. They walked on a while in silence.

Then Jack said, "You did it, then."

"What?"

"Interfered. My mum. She thinks you're Pete Burns."

"Oh. Yes." MapHead nodded. "I made up a story in her head. About Pete Burns coming to stay. And his parents don't mind a bit, because they've gone away to Greece."

"Why Pete Burns?"

*"Pete Burns' Seafood Kitchen,"* MapHead said simply. "I saw his fish-dish cookbook in the cupboard."

"You used to be Boothe once," Jack said, remembering. "When you came to Rubytown before."

"I used to be Boothe. Now I'm Pete Burns. When does it get there?"

"When does what get where?"

"When does this road get to school?"

Passing the grey-walled cemetery where the yews stood in rows like candles, a black-gowned figure overtook them briskly, paused, then crossed the road. MapHead stopped, confounded. The black-gowned figure flapped around a corner and disappeared, leaving MapHead with a vague impression of a face framed in white on top of a crisp black pyramid that cracked and snapped behind it as it went. It looked, MapHead thought, as it billowed around the corner, a bit like a manta ray. But manta rays didn't overtake people on their way to school. They didn't crack and snap as they walked. They didn't cross roads like swooping black crows. Mostly, they stayed in the sea.

Jack said, "It's only a nun. Nuns are—"

"I know," MapHead lied quickly. "I know what nuns are, kind of. It's just, I never saw one." And now it came to him what she – the nun – really looked like. Not a manta ray, or a swooping black crow, but – "I didn't know they looked like penguins.

"They live up the road in a big old house with a garden and a pond. The pond's always full of tadpoles. I go up there, but they scare me."

"The tadpoles?"

"No, the nuns."

"They do look like penguins, don't they?"

"Not that again. Forget about penguins."

"I can't, now I've seen them. No one should have to stand around in the cold with their babies on their feet."

"It's a joke, right?" Jack looked at MapHead.

As they passed the space the nun had taken up just a moment before, MapHead caught a whiff of saints and martyrs. He tried hard to ignore the ghosts standing sentinel between the yews bordering the cemetery. Some ghosts tried to be showy. These were the kind to avoid.

"So where did you go last night?" Jack asked, more casually than he felt.

"To see what penguins do."

"So what *do* they do?"

"I told you. The dads stand around in the cold with their babies on their feet. And they never, *ever* leave them, no matter what."

"Then what?"

"Then the babies hatch out."

"I mean, what did you do after that?"

"After that I slept in Holly's room. I like Holly."

"More'n I do," Jack said darkly. "That used to be my room. I thought you were sleeping on the roof."

"So did I, but I couldn't."

"When you went—" Jack stopped. "You jumped off the roof. I saw you."

"I know. But it's not what it looks like."

*"But I saw you jump off the roof."*

"I didn't jump *off* anything. I jumped *into* something," MapHead corrected soberly.

"Into what?"

"Subtle time, what else?"

"What *is* subtle time?"

"Like dream-time, only you're awake."

MapHead had a feeling dangerous things were unfolding between them. He held Jack's eyes until Jack looked away.

"This is weird." Jack blinked rapidly, several times together. "This is seriously weird."

"I told you not to look, and you looked. You didn't have to know."

"So you're telling me you went all the way to—"

"Antarctica. In subtle time. I'll map it up if you want."

Jack stared. "Maybe later. Not now. Now we cross the road."

MapHead crossed the road behind Jack with a feeling of dawning understanding. He knew the place they were headed. He recognized the sandwich-layer of concrete, the glaring overhead bulbs beaming orange light into dangerous-looking spaces, the many-coloured gleaming tops of cars, the sign that said CARE WHEN ENTERING.

"Why are we going in here?" he asked Jack.

"Dump our stuff. Hang out. You got a better idea?"

"But what about school?"

"Stuff school," Jack said, with feeling.

Was this the flushed-looking winger who stayed back for football after school? MapHead followed Jack up the foul-smelling concrete stairway and knew, beyond doubt, that his newly altered friend was in trouble. Some of it – most of it – was his fault. In filling Jack in on his, MapHead's, past life, MapHead had opened doors in Jack's mind Jack didn't know he had. Words like *you had no right* swam into MapHead's head. *Sorry* was in there somewhere. The meaning of breaking a golden rule began to tingle in his brain. Why had his father warned him not to interfere? Because there was a horrible reason not to. Everyone's mind was their own. You absolutely couldn't change them.

Newly mixed with exhaust, the morning air in the multi-storey car park smelled bitter and smoky and filled with things hostile to life. Cars stretched away in steadily filling ranks to the scabby-looking walls dividing every bay, walls which shouted the now-familiar marching letters which MapHead knew would spell out things he would never entirely understand. Jack considered them, too. He brought out a spray-can and shook it. "See this? Dad won't miss it. Know who I am?"

"Who I am?" MapHead echoed, confused.

Jack Stamp popped the top off his spray-can with the air of a gunslinger. Then he sprayed:

## ! DJ BLACKJACK !
## NEW NAME OF OUTRAGE

in angry black capitals on a wall shouting monster TRIFFS tags. He stepped back to admire the effect. Then he added:

## BIG SHOUT 2
## I WOULDN'T B U

Jack wrote it big and with meaning, shaking his spray-can, enjoying himself, with a new kind of glint in his eye.

MapHead watched uneasily. "But shouldn't we go to school?"

"We can do anything, right?"

"Right."

"So why would I go to school?"

Somewhere there was a reason. MapHead tried and failed to find it. Big – enormous – things were adrift with Jimmy-Jack Stamp, and he, MapHead, could hardly hope to explain them. But maybe he could contain them. Maybe he could watch and wait. Maybe things would get better. With his usual rising optimism, MapHead hoped the change in Jack Stamp would clock out with that day's traffic. Until then, he knew with dreadful certainty this was one ticket that could jam the machine. Largely thanks to him, the boy with the flame-coloured hair was well and truly up the multi.

# Valet Packing – May I Help You?

The day up the multi began quietly enough, with no hint of what was to come. Even Jack – though he wouldn't admit it – was bored. First he took off his school sweater and stashed it in his bag. Then he tied his coat around his waist and swaggered up top, where G deck met the sky.

MapHead was glad to follow. The stench of exhaust made him tired of life. B deck was filling rapidly. He found Jack leaning over the parapet that ran, two rails thick, around the top of the wall crowning the whole concrete-and-metal layer cake, seven stories high, which made up the car park beneath them. MapHead looked down. Way below him morning shoppers beetled around the market square like purposeful pinheads with Important Things to Do. Unlike him and Jack.

"Starkey! Starks! Up here!" Jack whistled piercingly, then cupped his hands and yelled below, *"Surprise, surprise! Late again, Starkers? Take a misdemeanour!"*

MapHead searched the pinheads below, some of them kids late for school. One of them – the one looking up now – was Starkers. In the time it had taken him to match the name to the face, Jack Stamp had scraped up a bomb from a SuperFare bag and a puddle.

"Starkey!" Jack cupped his hands around his mouth. "You, Starkers! Cop this!"

Extending himself dangerously out over the parapet Jack dropped the mud-filled carrier bag, craning out still further to see it burst over Martin Starkey.

"*Starkey! Starks! Tell it's raining?*" Jack hooted and bawled like a madman.

It wasn't a good thing to do. Dropping things on people. Leaning out over the edge of a very high building in an excitable sort of way wasn't good either, MapHead knew. With rising anxiety, MapHead watched Jack. A tide of empire red washed over his scalp in the shape of northern India. He saw his hand going out to take the back of Jack's shirt in a safety grip. He couldn't help himself.

"Leave it out." Jack shrugged him off, eyes flashing.

"I only—"

"Well, don't. I can look out for myself. Who are you, Mary Poppins?"

MapHead considered this comment carefully. He desperately wanted Jack to slide back down off the edge of the wall and stop leaning out over the dizzy morning streets. Another centimetre further – just a tiny amount – and Jack would drop like a fruit off the multi and smash on the pavement below. Jack was in danger. What was he to do? What would the Poppins woman – whoever she was – have done in the same position? Jack's mother would want to know her son was here, seven stories high, on the topmost edge of the railings. Shouldn't he let her know? What should he do in the meantime? Shout? Faint? Eat?

"Mary Poppins says, Keep In," MapHead tried, sepulchrally.

"Do me a favour." Jack eyed MapHead scornfully. "Anyway," he said, "if I wanted to walk all around the edge of this wall, you couldn't stop me."

"But you don't. Want to walk around it."

"Who says?" Jack looked at MapHead intently. Still looking at MapHead, he swung one leg, then the other, up onto the parapet. He pushed up his chest with his arms and brought up his knees.

"What are you doing?" MapHead asked quickly. "Lie flat, I should. Flat's best."

So far from lying flat, Jack straightened suddenly. Extending his arms he stood, with an effort, on the very edge of the parapet. "You could jump off this, couldn't you? Like you jumped off the roof?" Slowly he turned to look at MapHead. "And if I jumped off now, you'd have to save me."

MapHead flushed up the colour of turkey wattles. "Please," he said, "don't. Please, don't."

Jack wavered on the edge. *"Wouldn't you? I know you can. You couldn't let me fall."*

MapHead's scalp plotted the Great Lakes in garbled detail. The Yucatan Peninsula cut into and overran them and spread like a flood down his neck. MapHead felt himself beginning to come unstuck.

"Please," he said, "you don't understand. My first time on my own. I don't know what I'm doing, and I can't have it on me, and I don't know what's right when you know you can choose and it's turned out fine today, how do you do? I say pleased to meet you and I don't like Jack going out where he might fall down so then I say, Please, Jimmy-Jack, I want you."

MapHead stopped, trembling. Jack stared, then shuddered. When he opened his eyes again after, he seemed drabber and smaller, somehow. Somehow more like a frightened kid on the very edge of something he couldn't understand. He even took MapHead's hand when he offered, climbing wordlessly down and enfolding MapHead, without embarrassment, in arms that were suddenly shaking.

"Hey," Jack said, "it's all right. I don't know why I did that. I'm sorry, I'm really sorry."

MapHead squeezed Jack tight. Something relaxed inside him. It had been a close call, he knew, if Jack didn't. How close, he wasn't sure.

"You won't say anything, will you?" Jack said in his ear. *You and me together. We're OK.*

MapHead nodded. Then he sat down. A new change had gripped Jack already.

Slicking back his hair, Jack considered G deck with

227

its ranks of family cars. His eyes swept over them shrewdly. A tight little smile lit his face. MapHead's heart sank. What next, after near-death by falling? Jack Bradley Stamp changed course with the wind, a bit like April weather. Sun and thunder together. No breeze, no clouds, no warning.

"Look at these suckers." Jack turned to MapHead. "All these happy shoppers. Now we're here, let's do some business. Are we ready to make some dosh, or are we ready?"

"I don't know. *Are* we ready?"

"Ready, big time. What are we waiting for?" Jack said. He was actually rubbing his hands.

"Valet Packing. May I help you?"

For a while things went rather well. MapHead had his lines off nicely. What he lacked in looks, he more than made up for in efficiency. Packing people's shopping into their cars for them was clearly a good thing to do. *Valet Packing. May I help you?* He had to ask them the way Jack had told him to. That way they'd want him to help. But why *did* he have to ask them that way? What did the formula mean?

"Val-ay packing. What *is* val-ay?" MapHead asked Jack.

"It's where you look after people," Jack told him. "Like valet parking where someone parks your car? Only we're doing valet *packing*."

"I knew," MapHead said quickly, deeply unsure of

the difference. "It's just, I forgot for a moment."

The whole trick had been to convince shoppers that they – MapHead and Jack – were part of the SuperFare service. Once Jack had straightened his shirt and fished out his sweater for MapHead, they passed for staff no problem in their navy, green and white. Luckily the SuperFare trim matched Hubert Sewell Community College colours. It was *pimps* cutting the SuperFare logo off a couple of bags. Jack took his time with the edges. They had to look convincing or it wouldn't be worth them wearing them on their chests. Jack seemed highly focused. He even found a Pritt Stick in his bag.

MapHead looked down at his SuperFare badge. Jack looked down at his. Then he looked up. "Let's go get 'em."

"How?" MapHead asked.

"Don't worry. Just do what I do."

MapHead soon got the hang of it. First you hung around the big metal lift from the first-floor SuperFare store. Soon as the metal doors parted revealing two, maybe three, loaded trolleys, you put on your best smile and said, "May I pack your shopping? Valet Packing?" Then you wheeled the trolley and put all their shopping in their car. Then they said, Thank you and left.

"Didn't you ask for money, you dope?" Jack shook his head over MapHead's latest – departing – client.

"Money? No. Did you?"

First Jack relied on tipping. Then he brazenly announced a service charge of ten per cent of parking fees. Most people paid up, amazingly. But MapHead flinched a little. He hadn't realized Jack was charging. He'd thought, a little fondly, they'd simply been adding to the general sum of *helpfulness* in the world.

Jack took MapHead aside. "Look. It's better telling 'em straight out it's ten per cent of parking fees than hanging around trying to grease 'em up, OK?"

MapHead had a feeling the guy in official SuperFare colours smashing empty trolleys together over by the lift might take a different view. He had his beady eye on them already.

"Maybe we shouldn't do this," he said.

"So you don't agree. So your cut can be less. That make you feel any better?"

Cut-throat businessman Jack Bradley Stamp was a tough guy to deal with. He only got tougher as the afternoon wore on.

"I'm hungry and I'm stopping." MapHead sat down at two.

"Here." Jack tossed MapHead a Twix, then a Crunchie.

"Where'd you get these?"

"I lifted 'em."

"Lifted them?"

"I borrowed 'em from people's shopping."

MapHead felt a wave of peculiar anxiety. That feeling again. Right and wrong, and all the stations in between. He opened his mouth, then closed it. Then he asked Jack, "Aren't you stopping for lunch?"

"Money doesn't eat." Jack scanned G deck for punters.

MapHead dealt with the picture *that* conjured up. Then he said, "No. But you do. Anyway. Why are you like this?"

"Like what?"

"Cross all the time. You weren't cross before."

Jimmy-Jack shrugged. "Time is money. I know more things now."

"Why does knowing things make you horrible?"

"It doesn't. I mean, I'm not."

"*I* could be horrible if I wanted, except I don't," MapHead said earnestly. "Like my dad, when he – when he melts things with his eyes."

"Can you?" Jack asked.

"What?"

"Melt things with your eyes."

"Power is responsibility. No taking advantage. Respect," MapHead intoned, like a lesson. "You might want to think about that."

"I might, but I don't." Jack looked away, bored. "I was stupid before. Now I need money to travel and *do* things, all right?"

"I liked stupid."

"What?"

"The way you were before."

"Well, now I've changed. So you can get off giving

231

me a hard time about it."

MapHead took refuge in his Crunchie. He'd seen the ad. *Thank Crunchie it's Friday*. He especially liked the honeycomb bit in the middle. Then he said, "What does Lois do at lunchtime?"

"What?"

"Your sister Lois. Where does she go to eat her lunch?"

"Who cares? She doesn't eat either."

"Lois doesn't eat?"

"She never sits down to a meal. She's always yakking on the phone."

The next few customers were the worst yet. An old gent with a bag Jack snatched, then thought better of it. A mother and kids with an overflowing trolley and a sarcastic laugh instead of money. A middle-aged woman who backed away when MapHead approached, a kindly smile on his face.

"Get away from me. You punkers."

"Punkers? It's Valet Packing." MapHead smiled some more.

"Well, you can pack yourself off," the woman said, waspishly. "Writing on walls. Vandalizing toilets. You punk types are all the same."

MapHead felt badly shaken. What they were doing seemed silly. The people who fell for it under the dim orange box-lights seemed silly. Maybe they liked having their cars loaded for them. Maybe it was the bad light. Maybe it was the multi itself, a world away from real situations. Couldn't they see they were school kids? That they should, after all, be in school?

One woman could. She eyed them both coldly and pushed her own trolley. "Shouldn't you both be in school?"

"He should, I shouldn't," Jack countered. "Don't you know? It's work experience week."

"And you are?"

"Executive packing operative. Till-to-car service. Personal Packing at a Price."

"You don't look old enough to me."

"You're the sixth person who's said that," Jack said smoothly. "Any more, and I'll start to believe it."

The woman looked at Jack. Then she said, "Well. Would you like to unload my shopping?"

"You don't look," Jack said coldly, "like a person that needs any help."

"Oh, but I—"

"Have a nice day."

Jack showed MapHead afterwards the coffee he'd lifted from her bag. It wasn't that he wanted it; just that coffee was expensive. MapHead watched as Jack poured the coffee into a puddle. Then he kicked the puddle up the wall so that dark brown fingers of Continental Blend dribbled expressively down it.

"What did you do that for?" MapHead asked.

Jack Stamp raised his eyebrows. "Because I wanted to?"

The row blew up out of nowhere. But somehow the

coffee had brewed it.

"Let's go now. Shall we go now?"

It seemed like a good time to go. MapHead eyed the trolley-smasher, talking now with a suit. The suit listened and nodded, looking at MapHead and Jack.

"This is good." Jack kicked the empty coffee jar. "This is different. Everyone should do what they want."

"You know you can't, Jack Stamp." MapHead picked up the jar before Jack could smash it.

"Put it down." Jack waited.

"Supposing you smash this jar. Supposing someone steps on it."

"Supposing they don't," Jack said. "I want to kick things over. I want to do something *radical*."

"Radical," repeated MapHead. "*Thorough; complete; drastic. Upholding far-reaching change.*"

"Whatever." Jack seemed bored already. "Anything – different, you know?"

"Revolution," said MapHead, "*a radical change.* Will you be like this tomorrow?"

"Maybe. What's it to you?"

"Some revolution. Valet Packing."

"What did you say?" Jack looked dangerous.

"I said, I'm going home to Holly." MapHead peeled off his SuperFare logo with as much dignity as he could muster. "And I'm not coming back, so you know I'm humpy."

"*Got* the hump, you mean."

234

"And *you* don't stop me going when I want to."

MapHead walked hollowly across D deck, head down, shoulders hunched, not avoiding puddles at all. Jack Stamp watched him go.

"That's right. Go home. Babies is all you're good for."

*Babies is all you're good for.* Jack Bradley Stamp's intended insult rolled around the multi and came back twice as nice. Remembering Holly, MapHead smiled. Jack could look out for himself. The baby Holly couldn't.

"What about your half of the take?" Jack shouted after him.

"Keep it. I don't. Want it."

MapHead dropped lightly into the stairwell, taking levels D to Ground in a single swooping free-fall. Once out on the street he quickened his step. The baby Holly needed him in a way Jack never would. If babies were all he was good for, MapHead thought with feeling, he was really quite good enough.

That afternoon MapHead found a reason to belong. Don't worry, be happy. It was really quite simple, after all. The baby loved him, he loved her – what else was there to know? Once he'd speed-read *Dr Gillian's Cyclopaedia of Childcare* his happiness was – almost – complete.

Everyone loved Holly – Mrs Stamp's visitor; Mrs Stamp's visitor's baby, Daniel; the dog Weg – everyone.

Back at the house the quiet of the afternoon settled around MapHead like a blanket. Home life agreed with MapHead. He could take any amount of warmth and quiet and well-meaning household ghosts, like the biddy who lived in the stairwell or the old man behind the bathroom door. After he'd fixed the unsettling clock in the kitchen so it wouldn't bother anyone ever again, MapHead joined Valerie Stamp and her visitor in the living-room over two cups of half-drunk tea. The babies made eyes at each other and hurt themselves on things not obviously dangerous and examined bright objects with enormous care before dropping them. MapHead listened carefully to the two mothers. He tried to pick up what he could from their conversation. Finding out all there was to know about babies wasn't going to be easy.

"So, Peter—"

"Pete. Pete Burns."

"So. Pete Burns." The visitor smiled. "No school this afternoon?"

"Pete's got leave to study at home," Mrs Stamp said automatically. "He doesn't normally go."

"He doesn't normally go to school?"

"That's right. Pete's very intelligent. He doesn't really need to go to school."

"I shouldn't laugh." The visitor covered her mouth. "I'm sorry. It sounds so funny."

"I suppose it does." Mrs Stamp smiled. "I don't know why it came out that way."

"I suppose that's the way it is. If he's so clever, I mean."

"He is. Very clever indeed."

No one said anything for a minute or two. Then the dog Weg appeared with a pot of cold cream in its chops.

"Oh, Weggie, no." Mrs Stamp sighed. "Holly doesn't need changing."

"Isn't that your doorbell?" the visitor asked, following a dim *bing-bong*.

Valerie Stamp felt Holly. "I don't know, maybe I'll change her. Wegs, fetch my basket, will you?" She got up, looking harassed. "Won't be a moment. I'll just get the door."

"I can unpeel the baby," MapHead offered. He picked her up. She smelled. MapHead tried not to mind.

But when Jack came in, MapHead minded. When Jack Stamp came bloodily in at the door, MapHead minded quite a bit. He minded the way someone had turned out Jack's pockets and robbed him of every last penny he had, plus his door key; he minded the way they'd ripped Jack's shirt and thrown away his shoes; he minded the way they'd head-butted his nose so it wept all over his face. When he heard what had happened to poor old Jack Stamp when he'd not been there to save him, MapHead minded a lot.

# Surfer Moe

"*You* look bad, you should see the other guy, right?"

"Right." Jack Stamp nodded, approving his version of events that afternoon up the multi. He had given a good account of himself. The other guy had come off badly and wouldn't, for sure, mess with Jack Bradley Stamp again.

"And you clumped him a good one," MapHead repeated dutifully.

"Three good ones. I told you. Plus, I kicked him in."

"And you're not a bit sorry?"

"After what he did? Should I be?"

"So what did your dad say?"

"Lots."

MapHead went back to his book. "'Until emperor penguins are seven or eight weeks old,'" he read, "'they are kept and fed in their father's brood-pouch.'"

He stopped and looked at Jack. Jack's nose looked swollen and wonky. But he wouldn't be scarred for life. "So who was it hit you really?"

"I told you. Big Shout 2."

"Who *is* Big Shout 2?"

"You'll see when we beat him in. I want you to melt him with your eyes."

"Melt him with my eyes? Why would I?"

"So you *can* melt things if you want."

"I can do anything," MapHead volunteered solemnly. "Anything at all. That's the trouble."

No one said anything for a while. Instead of The Acid or Alkali Test, Jack wrote DJ BLACKJACK COOLEST SOUND AROUND in his science exercise book in overlapping jumbo capitals. MapHead read his *Wonderworld of Knowledge*. Jack's bedroom seemed suddenly suffocating. The dishwasher churned in the kitchen downstairs over odd bursts of *EastEnders* from the living-room as the living-room door opened and closed. The sound of the dog Weg scratching itself rhythmically – *thump, thump, thump* – on the kitchen floor rose steadily under the slap of Holly's bathwater. Someone put the kettle-lid on with a crash as Lois' confiding phone call wafted upstairs.

"*He's completely bald with this white face with eyes like a fish, and he stopped the clock in the kitchen and when Mum asked him he said, I fixed it so you won't be unhappy at breakfast. Yeah. Pete Burns. He's a trog. Do what? I couldn't. He might go mad or something.*"

"Don't mind her, she's a dipstick," Jack said.

"No," MapHead said, "I won't." But all the same, he

did mind. *Pete Burns. He's a trog.* He got up after a moment. "I think I'm going in the bathroom an' help put Holly to bed."

After he'd helped put Holly to bed, MapHead lingered on in her darkened bedroom. It wasn't so dark, after all. He loved the pink light filtering in through the curtains. He talked to Holly a long time. He told her all about subtle time, the gopher he'd had for a pet, chariot races in ancient Rome, the way you needed to see a map *once* and then you could plot it for ever. Holly chirruped through the bars of her cot and watched MapHead's face as he told it. Finally she forgot to kick and her eyes half-closed and her fists twitched. MapHead watched her enter a subtle world of her own, the world between sleeping and waking.

Just then, Jack came in. "Mappers," he called, "you there?"

MapHead brought a finger to his lips. "Hey," he said softly.

"Hey, yourself." Jack rubbed his swollen nose. "Want to watch *Memory Maestros* with me?"

"I don't know. What is it?"

"This game show where people beat experts remembering loads of things."

"Things like what?"

"Stuff. Lists. Facts."

"I can do that anyway." MapHead straightened. "Diseases of babies include: allergies; asthma; bronchitis; bowel movements, obstruction of; cot death;

cradle cap; croup; diarrhoea; earache; eczema—"

"How do you know all that stuff?"

"*Dr Gillian's Cyclopaedia of Childcare*. 'There is no need to wash your baby's bottom every time you change a wet nappy. If he is dirty simply clean him gently with cotton wool soaked in warm water—' "

"OK, OK – is she asleep?"

"Holly? Almost. Come and see."

Reluctantly, Jack entered Holly's room. They both looked down on the almost-sleeping Holly. Her drowsy eyes looked without seeing, her fists twitched, expressions chased one another over her face and faded again like dreams without troubling her at all. That, MapHead thought, was the way to be. Babies had a wisdom all their own. Holly's dolphins spun gently in the draught from the open door. The curtains moved very slightly at the window and shed their pink light over everything.

"It's like," breathed MapHead, "it's like, she's made of *pink*."

Jack looked at Holly's pink head; the way her pink fists clutched her blanket; the pink light bathing her cot. Holly turned her face, pinker still. MapHead was right. If pink was a thing you could shape babies of, Holly was made of pink.

Jack turned down her cover. "She's always wriggling down in her cot. Sometimes she gets covered up."

"She could get overheated." MapHead frowned. "It has been established that babies who become overheated are at greater risk of—"

Jack turned away. "See those?" He meant the stickers on Holly's drawers. "Those stickers used to be mine. Everything used to be mine. This used to be my room."

"Pretty old stickers," said MapHead.

"Yeah, well. I never come in here, do I?"

Jack was resentful of the baby – less so now, MapHead sensed, than when he came in. He would do a little something for Jack, he thought. While the spell of pink still held him.

"Here." MapHead lifted Jack's arm. "Choose a sticker. Go on."

*What do you mean?* Jack looked at MapHead. *What is it? Will something happen?*

"Go on. Touch a sticker. Any one you like."

*A pig eating a chocolate eclair, a Father Christmas, a toothy snake, a one-eyed monster in a spaceship, a strawberry ice-cream cone, a surprised octopus, a dog with a bone, a spaceman…*

Jack's finger hovered –

*…a sun with sunglasses, a juggling clown, a sad-looking ghost, a mouse gorging cheese, a witch and a moon, lips blowing bubblegum, two teddies, a surfing frog, an Easter egg, a pink rabbit doing a handstand, a smiling python, a planet Saturn, a bee, a tarantula, a skeleton…*

– and chose. MapHead joined his finger with Jack's and the sticker-image Jack chose filled both their fingers, their arms, their chests, their shoulders, their heads, their *minds*.

"Wow," Jack said, "oh, wow."

MapHead couldn't sustain it long. But while it was there, the surfing frog filled the room with its surfboard. It winked at Jack and showed him how it hung five, then ten toes over the edge, even though it had frog's feet.

*You know*, Jack grinned, *I always liked you best.*

The surfing frog grinned back, plus it showed Jack what the other side of its T-shirt was like, which Jack had always wondered about, and it turned out the other side was just the same as the front, which said Surfer Moe. Finally the frog faded so that all that was left was its big old cartoon-like eyes, then they faded as well and Jack was simply standing there in the pink light of Holly's good-night time with his finger on a babyish sticker once his, in a room once his, in the evening, about eight o'clock. And that was all there was to it.

Jack put his finger away. "We're not going to talk about this ever, right?"

MapHead nodded. "Right."

He followed Jack out of Holly's room. Jack looked back at the sleeping room, at the curtains and stickers well-remembered. Then he closed the door on it.

"Good though, wasn't it?" he said.

Watching TV downstairs they hugged the secret between them. During *Memory Maestros* – MapHead turned out genius at remembering things, beating all the maestros hands down, especially the ones trying place-names – during *Memory Maestros*, Mr Stamp seemed more talkative than usual.

"So," he said, "Pete. Where were you when Jack was being robbed?"

MapHead swallowed. "I was here. I came home."

"Leave him alone. It wasn't his fault," Jack said smartly.

"You came home." Jack's father's eyes locked with MapHead's. "Yes," he said, after a moment. "You study at home. I see."

The rest of the evening's viewing slipped away uneasily. Supper was cheese straws and cocoa. MapHead politely declined a sausage roll. He didn't eat animal protein these days, not ever, unless he *had* to. He drank his cocoa cold. Then he ate twenty cheese straws, one after another, like a train. Then he went into the kitchen and ate some Wegbiscuit. Wegbiscuit came in a packet which said *Packed With Calcium – Best for Your Dog*. The hexagonal biscuits were pink and pale green and pretty hard to snack off if anyone else was around. Up on the roof again after, Jack said, "Could you do that for me?"

"Do what?" MapHead opened his book.

"That thing you did with my dad. Making him think what you want him to. I mean, could you make 'em think what I want 'em to? Like I'm, you know – make Dad like me a lot?"

"He likes you already."

"You think?"

Jack had his geography homework, MapHead the

*Wonderworld of Knowledge* he'd been reading earlier in Jack's room. Leafing to *Penguins, Emperor*, he chocked himself comfortably into the *V* between the chimney and the roof and took up where he'd left off.

For a while MapHead drank in facts quietly. First the female emperors laid their eggs. Then they passed them over to their mates and went to sea. Then the Antarctic gales closed in, and the emperor dads sat them out. It was hard to believe what he was reading, except he'd seen it himself – the huddle, that few men had ever seen; a mass of thousands of male emperor penguins shuffling around like little old men in cardigans so they each faced the wind in turn, in temperatures cold enough to crack beaks. And they stood there for up to two months. With eggs on their feet. In darkness. Without any food.

It was incredible how they did it. Many froze or starved. Those that didn't, did it all over again next breeding season. On it went, and on – and no one knew they were doing it. No one knew to this *day* – MapHead read – no one knew to this day how many emperor penguins there were, nor how many emperor penguin Huddles, because no one knew how to count 'em. The only reason they could huddle at all was, they were in it together. Shared heat. Fitting in. Each of them one among hundreds. And every single one of them had their dad.

*They have to hand 'em over in ten seconds, see?* he sent Jack Stamp.

"Who?" Jack picked up the thought without thinking.

"The dads," MapHead said. "Once the chick hatches, the dad keeps it warm in his pouch. When the mums finally come back the dads have to hand over the chicks in *ten seconds or less*, else they freeze to death while they're doing it. The chicks I mean, not the fathers."

"We're talking penguins here, right?"

"Right. Babysitting for two or three months with nothing to eat in the freezing cold wind in the dark. King of Dads, or what?"

Jack shrugged. "King of Babysitters, I guess."

MapHead flashed up a map. *I'm thinking about Cape Crozier. That's where the first huddle anyone ever saw was. Know where it was near?*

"Surprise me."

"Scott's hut. Mr Scott who went to the South Pole and never made it back?"

"You should come into school," Jack said darkly. "You'd do Rickers' head in, you would."

"Rickers?"

"Mr Rickman. Year 8 Geography. You come into class, right, do Argentina all over your face, see Rickers do his loaf."

"His loaf?"

"His nut. Do his head in." Jack sighed. "Go mad."

"Right." MapHead nodded. Mad he understood. "Want some help with your geography? Anything you

246

want, I can map it."

"Nah. What I'm doing about homework is –"
Gripping his exercise book between thumb and fore-
finger like a shoe that had stepped in something, Jack
held two terms' geography work, up to and including
Shales and Demographic Displacement, at arm's
length. Then he dropped it down the chimney.
"– what I'm doing about homework is, I'm winging it."

"Don't do that. It's a *book*." MapHead was scandal-
ized.

"Right," Jack said, "a *dead* book."

Shales and Displacement, Igneous Interludes plus
Marshland Regeneration fluttered away like dead birds
in the soot-smelling mouth of the chimney. Jack
brought out Physics with Mr Wiseman. Maths with
Mr Rains. Chemistry with Miss Preston. French and
German with Brownsie. One by one, Jack Stamp
posted his entire stock of Year 8 school books down a
blocked-up chimney no one used. The books, Jack
knew, would back up into a fusty heap behind the
blocked-up fireplace in the dining-room downstairs.
No one would ever find 'em. Else he wouldn't have
done it.

"What did you do that for?" MapHead watched,
aghast. Hugging the *Wonderworld of Knowledge* he
flashed up an anxious little map of the Zuider Zee.
"What did you do that for? How will you do school-
work now?"

"I won't." Jack grinned. "I'm quitting."

"But you can't just stop going to school."

"Why not? You can do anything you want, and I can't?"

"You can do anything, but – I don't know – you have to *choose*."

"I can choose, all right," Jack said. "I choose life over brain death, freedom over school."

"Sometimes it isn't," MapHead said, desperately.

"Isn't what?"

"Freedom. Sometimes it isn't what you thought it was when you wanted it to start with. When you can do anything you want, *choosing's* not so easy."

"*Choosing*." Jack mimicked MapHead. "Choosing what?"

"The right thing to do."

Jack shrugged. "Nothing I do makes a difference."

"*Everything* you do makes a difference." MapHead held Jack's eyes until Jack dropped them.

Long after Jack Bradley Stamp had gone to bed, MapHead sat drinking in the nightscape. Growing tips of plants made a criss-cross grid of energy stretching way off to the moon. Way off, the sewage farm hummed. A bird buzzed by. A fox called. The green-winking night ticked and glowed. MapHead cast his eyes around. Nothing in the world escaped him. MapHead had eyes for everything.

Frosted in flooding moonlight at the highest point of the roof, MapHead stood alone in an attitude of power. Beneath the slates beneath his feet, the family

Stamp slept fitfully. He threw back his head and arched his back. The object of power was smooth in his hand.

With both hands MapHead raised the smooth, meshed dish – the dish that messed up the telly, so mysteriously lodged on the roof, almost, it seemed, just for him – and ran his thoughts around it and with it made a point of desire. The point of desire would attract whatever he wanted. It would poke up in the soupy stuff of the Subtle World like a raised toe under the sheets. And when it did, something would happen.

*I need you, Dad*, MapHead sent out like a pulsar, without much hope of an answer. Hadn't his father told him he must solve his own problems, sink or swim? Probably Powers wouldn't come, no matter how hard he – MapHead – pleaded. But maybe he would help.

Help wore many disguises. MapHead dreamed he met Powers that night in a fiery place subtly real. They walked through curiously textured landscapes together. Powers burned like a brand. MapHead held out his arm. Livid spots ran over it. He wanted more than anything to brush away those spots. *I don't like them, Dad. Help me brush them off.*

*You put them there yourself. Only you can brush them away.* His father held his eyes and questioned, always questioned. *Are you doing the right thing? Can you be sure, my MapHead?*

# Fear of a Kids' Planet

*"Pete! I forgot to ask you! Can you swim?"*

*"'Course I can! Don't worry!"* MapHead waved back to Valerie Stamp across a swimming pool filled with heads and shoulders. Then he walked up to the deep end with the heat and the noise pressing down on him like ten atmospheres of Jupiter.

The swimming pool was loud and bright and filled with turquoise water and many-voiced echoes that flung themselves into the roofspace and stayed there, booming and hooting. Children dressed in not very much yelled and shrieked and swam into irritable adults. Others popped, surprisingly, out of a green pipe the shape of an intestine. MapHead watched intently. A girl in black and white stripes climbed a spiralling staircase over the pool and disappeared at the top. After a while the same girl popped out of the green intestine, rather more surprised than she'd started. MapHead grinned. It really was a funny thing to watch. He couldn't have imagined, when swimming pools were mentioned, that this – this *intestine* place – would be what Jack's mother had in mind. Pools, MapHead knew, were generally green and rock-strewn. He must have heard it wrong. This must be a swimming *flume*. Meadowpark Sports Centre. FLUME OPEN TEN TO TWELVE-THIRTY. That, at least, was what it had said outside.

The noise and confusion were incredible. The changing room – for changing your clothes, not your mind, Jack's mother had carefully explained – had been bright and hot and noisy. So noisy, it had filled MapHead with a longing for wide, open spaces with anything soft underfoot. Jack had lent him a pair of blue shorts for swimming – Jack called them trunks, nothing to do with elephants – and warned him three times *no maps*, but things had not gone entirely smoothly. Already MapHead had locked his clothes in a locker and lost the key, mainly because he'd panicked when required to wear it on an orange rubber band around his wrist. He felt hot and on edge and pretty near a life-threatening tantrum. If it hadn't been for the water, MapHead might yet have run away.

The wonderful water waited. Crystal blue and curiously chemical-smelling, the deep end had signs saying DEPTH 2 METRES and other signs saying NO BACK-FLIPS, NO BOMBING, NO SPITTING, NO SPLASHING, NO SNORKELS. PLEASE. MapHead peered worriedly down, afraid he might do some, or all, of the things on the sign should he once get a foot in the pool. He cautiously dipped in a toe. The water was warm and used-feeling. Wavering red lane-lines marked its bright blue depths. MapHead slid gratefully in. He didn't wave to Jack, racing Saturday morning mates under the clock. He didn't wave to Holly, floating, amazed, in her bright yellow seated plastic ring. Instead he sank coolly to the bottom, tasting the water as he went. Chlorines were present in alarming amounts. No need to worry. Cool and blue would do. Through the wavering water on top of him, MapHead watched the hot red lines of a chair on extra-long legs with a man in blue on the top of it. There were several men in blue, MapHead had noticed; one by the green intestine, one on the long-legged chair, one who walked around and around blowing a whistle now and then. They had MEADOWPARK CENTRE in gold on their shirts. They didn't go in the pool at all. Maybe they couldn't swim.

After he'd been six and a half minutes on the bottom, MapHead turned lazily over. Divers plunged over him with sleek hair and bodies, trailing streams of bright bubbles from their mouths. Children exploded into the water sensationally under the intestine. A forest of interestingly shaped legs waggled and jumped in the shallow end. MapHead closed his eyes and felt better already. The pool had cleared his head no end. It made an entertaining spot to relax for an hour or so.

All at once the tone seemed to alter. MapHead opened his eyes. The waggling legs were standing to attention. A whistle blew. Voices belled over the water. A face appeared and stared down at him, hair fanning around its goggle-eyed edges. MapHead tried to sense what the trouble was. Something – what? – had gone wrong. Maybe a man in blue had fallen in the pool, after all. *Deep panic vibrations overhead.*

Suddenly a spear of white bubbles lanced into the water. As MapHead watched wonderingly, it turned into a muscle-bound man in blue trunks. The man in blue trunks kicked down to him purposefully. MapHead's heart jumped up. A man in blue trunks was swimming down to get him. What had he done? Was it bombing, spitting or snorkels? He hadn't meant to. He didn't know. All, or none, of these?

The man in blue trunks dived right down and seized MapHead forcefully under the arms without even asking if he minded. He kicked with him back to the surface. MapHead fought all the way. He tried to go back to the cool turquoise depths he'd been dragged from, but the muscle-bound man was stronger and determined to have his own way. Thoroughly panicked and outraged, MapHead fought more on the surface, grabbing anything he could get hold of to get away. Somehow the long-legged red chair got involved. So did the man with the whistle. So did Valerie Stamp.

The struggle involving three lifeguards, the lifeguards' red chair and the manager took quite a long time to sort out and the sparkling turquoise pool was pretty much spoiled for MapHead in the end. It wasn't that they weren't understanding, it was just that he felt so hot and cross. Drowning. Of course he hadn't been drowning. He had, MapHead insisted, only been *resting* on the bottom. Couldn't they *see* he was fine?

"Don't worry, it wasn't your fault." Jack's mother parked the car and smiled. "Home at last. I expect these things happen all the time."

"They do to *him*," Jack said. "They don't to anyone else."

MapHead took Holly indoors and put on the kettle for tea. Jack hung towels and costumes out, grumbling as he did it. Mrs Stamp answered the phone. She twirled the phone flex round and round her finger, listening, nodding, understanding. MapHead pricked up his ears.

"What about Pete Burns? He's a treasure. He can do anything with the baby. Holly adores him. Yes. Looks a bit strange, I know, but – of course he does, yes, don't worry. *Really* good for a babysit."

Valerie Stamp beckoned to MapHead over the phone.

"Lois? Lois can't do it. On a Saturday night, are you kidding? Yes, but Pete Burns can. Give him a go. You'll like him."

She gave a thumbs up to MapHead. MapHead grinned, he didn't know why.

"Seven-thirty OK? I'm sure he would. I'll send him

over. Are you swimming next week? We've just been to Meadowpark. Not really, no. Boundary Road Baths is better. See you there Tuesday? Great. OK. Got to go." Valerie Stamp replaced the phone. "Well," she said, "that was nice, wasn't it?"

"Can we go swimming again?" MapHead asked. "I won't do any more resting."

"Not the Meadowpark Centre again, I don't think." Mrs Stamp winced, remembering the scene. "But swimming somewhere, of course. Meanwhile, how about a job?"

"A job?"

"Seven-thirty tonight. My friend Tanya needs a babysitter at short notice. I told her you were good."

"I am, aren't I?" MapHead was thoughtful. "She might think I'm funny-looking."

"I told her that."

"Oh."

"She knows it's fine if I say it's all right. She'll make it two-fifty an hour. Unless, of course, you'd rather not?"

Valerie Stamp looked anxious and drawn, MapHead thought. Probably on account of Jack. Jack being beaten in had really upset her a lot. Plus, he was being a pain. Jagged, edgy, demanding things, breaking things, slamming out of the house, not – MapHead couldn't let on – not really going to school much more than the odd day here or there "to stop Rickers going ballistic", Jack's act couldn't go on, yet it couldn't seem to stop. MapHead tried not to worry. Worrying didn't help at all.

"I can easily say you can't do it. Would you like me to say you can't do it?"

MapHead threw Valerie Stamp a smile that widened to include all her problems, all his and most of the world's. It doesn't, said MapHead's smile, it doesn't really matter *at this moment*.

*It's fine*. The smile widened. *Don't worry. Be happy.*

Valerie Stamp looked at MapHead. "You know, Pete, we'll miss you when you go. Especially with Jack acting up." Tears welled in her eyes. "I don't understand what's made him like this. I really wish it would stop."

MapHead's heart did a double flip. "It – I mean, he – will. Stop, I mean, I'm sure."

"I hope so. He's not a bad person."

"How much did Jack weigh?" MapHead asked, after a moment.

"When he was born? Eight pounds, ten ounces, exactly."

"Heavier than Holly."

"Yes, I suppose he was."

"Maybe you should tell him sometime."

"I think he knows."

"He'd like to hear it," MapHead said sagely. "Trust me. I know about these things."

Valerie Stamp wiped her eyes on her sleeve. Pete Burns had such a funny take on things. She smiled half-crossly through tears. She couldn't help herself.

"Anyway," she said, "it's 29, Rhames Terrace."

"What is?"

"Tanya's house. Jack can show you this evening."

MapHead nodded. "Fine." Then he went to find Jack.

After lunch Jack's mother finished the washing-up still smiling over Pete Burns, thinking what an extraordinary person he was, how he always made her feel better, how magic his touch was with the baby. If only Jack could be more like him. Jack was the only trouble.

Then she made a cup of tea, thanking her stars the kitchen was straight as she did it. No need to look for the biscuits in the muesli bin any more. It had taken a while, but at last things were back as they were. Good job whatever had happened – what *had* happened? – wasn't likely to occur again since she'd fixed up a visit to the doctor. It's all down to stress, the doctor had said. Take things slowly. No need to worry about it. Plenty of people moved things and couldn't remember they'd done it. Valerie Stamp bustled around for tea bags. Immediately she opened the cupboard over the kettle, *Pete Burns' Seafood Kitchen* jumped out and hit her smartly over the head.

She picked up the book and looked at it. What an extraordinary person Pete Burns was. How extraordinary he should have the same name as – as this cookery book in the cupboard. Valerie Stamp sat down. She felt subtly different since the knock on the head. Cogs in her mind long silenced started to turn over slowly. A flood of questions welled up.

How much did she really know about Pete Burns, anyway? How long would his parents be away in Greece? Why couldn't she picture his parents? Remember how she'd offered to put him up while they were away? Any arrangements that were made?

Valerie Stamp looked into her tea. Maybe she'd forgotten it all. These days, she couldn't be sure of anything. She got up and looked down the corridor to see Pete Burns, plainly eavesdropping, flattened against the wall outside the living-room door. She withdrew quickly, heart thumping. Pete Burns was really quite strange. She would have to have it out with Jack. Who was Pete Burns, really? What was he in their home *for*?

"I need decks and a mixer." Jack Stamp stood over his father. "I need some decks like, *now*."

"Decks?"

"And a mixer. Like I need them *yesterday*, all right?"

MapHead flattened himself against the wall outside the living-room door. These voices had business together. Business that didn't need him. MapHead applied his eye to the slit where the door met its frame. Through the slit he could make out an armchair and two figures, one sitting, one standing. Mr Stamp and Jack. Father and son. Not so much together, as on different sides of a wall. That's what it seemed like, at least. Alan Stamp looked up over his paper.

"No, it's not all right. What d'you mean – decks?"

"Twin turntables. For mixing. Techno, Hardcore, Hip-hop."

"Like a disco set-up? For music?"

"That's the one."

"What for?"

"I want to be a DJ – so can you front me something for it?"

"Front you something for it?"

"Can you lend me the money for a deposit?"

A week or two had gone by since Jack had come home bloody, days in which Jack's mood had darkened. He'd not seen MapHead much. MapHead babysat, Jack brooded – in various depressing places, sometimes in school, sometimes not, mainly up the multi, despite what had gone down before. He needed dosh *big time* now, Jack had tried to explain to MapHead. Especially since he got ripped off for the Valet Packing take. But MapHead didn't like money. He wouldn't go Valet Packing. Money didn't eat, he knew already. What he'd learned with Jack was that as well as having no appetite, it had no conscience. MapHead didn't – wouldn't – listen to Jack about money. Neither would his father.

"I don't want to hear it, Jack."

"Just *listen* a minute – "

"How much are these things, anyway?"

"Ben Pringle's brother's selling his."

"How much does he want for it?"

"Them. A hundred and fifty, maybe two."

"Is that all?" Jack's father lowered his paper. "Look, I know you've had a rough time lately, but this isn't the way out of it, all right? I still don't understand what you were *doing* on the estate."

"I told you. I went to see Starkers."

"But Martin Starkey lives on Smucker's Row."

"It was the Smucker's Row end of the estate."

"You're sure about that, are you? You don't seem very sure about anything else that happened to you."

"I'm sure."

"And you didn't recognize the boy who hit you?"

"I told you. No, I didn't."

Greenslades Estate – not the multi – so far as the Stamps were aware, the scene of their son's assault, hadn't recommended itself to MapHead on first acquaintance. He'd visited it once or twice with Jack. But he hadn't liked it very much. Greenslades had the same air of cold and neglect as the multi, like nobody cared very much what happened to it – or them – while they were there.

"Well, next time don't hang about." Alan Stamp returned to his paper. But Jack wasn't about to give up.

"He'll take a deposit."

"Who will?"

"Ben Pringle's brother. That's why I'm asking. So can I have something up front?"

"Can you have something up front? How about a

kick in the pants?"

"I'm serious. How can I be a DJ without any decks?"

"I'll deck you myself in a minute. Give it a rest."

"Up the Revolution." Jack looked down on his parent with naked hate in his eye. "Fear of a Kids' Planet. One Nation Under a Grouch."

Jack swept icily out. Jack's father thought a moment. Then he folded his paper and shouted after Jack, *What was that you said?"*

Jack paused at the front door. There were other rap titles he could've pressed into use for insults, but none his father would understand, so there wasn't really much point. MapHead followed Jack out of the house, more than a little puzzled by what he had to do. For one thing, he had to calm Jack. Jack was well out of order. It wasn't what he wanted to *do*, so much as the full-on way he wanted to do it. DJ BlackJack, New Name of Outrage, was one cool dude – when he wasn't blowing the lid off the whole of his life to date. He had a family and a dad to himself. Wasn't that enough?

"Hey," he told Jack, "don't puff it."

"Puff it?"

"Blow it, I mean."

"MapHead, leave me alone."

"My name's Pete Burns, if you mind or if you *don't* mind."

Jack Stamp and Pete Burns crossed the street

261

together at the crossing – a pelican crossing, Jack said – more than a little aggro with each other. First Pete Burns had wanted to know why there weren't any pelicans. Then he'd wanted to wait for the green man to light up. With a clear road either way, Jack Stamp had grown impatient.

"You don't *have* to wait for the green man, all right?"

"Why's the green man *there*, then?"

"He's just like, *extra*, OK? You're really teeing me off. Mary fussing Poppins, or *what*?"

MapHead pricked up his ears. The Poppins woman again. Clearly an expert on Road Safety as well as Safety at Height, she certainly put herself about. He pictured a strapping woman hung about with ropes and picks and torches. Then he added a lollipop stick and a hat. It made a strange sort of image, not entirely friendly. MapHead mentally filed it. If he could find out more about the Poppins woman, there was a chance he could flesh it out later.

"I'm babysitting Saturday," he told Jack as they walked on.

"It's Saturday today."

"It's seven-thirty. Tonight. And you're supposed to show me where it is."

"Is that right?"

MapHead nodded. "So will you?"

"I've got better things to do," Jack said grimly.

"Like what?

"Like Big Shout 2."

MapHead felt his pulse race. "When will you do him?"

"Now."

Jack turned in at the multi. With his stomach lifting like it was about to show him his breakfast again, MapHead turned in after him. Immediately the growl and stink of manoeuvring cars made MapHead's nostrils contract. Scorning the stairway, Jack marched straight up the concrete ramp to the heart of level B. The concrete ramp led them steeply up clockwise with the kind of defensive twist a castle stairway might have, so no one could draw their swords on their right-hand side. With its passages and levels, its echoing stairwells and lift-shafts, its painted nooks and chambers, the multi wasn't so different, MapHead supposed, from a kind of medieval castle. A castle and a kingdom, for those lonely enough to soldier it.

Jack Stamp was all eyes and vengeance. Rapidly he scouted level B. Then he signalled to MapHead across an orange-lit crypt of car-tops: *Nothing – You?*

*Nothing*, MapHead signalled back, sweating at every pore.

"On up," Jack said, rejoining MapHead with a hawk-eyed, military air. "Level C. Let's go get him if he's there."

"Let's not. Let's do Nuns and Tadpoles instead." MapHead pulled Jack's sleeve really quite hard as they went. "Can't we do fishing in that nuns' pond? Like we

263

did the other day?"

"No," Jack said, "we can't. I'm not doing Nuns and Tadpoles. Nuns and Tadpoles is stupid."

"Let's go up the estate. Go and see Starkers, can't we?"

"Stuff Starkers." Jack shrugged his arm free. "This is serious. He's got my key, you know?"

"Who?"

"Who do you think?"

"Big Shout 2 has your door key?"

"That's what I said. He stole it, remember?"

"I don't think we ought to do this." MapHead blocked Jimmy-Jack bodily. "I think we ought to go home."

Jimmy-Jack coldly sidestepped. "So go home if you want to."

MapHead gripped Jack's mind with his. *We should stick together always. Remember what you said?*

"So?" Jack stared. "What did I say?"

*You and me together. We don't need anyone else.*

"Yeah, well," Jack said, "that was then." But he wouldn't meet MapHead's eyes.

"I could stop you," MapHead said. "I *could* get inside your mind and make you want to go home, except you're free to do what you want."

"I'm free," Jack said, "that's right." And walked away.

# The Babysitter

MapHead felt bad all afternoon. Supposing Big Shout 2 were six – or seven – feet tall? Supposing Big Shout 2 beat Jack up, and he – MapHead – wasn't there to help him *again*? But Jack was free. He had to *choose*, and he'd chosen.

Pretty soon MapHead spotted Lois. It wasn't too hard, in a high street of shops fizzing with Saturday shoppers. Lois went shopping every Saturday. There weren't a million other things to do. At about the same time MapHead spotted Lois, Lois spotted him back. Off she went in a gaggle of friends and pretended she hadn't, but her laugh took on a self-conscious note all the same. MapHead followed as if attached by a string to Lois' back, deftly dodging pushchairs and ladies in too-tight dresses.

Lois flounced as she walked. She looked, MapHead thought, kind of *fluffy*. Lovely, fluffy long hair flounced and bounced behind her and her shirt fanned out beneath it as she walked. MapHead followed Lois and her friends through Top Look, where they all browsed dresses and disappeared for quite a long time into the changing rooms and came out again more or less the same as they went in, only pinker; through Crystal Cauldron Candles, where they smelled every essential oil in the place and came out really quite fragrant; through Boots, where he watched them test make-up until the woman on the checkout who'd been staring hard at him for some time made a move to approach him around the counter. MapHead bolted next door into Woollies, where he waited under Irish Sphagnum Moss Peats, heart thumping, in the garden accessories section.

Soon Lois and her satellites drifted by like the centre of the universe. MapHead slipped after them into Smiths. Smiths was bright and many-coloured, flagged with magazines and posters and cards and stands with a multitude of books. First MapHead looked at the pencils. Every kind of pencil was represented, from childish thick red crayons to steely refillable stilettos. He spent a while with spiral binders and document wallets. What were all these things *for*?

Suddenly Lois rounded the stand. She looked kind of *confrontational*, MapHead thought.

He put on a smile for her anyway. "Hi, Lois. I'm doing shopping."

Lois' eyes snapped. "Are you following me?"

"I'm looking at pencils. Why would I?"

"Yeah, right. Coincidence you're *here*, like you haven't been in *every* other shop I've been in."

MapHead eyed Lois sadly. "You don't like me, do you?"

"I don't *not* like you. I don't think about you either way, all right? So stay away if you don't mind."

"I really don't, if you—"

"And you can *stop* following me around all the shops."

Lois marched off to look at magazines. MapHead wandered sadly into books. *Teach Yourself Italian* failed to shed much light on whatever it was he'd done – *was* doing – wrong. Pretty soon he had to look at Lois. Lois' warning to stay away went around and around in his head. Did she mind him so very much? She'd bothered to come and tell him so. It seemed as though she did. MapHead wasn't the only one to think about Lois' warning. Lois turned once to see what the effect had been, just as MapHead turned to show her he didn't bear a grudge and wasn't about to follow her any more. Their eyes met over Junior Fiction.

A peculiar moment passed.

*You think I haven't been watching you?* Lois' eyes held MapHead's. *You think you can just arrive out of nowhere and live in someone's house when they don't even want you and be totally weird and creepy and they're just like, going to* accept *you?*

MapHead opened his mouth, then closed it again. He would've given a lot to look like a bookstand. He didn't have to read Lois' thoughts. Her eyes spoke clear across the shop: *Mum's changed. Jack's changed. You think you can make me think what you want?* Lois' eyes widened. *I know it's down to you. What are you going to do about it – change me as well?*

MapHead flashed up a big, loose map over his head. Then he backed away. The map pulsed over his scalp, crazing his face with rivers. A space around him widened as people turned to stare. MapHead tried to smile, but the loose map ran on the smile and made it lunatic and blue around the edges. A stand which said CLASSICS AT BEDTIME: GEORGE ELIOT, MRS GASKELL, JANE AUSTEN fell down with a clatter behind him. MapHead slid around on the shiny slick covers of *Emma* and *The Mill on the Floss* while alarm bells sounded all over, both inside his head and out, before gathering himself and running out. The bright lights hurt him. Lois' eyes hurt him. The names on the stands, the colours, the shapes, the books themselves, the people staring after him, hurt him most intensely.

MapHead ran and ran. He ran past the Co-op, he ran past Spar, he ran past Do-It-All. He didn't stop running until the nuns' pond. Sinking gratefully into the murky, tadpole-speckled water deep in the flower-flagged terraces where the nunnery brooded on Jack's street, MapHead let out a long string of bubbles and allowed his sense of self to dissolve like an Alka-Seltzer.

Sister Wilhelmina noticed a ripple. Parting the curtains in the refectory overlooking the garden she said, "I thought I saw a fish jump. Quite a big one, too. My word. Did you see that fish?"

Precisely an hour later, MapHead sat up. Unlooping a long string of pondweed from around his neck, he got up and went into town refreshed. Then he remembered who he was. Then he remembered who else knew who he was – or suspected, at least, there was more to Pete Burns than met the eye. MapHead sighed. She'd never really trusted him. Lois was going to be a problem.

"Hey, Jack! Jack, wait!" It wasn't any coincidence MapHead met Jack leaving the multi. MapHead had a *subtle* sense of timing. Jack didn't look too subtle. In fact, he looked kind of shifty. Plus he was running full-out.

*Oweeee – oweeee – oweeee – oweeee – oweeee –*

The air vibrated with the sound of a car alarm, way up in the blaring multi. The sound beat down on Jack and MapHead and everyone else looking up or running away. MapHead felt vaguely panicked. He kept up with Jack with an effort.

"Is it thunderstorms? Why are we running?"

"No one asked *you* to. Bog off."

"Don't say that. You hurt me."

"Aah. I hurt him. Wibble."

"Jack! Wait! *Wibble?*"

"Yeah. Wibble. Feel sorry for yourself, why don't

you?" Finally Jack slowed a little. He looked MapHead up and down. "Why are you soaking wet?"

"I did Nuns and Tadpoles."

"Oh."

"What about you? Did you find him?"

"Who?"

"You know. Big Shout 2."

"Oh. Yeah. It's sorted."

"Did you get your key back?"

"He's bringing it. Next time."

"So is he big?"

"Massive. Almost did me in."

Jack ducked into Home Street. That was what MapHead called it, on account of its being the street with Jack's home in it. Really the street was named Gough Street, but MapHead thought Gough Street sounded like a noise you made in your throat. Way up in the tall trees cresting Gough Street the nunnery brooded with its pond. MapHead inched a slug of pondslime out of his sleeve. Exactly the place he'd come from, he was heading back towards. Funny how things went in circles. Except when they went in crossed lines, like the wires between him and Jack.

"So how did you pay him back?" he asked Jack quietly. "Big Shout 2, I mean."

Jack looked mysterious. "I got ways."

MapHead looked solemn. "He must've had a horrible life to want to hit people."

"That doesn't make it right."

"It gives it a *reason*."

"Maybe he's all mixed up. Maybe he doesn't know why."

Jack dashed an arm across his face. He seemed mixed up himself. MapHead tuned in, but Jack was blocking him out. They walked on in silence, threading the roads home in the half-dusk with the car alarm fading behind them and Saturday afternoon dying on the streets in thickening shadows pooling into one another to make up a still early evening. No one said anything much. There was nothing much to be said.

Teatime passed uneventfully. The only thing MapHead noticed was that Valerie Stamp seemed edgy. She looked at him in a funny way. She spoke a little coldly.

"Pete. I don't seem to have a note of it. When do your parents get back?"

MapHead looked at Jack. Then he looked at Lois. Lois raised an eyebrow. She got up and pushed in her chair. "I have to call Stiggy. Thanks for tea."

Mrs Stamp frowned. "Do you have to call him *now*?"

"I do if I want to go out."

Lois left the room. Soon they heard her voice on the phone.

"*Eight-thirty? Can't you make it nine? OK. Mandeville's. Maybe.*"

"So, Pete." Valerie Stamp returned to MapHead. "When did your parents say?"

"They said," MapHead said carefully, "they might not be back for a year."

"A *year*?" Mr Stamp looked up.

"To Greece," MapHead amended hurriedly. "They said they might not go back to Greece for a year. Because of having such a good time now."

"So when are they coming back *here*?" Alan Stamp gave MapHead his full attention. A pulse in MapHead's head began to jump. He looked at Jack for help.

"Here? About –" MapHead considered the ceiling, as though choosing his words with care. "Oh, about –"

"About seven-thirty, isn't it?" Jack Stamp checked his watch. "I thought Pete was babysitting. Won't that make him late?"

"Oh, no." Valerie Stamp covered her mouth. "Tanya's presentation dinner. That stupid clock. Of course it's not ten past four."

"I'll take him round now if you like," Jack offered. "Might stay and keep him company."

"I wish you would." Valerie Stamp looked at Pete Burns. Why had she recommended him to her friend? Tanya would think he was strange, mainly because he *was* strange. Too late to stop him now. But better with Jack than without him. "I wish you'd babysit together," she finished. "That way you won't get bored."

Jack and MapHead got up and went out hurriedly. But Valerie Stamp called them back.

"Pete. Before you go. Have I a number for your mother?"

"A number. No."

Valerie Stamp waited. "Well, can you give me one?"

MapHead smiled glassily. "Oh. Yes." Then he made up a number. "It's eight hundred thousand and two. And a half."

"I mean a telephone number. That doesn't sound right."

"800-0002," translated Jack. "Plus the code for Greece."

On the way to 29, Rhames Terrace, Jack said, "That was close. It's wearing off. You'll have to fix her up."

Well off fixing people up, MapHead nodded miserably. Things were getting complicated, the way they always seemed to if he hung around for a while. The travelling life stayed footloose and free. Footloose and free and lonely. Soon he would have – he supposed – to move on. But first he would babysit for Tanya. He could be the best babysitter Tanya ever had. A babysitter she would never forget. And Jack would be there to help him.

MapHead put his best foot forward. On the steps of 29, Rhames Terrace he set his chin and put on – what he hoped was – a sparkling smile.

Jack Stamp looked at MapHead. "Two-way split, right? How much are you getting?"

"Um, two-fifty an hour."

"We'll say we thought it was three. That way it's one-fifty each."

Jack Stamp knocked smartly at the door. Then he

stepped back and waited. MapHead waited too, improving his smile, so that it was quite fixed and taut when the door opened.

"Good grief. Are you the babysitter?"

Tanya Rhodes opened the door on MapHead's grimace. The grimace took her aback. She'd been warned he'd be funny-looking. But this kid looked like an apple.

"Sorry we're late, our clock stopped," Jack explained. "This is Pete Burns. Mum said to come together."

"Thanks for coming at short notice, Jack." Tanya considered MapHead. "So this is Pete Burns. You'd better come in, I've got to get my skates on."

MapHead smelled Tanya's heavenly scent on entering. Her eyes, her dress, her hair, were heavenly too. He watched her shrug on a coat. Where were the skates she'd mentioned? He wondered why she needed skates – wheels on feet, not fish – when she looked so perfect already. MapHead took in the vision that was Tanya done up to the nines. He really was quite bowled over.

So, it seemed, was his charge. The small boy in pyjamas in front of the telly had turned to stare at MapHead like his neck was permanently stuck.

"Must dash. There's coke in the fridge and sausage-flavour Krackles on the side," Tanya told them. "Maxie goes up at eight o'clock. I said he could stay down till then."

The small boy in pyjamas rushed across to his mother. He clung to her, wailing thinly. "Iss him," he wailed, "that funny boy. *An' I want to come with you.*"

"Now, Maxie." Tanya frowned and detached him. But Maxie wailed and wailed.

"Give him a drink," Tanya advised. "He'll settle down soon as I've gone."

As soon as she'd gone, Maxie settled. Only minutes after the front door had closed on his mother, Maximillian Rhodes was running a space-probe, experimentally, into Jack Stamp's feet. Jack Stamp turned up the telly. He put up his feet and flicked through the channels. Then he said, "Maxie. Get me the coke 'n' Krackles."

Maximillian Rhodes buttoned his lip and looked at MapHead. He turned on his heel and fetched the Krackles. Then he sat down on the furthest possible edge of the settee away from MapHead and stared at him fixedly.

MapHead smiled. "I thought you'd be a baby. But you're not."

Maxie edged further away. His mother might've forgotten the boy in the bubble of light in the multi-storey car park one Tuesday, at SuperFare, not so very long ago.

But Maxie hadn't forgotten.

# Makeover

"OK, Maxie. Bedtime."

"I don't want to." Maxie twisted away from Jack's hand and continued his game on the floor. It was the kind of game that crept under your skin and stayed there, involving as it did the frequent collision of Tonka tippers with the leg of Jack's armchair.

"Hey, Maxie. What did I say?"

"And-this-one's-coming-back-little-bit-too-fast-zaz-zaz-zaz-urrrrch! Tip-alla-stuff-up, oh no, it fell out! Captain's coming! Got to – urrch-urrch-zaz-zaz-ZAZ-an-off-he-goes-again—"

"MAXIE! BED!" Jack looked fierce.

"Nogunna." Maxie set his chin defiantly.

"Nog-unna?"

"Not going to," MapHead translated. "I don't think he wants to go to bed."

Jack plumped into his chair in disgust. He flipped a few channels. "Well, when then?"

"When what?"

"So when *is* he going to bed?"

MapHead inclined his head as Maxie's tipper negotiated the top edge of the settee and launched itself, rocket-like, across the fatal gap towards the armchair. ZAZ-ZAZ-ZAZ—

Jack wrenched the tipper-truck off Maxie and put it down coldly beside him. He coldly pushed the nose of Maxie's teddy with his foot. "Take that thing away, will you? I don't like the way it's staring at me."

Maxie considered Jack calmly. With icy dignity he turned to revisit his toybox in the corner. For a moment everyone forgot about Maxie. A re-run of the first series of *Beverly Hills 90210* washed smoothly over Jack and MapHead. MapHead helped himself to a banana from the fruit bowl. Then he ate another. And a third. They were nice, but – somehow bananas didn't quite hit the spot.

BEE-BAH, BEE-BAH, BEE-BAH – materializing with enormous violence and a realistic-looking fire engine with siren and flashing blue light, Maxie jumped up in Jack's ear. "BEE-BAH – EMERGENCY 999 – FIRE! FIRE! LOOK OUT!"

Jack leapt up like his chair was on fire. Maxie – wisely, as it happened – bee-bah'd on out to the kitchen. "BEE-BAH BEE-BAH, FIRE ENGINES COMIN' –"

"That's it," Jack said. "I'm killing him."

"As babysitters we have to preserve him," MapHead said worriedly.

"What did you think, I'm really going to kill him?" Jack looked at MapHead. "Of course I'm not going to kill him."

"I knew that." MapHead tried a smile. He didn't know what to think.

Maxie brummed back in. They watched him negotiate the furniture with a futuristic-looking rocket in fluorescent plastic and chrome. The rocket made a noise like a cross between television interference and someone with very bad phlegm. Also it had a laser gun. The laser gun made a noise like an electric gorilla coughing inside a video arcade. Jack watched telly fiercely. He looked, MapHead thought, a little tense. Jack was usually tense lately. Also, his mood changed a lot. Oblivious to its danger, Maxie's Intastella Explorer laser-gunned its way around the room. The angle of its trajectory from Planet Kitchen to touchdown brought it perilously close to an orbit around Jack Stamp.

"Can't you shut him down?" Jack turned up the telly. The combined noise sounded like a gorilla going mad in a gun shop.

"What d'you mean, shut him down?"

"Well. You could make him go to sleep if you wanted, couldn't you?"

"I suppose I could, if I—"

"Do it."

Something ticked inside MapHead's head. Hadn't he been here before? Wasn't there a point – or something – at stake?

"He's driving me nuts." Jack glared. "You can make him think he's tired."

"Yes, but—"

"So make him think he's tired."

"No." MapHead rose angrily. "I won't. You didn't want me in *your* mind. Now you want me in his?"

"He's just a kid. This is different."

"No," MapHead said, "it's the same. *And I'm not interfering in anyone's mind any more.*"

MapHead stormed out to the kitchen and looked in the fridge. He searched around impatiently. There was some dietary itch he needed to scratch. Margarine. Cheese. Milk. None of them were *it*. The food looked kind of grey and old and tired. Especially the cheese. The cheese was going mouldy. MapHead felt strangely angry with everything and everyone in view. There was so much Jack didn't understand. Maybe he should tell him. MapHead slammed up the fridge and stormed back in to Jack.

"Anyway," he told the back of Jack's head, "it's not so easy, doing these things. There's only so much around."

"Only so much what around?"

"Energy. In the Subtle World. It's all connected, see? What happens here, happens there."

"I don't understand what you're talking about."

"Where I come from – the Subtle World – see, it's only the other side of this one."

"What are you on?" Jack dimmed the volume on

*90210* and finally gave MapHead his attention. Maxie had melted away. "The other side of *what*?"

"It's like – " MapHead took a deep breath " – it's like another dimension, sort of. Invisible, but *around*. Side by side with everything, you know, ordinary."

"Invisible but around. Another dimension. Right."

Jack turned back to the television. Onscreen a guy in a black leather jacket spilled out his pockets onto the police department desk. A cop in blue braces picked up a book of matches. Close up, a name and number revealed the address of the Blue Hawaii Motel.

"You don't see many kids like me," MapHead continued sadly. "Less energy, see? What goes around, comes around. Maybe I'm one of the last."

Jack stared.

"That's why I like babies. They're like, beginnings we don't have?"

Jack stared some more. The onscreen cop behind his head moved quickly to seal off the bank.

"There *are* others like me. Like my dad, I mean, at least." MapHead smiled uncertainly. "Did you think there weren't?"

"I don't know. I didn't think anything." Jack's mouth felt numb.

"And things aren't so good any more. That's why they're coming in."

"Coming in where?"

"All over. You see 'em sometimes, in the sky."

The feeling that he was on the brink of something

280

huge grew upon Jack with every passing moment. What *was* it about MapHead? Undreamed-of possibilities seemed just within his – Jack's – reach. All he had to do was open his mind.

"I feel like my head's bursting." Jack's breathing came shallow, then shallower. "I know about star clusters. I know about spatial displacement in four dimensions. I know how to fix a baby's nappy three different ways. I know about *ancient Rome*. I know like, millions of things I never knew before and I haven't got *room* for them all."

"What's the chemical composition of a cat?" MapHead tested gravely.

"Ninety-eight per cent water, two per cent carbon compounds, plus calcium, minerals, trace elements. Nutritional content: fifty-eight per cent useable protein. How did I know *that*?" Jack held his head. "*I know too much and I want it all to stop.*"

"It's my fault," MapHead said sadly. "I swapped your pictures for mine."

"You swapped my pictures? How do you mean?"

"Mainly memories," MapHead explained. "I wanted to show you everything. I wanted you to *understand*."

"Understand what?"

"How I want to fit in." MapHead hung his head. "It seemed like a good idea at the time. Go ahead, if you hate me."

"You interfered." Jack's eyes glowed. "*I want my own pictures back.*"

"You will, and I'm going to fix it." An enormously sympathetic map of southern Australia lit up MapHead's head. He got up to reassure Jack. "Soon as I can, I'm fixing it. I never meant it to change things."

Jack sidestepped MapHead, his mind already on other things. "Mind out, will you, I can't see the telly."

"The thing is, I don't know what's wrong. I didn't know this would happen."

"This what?"

"You. Being weird."

"Me? Weird? And you're not?" Jack switched telly channels. "*Mad Max* re-run. Cool."

"I'll fix it so it's OK. I didn't mean to do it and I *promise.*"

"Promise me another coke, if you're going out to the kitchen." Jack waved MapHead out of the way. He draped himself over his chair. "Give yourself one too, if you get that kid in bed – where is he, anyway?"

MapHead's map subsided. He watched Jack watching telly. Unable to concentrate on anything for more than a minute or two, Jack was seriously strange. Hadn't anything he'd said meant anything at all?

Wandering back out into the kitchen, less angry this time, MapHead's attention was held by the large and imperious-looking plant on the windowsill. *Cyclamen*, his mind whispered. *Bulbous. Winter-flowering. Can be forced on throughout summer.* Immediately attracted by its juicy stems and imperial purple flowers standing up straight like butterfly wings, MapHead took a bite.

Then he took another and another, finally holding the wide-bottomed plastic pot in both hands and scything across the plant with an open mouth. MapHead closed his eyes and chomped on a mouthful of stems. This was it. Brain food. The trace elements he'd been lacking fell into place like the tumblers in a lock.

It was while he was finishing up that he noticed Maxie under the table. Maxie stood up slowly. Hurriedly replacing what was left of Maxie's mother's houseplant, swallowing down stems as he did it, MapHead turned to face Maxie. There was a long – a very long – silence.

Finally Maxie said, "You were angry, weren't you?"

"Just now?" MapHead nodded. "I was angry."

"You've got no hair."

"No." MapHead smiled. "I haven't."

"Would you like some?"

"I suppose."

"You're funny, you are."

"Yes," MapHead said, "I'm funny."

MapHead brushed away a suspicion of stem from his mouth. It said a lot for Maximillian Rhodes' composure that he didn't run off and hide. Most people didn't eat house-plants, MapHead realized. Especially not in that ravenous, scything sort of way. Most people would probably have run off and never come back. But Maxie hadn't. Plus, he had something to say. MapHead waited. Maxie would spit it out in his own good time. In the meantime, he couldn't honestly say he regretted the cyclamen. The cyclamen had really hit the spot.

"When I was in the car park –" Maxie edged a little closer "– when I was in the car park, I saw you in the light."

"You saw me in the light." The boy in the car in the multi – how many weeks ago now? MapHead looked at Maxie. How much could Maxie understand? "I waved to you, did you see?"

Maxie nodded a lot more than he needed to. Then he nodded some more.

"That's the way I travel from place to place," MapHead explained. "The light takes me where I want to go."

"Is it hot?"

"No, it's not hot."

"Did it make your hair fall out?"

"That's right. It falls out every time."

"You better not do it then. Maybe you'd have some hair."

"Maybe –" MapHead said, enjoying himself now "– maybe I would."

A longish pause followed.

"'F you want hair –" Maxie held up a felt-tip pen "– 'f you want hair, I can do it."

MapHead considered Maxie. "Do I have a choice?"

First Maxie drew on moustaches. Then he carefully coloured MapHead's scalp in running lines of broad-tip dark-brown paint-stick. He made a careful parting.

How about burners? Could he do burners? What are burners? MapHead asked. Soon he knew, because he had them. It seemed they were bits of beards. Side beards, down from his ears. Soon Maxie wanted to join them under his chin. But MapHead drew the line at a beard right down his neck.

MapHead wanted a mirror, but Maxie grew stand-offish. Not yet. It wasn't finished, all right? Maxie raced upstairs and returned with a silk-finish zip-up that smelled the same as Tanya. Tipping it out onto the settee, he picked out a flat pad of powder and patted it over MapHead's face. MapHead picked out a tube or two from the jumble on the settee. Most said: COVER LIPS MOISTURE PLUS. One or two said things like CINNAMON CRUSH or PINK TWIST or GINGER UP as well. Others said: EYES HAVE IT, MOONSTRUCK BLUE – disconcertingly, MapHead thought.

It turned out Moonstruck Blue was exactly the shade Maxie had in mind for MapHead's eyebrows. After the eyebrows he had a bright idea. Racing upstairs for a scarf and a hat, Maxie finally displayed the finished effect to MapHead in front of the mirror.

MapHead stared back at himself. He was forced to admit Maxie had made a difference. He looked like an eccentric forties' film star forced to cover up due to some frightful disease of the skin. Maxie held up a plastic case. He forgot the false eyelashes. Where were they, anyway? MapHead covered his mouth. He'd only eaten one.

Jack said, "You look stupid. What d'you let him do that for?"

"He's tired," said MapHead. "Look at him."

"Look at *you*, you mean."

MapHead put Maxie to bed, meekly, in his own little darkened bedroom replete with a glow-worm night-light. He kissed him and closed the door. Then he opened it again.

"'Night," said Maxie, the top of his head just visible beside his ted's.

"'Night."

"Pete." Maxie called MapHead back.

"What?"

"Nothing. You look really funny."

MapHead grinned. "Wonder why?"

"Will you come again?"

"Maybe. I don't know."

"In the car park, maybe? In the light?"

"In the light," said MapHead. "Goodnight, Maximillian Rhodes."

"'Night, Pete Burns. G'bye."

Goodbye. MapHead stood uncertainly outside the door. What should he reply? Should he lie and say, See ya soon? In the end he stood silently, choked, for a long time. Then he went downstairs again with a totally satisfying warm feeling halfway between pain and tenderness burning inside his chest. He drank a litre of milk to damp it down a bit. Then he put his decorated head around the living-room door.

"I'm having a bath. Wash this stuff off."

Jack grunted. "Good job, 'cos I'm not being seen out with you till you do."

With his arms folded in front of the telly Jack looked, MapHead thought, quite a lot like his father.

Tanya got in at eleven-fifteen with very bright eyes and a collapsing hairstyle. She expressed her surprise that Pete Burns and Jack had had no trouble with Maxie. Usually Maxie played up. The dinner? *Really* good. Steak in peppercorns and sorbet. Plus she won Ferrero Rocher in the raffle. Talk about whacked. She'd call Jack's dad to pick them up. Thanks a million, how much did she owe them?

Soon after they got in and climbed the darkened stairs to bed, MapHead rose off his supposed bunk in Jack's room and lay down at Holly's bedside and went instantly to sleep with no trace of guile or guilt about him. Maxie would be sleeping deeply, too. It was a job well done. MapHead smiled in his sleep, curled like a hedgehog on the floor. He'd made, he thought in his dreams, a *proper* babysitter. Better'n the Poppins woman, any day.

"Mappers. You awake? It's me."

"What?" MapHead looked up groggily. Jack's face loomed above him. "What is it? Don't wake Holly."

"Why are you always in here?" Jack asked, bug-eyed in the light from the landing.

"I don't know. I like it. What's the matter?"

"Nothing. Only – I wondered."

"Like me to come in with you?"

Jack nodded manfully. "Yeah, I really would. I sort of felt – frightened, you know?"

"Frightened of what?"

"Being alone."

"Alone is scary. I know what you mean."

"Plus, I'm scared of myself."

"You're scared of *yourself*?"

Jack nodded. "All these things I'm thinking. And I saw a ghost, you know? Behind the bathroom door."

Back in the attic room under the stars, MapHead watched Jack sleeping. His open door said JACK'S ROOM, ALL RIGHT? If only it really were. Poor Jimmy-Jack Stamp knew too much, yet too little, and none of it was his fault. His own part in Jack's dilemma hit MapHead between the eyes. He would have to set it straight, and soon. How was another matter.

Long before morning ruddied the sky, MapHead had decided. The hollow place in the runner beans, where he'd sat and thought long and hard, was hours since cold and abandoned. The morning light shone in at a certain bedroom through a certain denim-blue blind. It shone on Jack Stamp's bed, it shone on Jack Stamp's books and clothes, it shone on all the sticky bits in Jack Stamp's bedroom carpet. It shone most especially on Jack Stamp and the freshly painted message on the wall beside his bed. Jack Stamp opened his eyes. The smell of spray-paint hung in the air. Letters sprayed in spray-paint marched beside his bed. Jack

Stamp sat up. The wall beside his bed read:

JACK–
  GONE 2 FIND DAD. GARD HOLLY 4 ME.
  CATCH U LATER. PETE.

*Gone to find Dad. Catch you later. Pete.* Where in two worlds had the oddball with the agitated scalp taken off to so suddenly? MapHead, gone? Where? Jack held his head. He ground his teeth. He buried his face in his pillow. He writhed and rolled in bed. Finally he flipped up the blind. A day without MapHead flooded in. A day without friends or purpose.

# Wibble

"Dad! Dad! Where are you? I need to know what to do!"

Through all four dimensions and all through a whole subtle world, MapHead searched for his father. His father watched him do it. He curled his lip and wondered, When will he ever learn?

"Dad! I know I'm not meant to. But I need you to tell me. Please, Dad! I mean it. Can you only tell me what to do!"

It was a little painful for Powers to listen to his son bleating in all four corners of the globe. Painful, but unfortunately necessary. He launched away in space, as MapHead got too close. His son had almost caught him in South America. Only the dusty summit of hill-fort Machu Picchu had got in the way. It had been a close shave, too, at the pyramids. Lucky King Cheops had built in a place to hide. And the misty mountains of Mourne had posed a problem or two. At the misty mountains of Mourne, MapHead had been close on his trail. At his son's approach,

*Powers had flashed away to the Giant's Causeway on the northernmost coast of Ireland. The Giant's Causeway surprised him. A layer-cake of odd-shaped rocks tilting out to sea, it looked, Powers thought, like the scene of some wild party. Someone – giants – had partied wildly and left behind their giant cake topped with shattered candles. Powers sat down to wait. Presently his questing son glowed among the candles.*

*"Dad! Are you there? Is that you?"*

*Powers sighed and flashed away. There would come a point when he'd take a hand in MapHead's affairs. Until then every appeal, every cry for help or advice, must fall on stony ears. His son had come of age. He must solve his own problems, sink or swim. That was the point of leaving him, no matter how urgent his cries. Even the one that followed him, faintly, on the wind:*

*"Dad, wait, don't go! I did this thing I never meant to! Now I know what you meant and I'll never, ever – Dad! I know you can hear me! Wait for me, Dad – are you there?"*

MapHead took a deep breath and sat down heavily on a rock. The Spartan sea rocked in a basin before him. The Spartan hills, with Spartan valleys under them, looked down. Cypresses stood cool and tall and gracefully spaced, wherever the sky needed lancing. Wherever it didn't, rounded clouds of olive groves rolled away into the distance.

MapHead sighed. He was going to stop somewhere. With its tranquil light and brilliant blue bays, Greece was as good a place as any. As good a place as any without a father or a conscience he could live with, which no amount of *travelling* would discover. He would never find his father. Not while his father didn't want him to. Instead, he must find something else. Self-respect, for starters. It wasn't fair that he should have to do everything without any help. It wasn't fair that he was always alone – why *was* he? He only had all the power in the world, yet here he was lost on a hillock, somewhere in Spartan Greece. Aah. Poor MapHead. *Wibble*.

Feeling a bit sniffy and more than a little sorry for himself, MapHead walked alone along the shore. Silvery fishes darted as one in needle-bright shoals when he feinted throwing them food. They even sucked his toes, for want of anything tastier. MapHead looked up. The brilliant sun beat down on the Spartan hills. Sparta, home of the brave.

MapHead knew about Sparta. It had something to do with leaving babies on hillsides to die and sending young boys away to nasty-looking camps with not enough clothes or food, and they mustn't complain. And they combed their hair before battle, and their mothers had rather they came home dead on their shields than come home ashamed. Spartan boys stole what they could or they went without. It was a point of pride not to get caught. They wore a thin shift no matter how bitter the weather and never said, Mum, where's my jumper? or, Chilly today, don't you think? They slept on hard pallets and washed in cold water and – probably – dried themselves on bushes or something else prickly. They probably sharpened knives on their thighs. Probably they rolled on thorns or opened sores for fun. MapHead looked out on the china-blue bay. Here the Spartans had raided fisherfolk and robbed them of conger and octopus. They didn't farm or fish themselves, why would they? Wherever they went, they simply took whatever they wanted. Strength. Courage. No regrets. No matter what happened, they wouldn't complain. The Spartans had to be the most wibble-less people on earth.

*And* the Pass of Thermopylae. At the Pass of Thermopylae, Spartan King Leonidas had held off King Darius' *whole Persian army* with only three hundred men. Way to go, thought MapHead, reaching the broad promenade. Here the little seaside town traded its fish with tourists. MapHead, a tourist in more ways than one, felt he should do some shopping. Plus, he felt peckish at last. Following the smell of bread just out of the oven, MapHead entered a stooped little shop with not much more than a smile to pay his way.

The baker looked up. *"Kalimera."*

MapHead swallowed. It was all Greek to him. Maybe the baker said, Good day. Maybe he said, Get knotted. It didn't really matter much. Nothing MapHead said back to him was going to make much difference.

MapHead held the baker's eyes. He pointed, slowly, deliberately, one after another, to a golden loaf topped with sesame seeds, triangle-shaped pastries gleaming with something very sticky indeed, and an amber pot of honey with a picture of bees in clover. The baker handed them over one by one, not looking, his eyes firmly locked on MapHead's.

"Thanks a lot." MapHead smiled. Then he said, slowly, deliberately, "You've done enough. You should retire and go fishing with Eric. Eric wants you to."

Then he let the baker go. Baker Stoupos scratched his head. He watched the boy with the bread and honey leave his shop and trail away up the hill out of town. Then he took off his apron. The sky and the sea were a lazy afternoon blue. Tonight he would take the boat out with a bright light to draw octopus. He would stand in the bow with a spear and jab out their brains. His friend Eric Christos was right. He should fish, while the fishing was good. It was time he retired and enjoyed himself. Hadn't he worked all his life?

The smell of oleander and hibiscus followed MapHead as he climbed the village road to the hills. Beside a vivid field of poppies he passed the village school. The children tumbled out and made their way home for siesta, chattering noisily – very much, MapHead saw, like children anywhere else. They didn't notice the poppies or the oleander, the swooning hibiscus or the cheeses hanging to dry under flower-laden verandahs. These were things they passed every day, why would they notice them now? Plotting and unplotting the surrounding hills and coastline over his increasingly active scalp, MapHead climbed sweltering foothills through hot sage and wild oats, pausing only once or twice to look down on the dwindling blue bowl of the bay.

Way up in the Spartan hills, long after the bread and the pastries were gone and the honey all dripped, luxuriously, into his mouth, MapHead fell in with a man dressed all in purple. At least, the man was very far ahead when MapHead heard a yelp. Reaching a beautiful garden, MapHead saw a fox. A little fox with bewitching yellow eyes and deep-fat puppy fur. The fox cub yipped. MapHead's pulse beat fast. Then he remembered Spartan boys took whatever they wanted and died before they got caught. Reaching over the fence into the beautiful garden to tickle the fox pup where fox pups most needed tickling, MapHead weighed its weight in his hand. He wanted it, no question.

By the time he reached the man dressed all in purple, the fox cub was safe in his shirt. More than a little wild and scratchy, he thought – he hoped – it would quieten down in time. The man in purple turned as MapHead drew smartly abreast. His mouth widened and smiled under sea-blue eyes, saying something, anything, friendly.

*Kalimera*, MapHead returned. The fox cub stirred in his shirt.

"I said, are you going far?" The man in purple repeated.

MapHead had the feeling that the man had spoken in Greek. But strangely, his greeting made sense.

"Far as I need to. Not really."

"What do you mean, not really?"

"I'm not really going anywhere. I don't have anywhere to go." MapHead heard the self-pitying note in his own voice with something like surprise. Did he really feel so hard done by?

"It is better to travel than to arrive," the purple sage advised.

"I hate that." MapHead sighed. "That's what my father says."

"Better, by far, to find your own way than to have someone else choose it for you – don't you think?"

MapHead scanned the road ahead for a fast way to lose the man in purple. He didn't feel like a lecture. Plus, the fox cub was murder. Squirming and wriggling under his shirt, the fox cub meant to escape. For something so cute and appealing – *ow!* – it felt pretty vicious close up.

"Who knows what decisions we may have to make, what we might have to do?" the purple sage was saying. "These hills, this path – that next turning, up ahead. Who knows what – or who – may lie around it?"

"May lie around it," MapHead echoed, his attention anywhere but on the man in imperial purple. He'd have thrown down the wriggling fox cub then, except that Spartan boys *didn't get caught*. They'd both passed the beautiful garden. If he threw down the fox cub now, the man dressed all in purple would know that he was a thief. A thief, as well as someone who played with people's minds, then didn't know how to set it straight. MapHead felt like crying. He held the fox cub tightly under his shirt. Wasn't he in Sparta, now? He mustn't – *wouldn't* – complain.

"I'm sorry," MapHead continued, "but I've been on my own a long time. I don't know what to talk about when I bump into other people."

"Talk about yourself," the purple sage invited. "What better thing is there to talk about?"

"About a million better things," MapHead answered darkly. "I'm not so great that I want to *talk* about anything I've done."

The man in imperial purple stopped. "What *have* you done?" he asked MapHead.

The blue Spartan sea swam behind the sage's gaze. His sea-blue eyes questioned MapHead. MapHead swallowed. Was it *that* obvious? Did he wear his guilty feelings all over him like livid spots he couldn't brush off, not even – especially – in dreams? Did they swim on his face like contour lines? Did they ring like a leper's bell? The matter of answering the man in purple honestly and *not dropping the fox cub* had become as thoroughly entangled in MapHead's mind as Jack Stamp and wrongs unrighted.

"What have I done?" MapHead took a deep breath. "I only messed up my friend's mind, plus the whole rest of his *life*, plus the whole rest of his *family*. Then I ran off and left him, just when he needed me most."

The purple sage inclined his head. "And?"

"And what makes it worse is, my dad told me not to. Interfere, I mean. So now I want to put it right, but I don't know what to do."

"So you knew it was wrong when you did it?"

MapHead opened his shirt. He took out the fox cub lovingly. The fox cub regarded him with golden-yellow eyes with a pinprick of black in the middle. It tried to wriggle down through his fist. Its pink mouth tried to bite him.

*"So you knew it was wrong when you did it?"*

MapHead set down the fox cub. It scampered lightly away. MapHead watched its silly little brush-tail flickering away through the dry grass under the olives. *Power is responsibility. Don't take advantage. Respect.*

"Yes," he said with a full heart, "I knew it was wrong when I did it. And I'm," he added, "the only one who can fix it. And that's just the way that it is."

It hurt him so much to say it. MapHead held the feeling close and knew it for a friend. Some things were good for you, like medicine. The fox in the beautiful garden – the purple sage, the china-blue bay, the dream of Spartan Greece – were things in the order of these. He hadn't complained, after all. He'd faced up to himself like a hero. Wibble-less at last, he was free to act as he chose.

Flushed with triumph after all, MapHead glowed on

the path. The last thing he remembered was the hot smell of sun-dried grasses, bright with butterflies, murmurous with honey bees. Then something broke inside his head, and Spartan Greece flashed away.

# No Love No Home This Summer

The dog Weg looked at the digger. MapHead looked through Weg's mind's eye. It was a long time – had he ever? – it was a long time since he'd tried to see things from a dog's point of view. The digger roared, churning up mud as it lifted a log with its bucket-that-opened-in-the-middle. The bucket-that-opened-in-the-middle swivelled. Then it set down the log, gingerly, on the topmost tip of two other logs, balanced one on top of another.

The scene was a strange one to start with. Through a dog's eyes – through Weg's eyes, at least – it made no sense at all. As if it weren't all confusing enough, when he'd looked around after materializing as close to Jack Stamp as he was able, MapHead had had a job to work out *where he was at all*, never mind at some kind of show. At Rubytown & District Agricultural Show, as it turned out. At the Digger Competition, to be precise.

The Digger Competition seemed to involve enormous

earth-moving machines with limbs like crabs moving tiny objects in impossibly delicate situations. After the competition to set one log, end up, on top of another without toppling them, the diggers moved on to a line of empty bottles. MapHead watched incredulously as a digger-driver picked up a single bottle with his crab-claws. The excavator's huge serrated claws, as big as a dinosaur's jawbone, held that bottle as lightly as an egg. Hugely straining and roaring, the digger set the bottle on a plank. Then it went back for another.

After MapHead had witnessed competitor Dean Stockwell's digger levering itself over a pole with much crunching of gears and insect-like manoeuvring of arms and struts and buckets, he still didn't understand it. The dog Weg didn't understand it either, MapHead could see. Jack Stamp and his family understood it, but waited to see what would happen. It was good to see Jack and his family again. Wasn't that Martin Starkey, as well? MapHead dodged their eyes. He would join them when he was ready.

"And Dean Stockwell ... going well now against the clock," droned the loudspeaker. "Three bottles in position ... lovely job, Dean ... and going on now to tackle the Floating Balls in the Skip..."

Fruity smells wafted into MapHead's brain as the dog Weg sniffed its way into the Rare Breeds and Ewes Enclosure. MapHead checked the family Stamp. Surely they'd notice their dog had wandered off? Apparently not. Totally involved in Dean Stockwell's bid to skim balls out of a water-filled skip with the business end of his digger, no one seemed to have noticed the Wegster's move. MapHead wrinkled his nose. Then he followed Weg, seeing what Weg saw, smelling what Weg smelled. And was there ever plenty to smell in Rare Breeds and Highland Ewes.

Odour-radiating sheep of every size and texture eyed MapHead fearfully over the tops of their pens. Black-face sheep, white-face sheep, Jacob's Sheep, rugged moorland crossbreeds and sculpted-looking show queens with flat backs the width of Welsh dressers – such a bewildering mass of heaving, lanolin-smelling bodies brought MapHead up short in his tracks. All of them were sheep. And all of them were smelly. Smellier than anything MapHead had ever niffed before, they weren't at all unpleasant. In fact they smelled quite – exciting.

Wagging with joy from head to tail, the dog Weg sneezed three times. MapHead sneezed three times in sympathy. With a sense of smell so sensitive a million whiffs a second swamped your brain like a funfair you could niff but couldn't ride, pulling you this way, then that, filling your head with a hundred edible scents, the sheep tent was Niff-It Heaven. The dog Weg thought so, too. No one noticed Weggie Wegsford approaching an aisle of ewes. He wandered between them, sniffing. MapHead searched the ewes' minds. He probed their syrup-coloured eyes. Nothing. Worse than Weg. Just *nothing* but fluff. And fear.

"Get that dog out! Now!"

A large agricultural type, with a red face and a white coat with bursting buttons so tense they'd explode any minute, bore down on Weg. MapHead sidestepped to avoid him. Then he sidestepped again.

"Don't dance with me, boy. *Get that dog out!*"

Bursting out of Rare Breeds and Highland Ewes hot on the heels of Weg, MapHead turned a corner, then another, finally dodging down a miry passage ankle-deep in straw behind a barn. Weg ran on, but MapHead didn't. Instead, he stared at the boy. A boy with a spray-can. Spraying big marching letters on a concrete-block wall. The concrete-block wall of the barn.

"And Frank Doidge bringing years of experience to bear on these balls in the skip now..." boomed the loudspeaker, somewhere beyond the sheep tent. "Going on now to Stack the Can ... and Dean Stockwell building up an impressive lead in this event. It's going to take some beating... Is Frank Doidge the man to do it?"

"I went in the sheep tent. I just got chased out." MapHead smiled uncertainly. "It's pretty smelly in there."

"So surprise me." The boy spraying paint on the wall was really pretty skinny.

"What are you doing?" MapHead asked.

"What's it look like? Tags."

"Tags?"

303

"Tag lines. IDs. Riffs, you know?" The boy continued spraying. He didn't miss a beat.

"But why are you?" MapHead persisted.

"Why am I what?"

"Why are you writing it on the wall? Why don't you write it on a piece of paper or on a computer or something?"

"I dunno. Because." Finally the artist looked at MapHead. "Why did old Leonardo de Thingy paint pictures? Why didn't he just doodle on bits of paper?"

"He did," MapHead said simply. "He did lots 'n' lots of doodles, all the time." *Leonardo Da Vinci, 1452–1519*, MapHead scanned in his mind. Then he added, "I could show you where he lived, if you like or don't like."

The artist stared. "*Don't* like."

MapHead controlled his scalp with difficulty. Probably plotting a map of the small Tuscan town of Vinci would be too much, anyway. Way too much, at this stage. Better not come on too strong. Not with some kid he just met.

Still looking at MapHead, the artist shook his spray-can. Then he turned away and finished spraying

no LOVE NO homE this
SuMMer biG ShoUt 2

"*You're* Big Shout 2?" MapHead boggled.

The artist sprayed on. "No prizes."

"You're not very big. Can you shout?"

"It's my tag line, all right?"

"Do you live here?" MapHead felt muddled. Was *this* the robber who beat up Jack Bradley Stamp?

"Oh, yeah. I'd live in a field."

MapHead weighed the tone of this reply. *No love no home this summer*. Then he said, "So where, then?"

"Where what?"

"So where do you live?"

"Over on Greenslades. What's it to you?"

"So you *do* have a home."

"Foster home. My mother, she don't want me."

A blast from a distant-sounding horn announced the end of the sheep-shearing contest. The *neee-yaw* of the Rotary Saw Display chewing through half a tree-trunk sounded peevishly over the *pom-pom-pom, tiddle-om-pom-pom* of the silver band playing the Floral Dance. Over the top of the hedge MapHead spotted Jack; then Mr Stamp, dragging Wegsy, disgraced, on a lead; then Mrs Stamp, with Holly, all trooping back to the car.

MapHead looked down. Then he said, "Those shoes. They belong to my friend."

"Says who?"

"I say. Me. 'Cos they do."

"Yeah, well." Big Shout 2 considered his feet. "Yeah, well, he owed me. Your *friend* put one over on me. Till my brother showed up."

"He did? I mean, Jack, he – did something?"

305

"Only robbed me blind."

"Jack was robbing you? And then your brother hit him?"

Big Shout 2 wiped his mouth. "Rob – that's my brother – Rob got my money back off of him. Plus we got all his. Then Rob smacked him a bit. Then he ran off and fell over."

"He lost his door key as well."

"Rob's got his door key. You better watch out. My brother, he – does things."

"What things?"

"Houses, mainly. Sometimes cars. Whatever he feels like doing."

"I do things too," MapHead said helpfully. "Mostly maps. Plus, I'm living with this family and trying to fit in? We're over on Gough Street. You should drop in some time."

"Maybe we will." Big Shout 2 smiled crookedly. "Rob likes dropping in."

"Is that why he's called Rob?" MapHead went on pleasantly. "Because he robs things?"

Big Shout 2 stared hard at MapHead. "Who are you, anyway?"

"MapHead," said MapHead. "Look. I can do tag lines too."

First MapHead tagged Verona. Then he tagged Ravenna and Bologna. Finally, the whole of northern Italy. Crisp in every twist of river, lake and bluff, the map was a physical map and one of MapHead's best.

The graffiti artist blanched. He capped his spray-can robotically. "I'm out of here," he said.

MapHead watched him back away, fast, then faster, so eager to go he'd go any way he could, no matter how much mud from behind the barn he took with him. It was funny what maps could make people do. It was funny what people did, anyway. It was funny – or tragic – the things that they wrote. A few words could say so much. When nothing of Big Shout 2 remained but his jumping tag line on the wall, MapHead finally emerged from behind the barn. *No love no home this summer*. A purposeful smile lit his face.

Jumping up onto the wall, MapHead looked down on Rubytown. A family town to MapHead; the place his own mother and half-brother and grandmother lived and worked and ate their meals and went to school and dried their hair and drank tea and broke their nails on supermarket blister packs, and watched their favourite soaps in. Home, with all that that meant. It gave him an idea. Suddenly filling his lungs, MapHead shouted with all his might:

*"Dad! I know what to do! You don't have to tell me any more! I know what to do about Jack!"*

Jack Stamp. Where was he? Popping out anxiously into the car-park field below, MapHead spotted a queue of departing cars in time to see the Stamp-mobile joining it. The Volvo looked so familiar by now, it felt like a toe or an ear. MapHead could make out Jack Stamp's head behind his parents'. Beside him,

Holly's car seat. On the other side of that, the well-disgraced and tousled head of the hound they called Weggie Wegsford. Jack wasn't looking back. But there was something about the back of Jack's head that made MapHead want to join him very much.

Vaulting a gate into the road ahead of the Stamps' departing car, MapHead stuck out his thumb, the way he'd seen hitchhikers do it. The slow-moving queue of cars rolled past him unhurriedly. No one stopped when they saw MapHead's thumb. Maybe they hadn't seen it. A sign saying HEAVY PLANT CROSSING worried him more than a little. He scouted the road. No heavy plants. Then he spotted the Volvo. He waved his thumb and waited. The Stamps pulled up obediently.

"Which way are you going?" MapHead enquired politely. He needed a cardboard sign, he knew. One that said ALL ROADS HOME.

"There you are, Pete Burns." Mr Stamp wound down his window. "We wondered where you'd gone."

"Where I'd gone." MapHead found Jack's eyes. Jack's eyes ate him up.

"I said we'd meet at the show," Jack improvised. "I told them you'd gone with Dave Wilkie."

"Dave Wilkie?"

"Dave Wilkie you went to have lunch with," Jack said, meaningfully.

"Oh." MapHead blinked. "Dave *Wilkie*. Right. I really like Dave Wilkie. 'Specially lunch with Dave Wilkie, then we meet at the show. And I say I've known

308

him a long time. And what I like is, to meet him. Mainly for lunch and a show. Then I say I've—"

"Pete." Alan Stamp checked the queue in his mirror. "Would you like to get into the car?"

Squeezing in between Jack and Holly's car seat, MapHead noted that Lois was absent with disappointment tinged with relief. He met Valerie Stamp's gaze inches from her face. Valerie Stamp smiled at him rather uncertainly. Then she faced front over a large bargain begonia with tasty-looking leaves. She exchanged a look with Jack's father. Then she turned back to MapHead. "Could we talk later, Pete? There's a few things we'd like to ask you."

"Talk. Later. I'd like to." MapHead squirmed. *Very* much later, he hoped.

Jack almost wept with relief. Except he kept it well hidden. First he pinched MapHead so hard he almost yelped, but didn't. Then the whispering began.

"Mappers. Where have you *been*?"

"Once round the pyramids. Twice round the Giant's Causeway. Plus I went to Sparta."

"Seriously."

"Seriously. How long have I been gone?"

"Last night," Jack said, "and today. Feels like a million years."

"A million years in *subtle* time. And anyway. You missed me."

"Not you," Jack said, "the maps."

"Just the maps?"

309

"I'm joking." Jack Stamp bit his lip. "I thought you'd never come back."

"As if," MapHead told him, holding Jack's eyes, letting Jack see where he'd been – if he wanted to, that was. *Pyramids. Sea-fog. A hill fort in South America. The candle-cake at the Causeway. A china-blue bay. An olive grove. The prickly hills of Sparta.*

"Oh," Jack said, "I see."

"What's that, Jack?" asked Mrs Stamp. "What did you say you see?"

"Nothing. I said, time for tea."

"Can you wake Holly? We're almost home. Teatime it certainly is."

MapHead shook Holly gently as Mr Stamp killed the engine on Gough Street. Holly's blue eyes opened, misted, focused. Her pink face puckered irritably. MapHead scooped her out of her car seat before she could start to cry. Holly examined MapHead's chin. She smiled in MapHead's eyes and smacked him on the head. MapHead smiled back. Holly liked him. She let him know. It felt good to know she missed him. Jack had missed him, too. It felt warm and right inside to reclaim his place beside them. It felt like fitting in.

"Hungry, Pete?" asked Mrs Stamp. "I'll bet you could eat a horse."

"No thanks," said Pete Burns seriously. "Egg and chips is fine."

# The Black Hole

Hubert Sewell Community College
Outlands Road
Rubytown
Tel: 01533 396876

16th June

Mr and Mrs A. S. Stamp
Rising Sun
Gough Street
Rubytown

Dear Mr and Mrs Stamp,

You will recall that I wrote
to you recently in connection
with Jack's erratic attendance
at school, suggesting a meeting

might be in order and proposing a
possible date for you to come in.
I'm sure you will be as anxious
as we are to discuss any problems
Jack may be experiencing. I will
be available next week any day
except Wednesday from 3.30
onwards. If you would care to
phone my secretary to make an
appointment I will look forward
to seeing you then.

Yours sincerely,

*A. Leary*

Ada Leary
Headteacher

Ada Leary. Headteacher. MapHead rolled the name
around on his tongue. It was a name he'd heard Jack
mention often enough. Ada Leary. Makes you weary.
Plus, she used to be a man. Supposedly. MapHead had
heard all about it. Someone had said it once, for a joke.
Now fantastical stories abounded, supported by anything as slight as an uneven bust-line or an extra nasal
hair. Poor Ada Leary. At any rate, she didn't sound too
cross – or manly – in her letter. More worried than

cross. But *how* worried? How long would Ada Leary smoulder before she blew?

Hearing Jack thump up the stairs, MapHead hastily folded the letter back into its stiff-looking envelope stamped with the Hubert Sewell Community College logo and slipped it under the carpet with the others. He'd learned to spot them a mile off, once he'd learned about letters. The first time the letters came through the door when MapHead – and no one else – was up, MapHead had blocked their passage through the letterbox and forced them all back out. In they'd come again. MapHead pushed them out. A tussle of kinds had developed between the postman and MapHead. The postman had got quite angry. Finally MapHead had opened the door and accepted the crushed-looking letters after the postman pointed out they were addressed to – and wanted to be received by – the people named on the front. Ever since then a wary truce had obtained between MapHead and the postman. The postman's name was Crispin. MapHead tried not to mind.

MapHead had recognized the letters from school as a threat the moment he'd seen them. Jack would be right soon enough. No need to discuss any problems. Even so, he couldn't hold it for ever. The situation re Jack had elements of coming to the boil. The threatened talk with Valerie Stamp hadn't materialized yet. Once or twice over the week since his return she'd looked as if she was up for it, but greeted with MapHead's candid gaze had somehow always backed off. Instead, she'd grown peevish with Jack. Jack couldn't do anything right. Hyperactive and cutting as acid in any reply to his mother, Jack didn't help himself. He looked pretty normal, but was he? What was normal, anyway? Just what had Jack been like before he – MapHead – had known him? MapHead couldn't afford to dwell on it. It would undermine his certainties. Certain hard-won certainties were just about all he had.

Jack put his head around the door. "So."

"So."

"What are you doing?" Jack joined MapHead on the spare bed, MapHead's bed, in his – Jack's – bedroom.

"Nothing. Just looking around."

"Want to look at my brochures?" Jack meant his travel brochures. Following a visit to Hoseason Travel in Fore Street, Jack had spent a lot of time, of late, poring over pictures of white beaches and extravagant purple sunsets. Sri Lanka, Island Paradise. Discover Turkey. Aloha Hawaii! Romantic Granada. Exotic Algeria. Unforgettable Algarve. Sun-kissed Canaries. Getaway Caribbean! Jack Stamp had read them all.

"Why don't you read things you're meant to?" MapHead asked.

"I'm not going to school, if that's what you mean."

"Something's going to happen if you don't."

"I've been in, now and then. What more do they want?"

Jack shovelled his brochures back under his bed.

Then he looked at MapHead.

"You won't go away again, will you?"

"Of course I'll go away."

Jack swallowed. "But you'll come back. Every time. Won't you."

MapHead smiled. Jack even *sounded* like him, these days. "I came back the other time, didn't I? Nothing ever really goes away."

"'Cept your dad. You said you never found him."

"I don't think he wants me to find him."

"You want your dad, I want mine," Jack said, simply.

"You've got yours already."

Jack raised his eyebrows. "Have I?"

MapHead considered Jack Stamp. Jack Bradley Stamp had had enough on his plate just lately without thinking his father didn't like him. Behind Jack's head his – MapHead's – funny marching letters still vaguely announced his departure. GONE 2 FIND DAD. GARD HOLLY 4 ME. Poor Jack Stamp. The scrubbed-out message on his bedroom wall was one more reason he was grounded.

"How do you feel?" MapHead asked Jack.

"Bored out of my mind. How would *you* feel if you knew what I know?"

"I *do* know what you know. Plus I know loads more as well."

"Well, then. You know how I feel."

"You know Big Shout 2," MapHead started. "I saw him the other day. You know you said he was massive—"

"He isn't, his brother is." Jack's eyes snapped. "I pushed *him*, his massive great brother pushed *me*, and I lost my door key, all right? It doesn't matter now, anyway. We're past all that. On higher ground, OK?"

"What d'you mean – higher ground?"

"We don't stick around much, do we?" Jack got up and paced around. "We flash around, don't we? From place to place. In subtle timing, I mean."

MapHead watched Jack carefully. "Travelling's not so great. Families are better."

Jack snorted. "Yeah, right. That's why your dad's avoiding you."

"I mean it. There's a place you fit in. You're lucky."

"Yeah," Jack said, "lucky duck. I'm grounded except for boring old family outings, no one understands I need dosh to like, *travel* and stuff and go all the places I want to, plus I know about a million things and I can't do anything about them."

MapHead looked at him. "Wibble."

"There's one thing soon. It's my birthday."

"It is?"

"I wonder what'll foul it up," Jack said bitterly. "Probably it'll thunder."

It might, thought MapHead, do a great deal more than *that*. Feeling the wad of letters under the carpet with his foot, MapHead pictured Ada Leary's advance in a rolling thunder cloud raining stiff-looking envelopes. Lightning flashed from her fingertips. The postman Crispin drove her vengeful chariot. Dogs of war snapped at her heels.

"What *was* that?" MapHead asked Jack, dreamily aware of a boom. "Is it thunder already?"

"Dunno," Jack said. "Sounds like something falling."

"JACK!" someone bawled up the stairwell. "JACK! I KNOW YOU'RE UP THERE!"

Lois put her head around the door. "Wonder what that noise was? Dining-room, I think."

"JACK! I MEAN IT! GET HERE NOW!"

"You better get down there." Lois smiled sweetly. "I wouldn't be you, Jack Stamp."

At the bottom of the stairs they found the front door ajar and Martin Starkey waiting stupidly on the doorstep. The phone rang persistently in the hall. Martin Starkey smiled.

"I rang the bell. Is it a bad time?"

"What d'you want?" Jack glowered.

"I just came to tell you they're gone. I thought I better tell you."

"What are?"

"Those decks you wanted. Ben Pringle's brother sold 'em last night. Someone local. They paid cash and fetched 'em straight off."

"JACK! I WANT YOU! NOW!"

"But I told him I'd pay a deposit."

"He never said. They're gone now. I thought you'd like to know."

317

"Great. Brilliant. I love you." Jack closed the door emphatically on Martin Starkey's face. Smacking the phone off the hook on his way through the hall, Jack Stamp entered the dining-room like anything might happen before he'd *care*.

"About time," Mrs Stamp's voice said furiously. "What's the meaning of *this*?"

MapHead took up his position by the door jamb. He saw Mrs Stamp put her hands on her hips. He heard the fury in her voice and knew it for what it was, almost – not quite – the last straw. The last straw but one for poor Jack.

"Meaning of what?" Jack asked.

"How can you ask? Look at this mess."

Things looked black for Jack. They looked pretty black mostly everywhere, now that MapHead came to look. A musty smell pervaded. There was black on the floor. Black in a fireplace MapHead had never even noticed before. A pile of black slabs on the carpet. Black over Valerie Stamp's armchairs. Black over Valerie Stamp.

"I never unblocked the chimney." Jack shrugged. "Why didn't you leave it alone?"

"I unblocked the fireplace to clean it," Valerie Stamp said wearily. "And what fell down inside? Apart from soot, I mean?" She bent to pick up the black slabs – MapHead saw they were books – and threw them down one by one. "Geography, Mr Rickman. Physics, Mr Wiseman. Maths, Mr Rains. Chemistry,

Miss Preston. Oh, and French and German. Mr Brown, I think." Valerie Stamp looked up. "Just about every subject. Let's hope they're not current, eh, Jack? Else what would you be working in at school?"

"What – would I be working in?"

"Yes, Jack. How can you work with no books? Perhaps you'd like to show me your recent school-work. Then we'll know where we are. Although I *have* got some dates on these." She picked up a book between finger and thumb. "Here we are. Shales and Displacement. Monday, 10th May – what do you know? They're not so old, after all."

"Yes, they are. They're duff ones. It's all new course-work now."

"Sines, Cosines and Tangents. Part One." Mrs Stamp flipped a maths book. "I wonder where Part Two is? Should we ask Mr Rains?"

"It's like this," Jack affected a laugh. "It's stupid, really, what happened. Some of them's not that old. But what happened was, what happened was I—"

"Yes, Jack?" Valerie Stamp waited. "Why *is* your Year 8 schoolwork down the chimney? I'd really like to know."

Jack seemed to blank out suddenly. "Isn't that Pete Burns? Pete Burns, listening by the door?"

Mrs Stamp whipped out to the doorway. MapHead blocked her vision, instantly, completely, with all the strength he had. It wasn't interfering. It wasn't going inside her mind. It was simply selecting what she saw.

319

He had the right, after all. He didn't *have* to be seen.

Mrs Stamp whipped back in. "This has nothing to do with Pete Burns. It has to do with *you*. But while we're on the subject." She strode rapidly out of vision. When she returned she had a book. MapHead strained at the door jamb. "While we're on the subject, take a look at *this*."

"*Pete Burns' Seafood Kitchen.*" Jack considered the Lobster Bisque on the cover. "A cookery book? So?"

"So why's he called Pete Burns?"

"Our guest, you mean?"

"Who else?"

"Because it's his name? Pete. And Burns. It's not so unusual, is it?"

"Funny his name's the same name as this book in the cupboard."

"Hilarious. So what?"

"Jack. I think you know what I'm saying."

"No. I don't. Why don't you ask him yourself?"

"I don't really think I want to know. The thing is, how will it end?"

"*You* brought him home."

"I can't remember anything about it. Where does he come from? What should we do?"

Jack Stamp shrugged. "Like you care."

"Of *course* we care. You've changed, Jack. It's something to do with Pete Burns. Don't ask me how, but I know."

Jack Stamp shrugged again.

"What is the matter with you?"

"I'm a person. I want to be free."

Mrs Stamp stared at her son. MapHead's heart raced. Everything seemed to be whirling, faster and faster, down a hole. Soon his whole life would go down it, and someone would put on the lid. And that would be – neatly – the end of it. Maybe not such a bad thing.

"That telephone number he gave me," Mrs Stamp went on softly, "the one I asked him for so I could ring his parents? The international operator said there was no such number. Too many digits. They're all 0030 numbers now. Even the first ones were wrong."

Jack Stamp edged his sooty books under a chair with his foot. His mother could ramble on ever so long, so long as the heat was off him. Happy to put the heat where it squarely belonged, on the shoulders of frail Pete Burns, Jack Stamp nodded agreement.

"Yeah. I know. It's weird."

"He's very strange. Did you ever see him eat a plant?"

"A plant? No way." Jack made a face.

"That babysit you did. I didn't say, but Tanya rang. Why didn't you tell me Pete Burns ran a bath and flooded the room downstairs?"

"He had a bath. I don't know what else. I didn't know it ran over."

"Ran over is putting it mildly. Tanya said it looked as though he'd filled the bath right up and left the taps running. Water went straight through the floor. You didn't touch any make-up?"

"Make-up? Please. Why would I?"

"Only Tanya said it was everywhere, as though someone had *used every single thing* in her make-up bag upstairs."

"Crime of the century," Jack mugged, unpleasantly.

"And Maxie told her – it sounds mad, but it was gone – Maxie told her he saw Pete Burns *eat her cyclamen.*"

"Her what?"

"Her cyclamen. A house-plant. Maxie saw him *eat* it."

"Oh. Gross. I mean, really?"

MapHead felt Lois coming downstairs before the scent of her reached him. He blocked her vision furiously as she blew past him like a dewberry-smelling wind, a wind he would follow if only – fat chance – she would let him.

"Mum. Quick. Take a look at this." Lois flung down a lunch-box triumphantly. "Guess where I found it? No? *Under Pete Burns' bed.*"

Jack took a sharp breath. "Lois. Lois. Wait—"

"See?" Lois spilled the box out. "Thirty quid. My money I've been looking for?"

"What money?" Valerie Stamp asked. "Since when have you been looking for your money?"

"Ever since my money went missing? I *knew* I was right not to trust him."

"Lois, wait." Jack looked flushed. "Maybe it's not your money."

"Oh, right. Take *his* side." Lois appealed to her mother. "Can't you see what he's doing to Jack? What he's doing to all of us?"

"I don't know," Mrs Stamp said helplessly. "He loves Holly. He cheers me up. What *is* he doing to all of us?"

"Think about it," Lois said. "This weird kid arrives out of nowhere. Strange things go wrong in the house. *You* can't remember what you're doing. Jack goes crazy, and no one asks why? And now he takes my money? My money I earned at Mandeville's?"

"What do you mean, at Mandeville's? Since when do you work at a nightclub?"

Lois stuck her chin out. "I'm waitressing. I told you."

"Just a minute. You most certainly did not. You can get on that phone right away and tell them you won't be in. It's a good thing your father's gone out. Don't think your father's going to—" Valerie Stamp stopped suddenly.

In listening, gobsmacked, to the whirling black hole of suspicion and counter-suspicion that threatened to suck them all in, MapHead had drifted out in full view of the open doorway. In the heat of the moment they saw him. Naked but for his clothes, full but for utter emptiness, MapHead stood in the doorway and stared at his adoptive family. His adoptive family stared back.

323

MapHead spread his arms in a kind of mute appeal.

"Show them, then," Jack ordered. "Go on, then. *Map it up.*"

They could have asked him anything. Anything at all. Obediently, MapHead set up a flow of maps over his scalp and face it would have defeated an artist to capture. He centred mainly on Spain. It seemed like the heartland he yearned for. Then he ran Antarctica. Mount Erebus; the Mertz Glacier; Cape Crozier, where the emperor penguins huddled that time when he'd longed to join in, but hadn't been able to, really. One of a kind when the icecap froze, he would never really fit in. The plots and contours rose and fell, swifter than MapHead thought them. The Amery Ice Shelf; Mount Terror; the Beardmore Glacier; Shackleton Inlet; Elephant Island; the Weddell Sea. The coldest names on earth.

MapHead stood in the doorway of the house called Rising Sun, on Gough Street, Rubytown, and glowed like an Antarctic sunset. The family called Stamp stood and watched him. And watched and watched and watched.

# The Multi Again

"Here. I brought you some breakfast."

Jack Stamp took off his Walkman. He waited a moment, then deposited his offering of cold Marmite toast in sandwich wrap and a carton of orange juice on the oily concrete deck next to MapHead. MapHead didn't turn around.

"I *told* 'em you didn't take Lois' money. I told 'em it was mine. Wish I hadn't, now. Now they think I took it. It *is* Lois' money, but what am I going to tell them?"

Jack Stamp paused. He looked at MapHead. MapHead continued staring out over the eight o'clock town. The past two nights he'd snuck home to curl up beside Holly's cot when the family Stamp were asleep, but he didn't want Jack to know that. Daytime, he'd spent up the multi. That was the way it had gone. But it couldn't go on that way much longer. Well and truly outcast now, he might as well make his move.

"The thing is, I only borrowed it." Jack Stamp

squatted beside MapHead. Cars spiralled up to level C behind them. The town below was waking up. A large delivery lorry nosed its way down Fore Street. The air was crisp, the sky light, beyond the stink of exhaust. It was going to be a nice day. Another nice day without MapHead.

"All right, I shouldn't have done it," Jack Stamp admitted. "I don't know why I've been doing weird things. It's just, I want something to *happen*." He looked at MapHead. "I've started a rap. Want to hear it?"

MapHead stared out over the town. A small vein pulsed behind his ear. The worst thing was feeling lonely. Sticking-out kind of lonely, like a sore thumb or an ugly piece of furniture someone put out for the dustmen. MapHead sighed. One of the family. As if. A map-flashing, plant-eating, mind-bending *traveller* like him. Please. What did he expect?

"Mum reported you missing last night," Jack said. "They wanted a photo. And a name that wasn't Pete Burns? The policeman asked me who I thought you really were."

Jack Stamp glanced across at MapHead. Then he unwrapped the Marmite toast and slowly began to eat it himself. "Like, what am I going to tell them? You're a super-powerful, inter-dimensional traveller sleeping rough up the multi?"

Jack polished off the Marmite toast. He lanced the carton of orange juice with its straw and began to drink it. "Anyway," he said, "it might be good if you rang 'em. Mum and Dad, I mean. Tell 'em you've gone to Greece. 'Least then they might stop worrying."

MapHead inclined his head. He might have been nodding agreement.

Jack Stamp rose, slapping crumbs off his Hubert Sewell blazer. "Got to keep 'em happy. You have to, really, don't you? That's why I'm going to school. I'm just like, marking time?"

MapHead gave no answer, nor any indication that he was listening. The rumble and growl of parking cars filled the hollow-sounding car-decks. Doors slammed. Office workers filed busily out towards the stained concrete stairwell. Others waited impatiently for the lift. Jack Stamp took it all in. Plenty of people around. But none of them looking at *him*.

"Here," he said, "cop this." Striking a pose he began to intone:

"Now we're *out*
and all *alone*
Say Maps
where *do*
you keep
your *home*

"Is it Cool Street,
is it *rude*
is it somewhere
in the *hood* –"

327

"Hood, that's *neighbourhood*, see?" Jack went on, intoning rapidly, popping his knees with the rhythm:

"Is it smokin'
is it *funky*
up – up – up the
up the *multi*…

"Multi-*plicity*
in the
*inner* city
multi-*tudi*nous
mighty-*rude*-of-us
multi-*milli*onaire
what me
*I* should care –"

He stopped uncertainly. "Then the refrain comes in."

"On cuh-cuh Cool Street
*Say Maps!*
On cuh-cuh Cool Street
*Say Maps!*

"Multi-farious
multi-*scarious*
multi-lateral
multi-*splateral*
multi-*cellular*

328

dig how *well* ya are
On cuh-cuh Cool Street –
*Say Maps!*

"Then I name-check DJ BlackJack. I'm working on the rest." Jack Stamp looked at MapHead. "So tell me so far. What do you think?"

MapHead shifted very slightly. Stiff-legged and straight-backed, he might have sat that way for hours. Jack took the slight shift kindly.

"Cool, isn't it? Not finished yet. But cool." Jack sighed. "It's a sickener Ben Pringle's brother sold those decks. I could've mixed a backing." He checked his watch, then shouldered his school-bag reluctantly. "I'm going to school now, worse luck. I'll bring you some dinner tonight." He walked around the front of MapHead to make sure he understood. "Dinner tonight, OK? I'll be round about eight, maybe half past?"

MapHead stirred. "Don't bother."

"It's no bother." Jack sighed again. "Crappy detention every day this week to catch up with classwork I missed. Plus I get no credits. Plus I have to pay for new school books."

MapHead looked out over Rubytown. "Anyway. Soon it's your birthday."

"I'm not having any birthday. I have to see Ada Leary instead. That's what Dad said, anyway."

"Grim." MapHead thawed very slightly.

"It's more than grim, it's tragic." Jack Stamp backed away. "I have to go now. See you later, OK?"

"I'll be round tonight to guard Holly," MapHead said rustily. "Don't bother bringing me food."

"Why are you always guarding Holly? Holly's all right. What can happen?" Jack Stamp shrugged. "Whatever you like. I'll see you. I'll have some food in my room."

MapHead considered the waking town while Jack Stamp walked away. It was a town it hurt him to look at. His mother and half-brother lived here. Somewhere, out over the houses, were the bedrooms where they'd slept. A kitchen they'd just had breakfast in. A front door they'd just walked out of. Their lives were complete without him. He wouldn't – would *not* – interfere. This had to be the last time. The last time he'd come to Rubytown, MapHead decided, as Jack Stamp's footsteps died.

Suddenly Jack was back. Jack's face was in MapHead's face, his anxious eyes on MapHead's. "Soon we're off on our travels, aren't we? Flashing from place to place. No limits, right? You and me. *Just you and me together.*"

Jack's fevered face searched MapHead's. His words had come out in a jumble no one else could have understood.

"We're only like, treading water just now. Aren't we? We're travellers, right? We don't stay long, wherever we go. And we jump – *flash* – and we're somewhere else, maybe Mauritius or Africa?"

MapHead looked at Jack. "Go to school," he said, evenly. "We're only treading water."

"Hello? Is that Mrs Stamp?"

"Speaking."

"It's me, Pete Burns. I'm phoning from Greece. I'm with Mum and Dad. So don't worry."

A longish silence. "How did you get there? Who are you, really?"

"Really I do hypnosis. I've been on Hypnosis Holidays. They place you with other people's parents? Now I'm at home I'm fine. My mum and dad say thanks."

"I don't understand. What do you mean – Hypnosis Holidays?"

"So if you think you saw funny stuff, remember it's only a trick. Things'll settle down now I'm gone. And your family's the best. 'Specially Holly. And I want to say thank you very much."

"Hello? Are your parents there? I don't remember volunteering for any holiday scheme." Valerie Stamp shook the phone. "Hello? Pete Burns? Are you there?"

After finally replacing the phone, Mrs Stamp sat down. How extraordinary she shouldn't remember a holiday scheme she took part in. How extraordinary she thought she saw squiggles and lines all over that boy's face. It must have been the hypnosis. *That* would explain a few things. How extraordinary he should suddenly ring her from Greece. *Things should settle down now I'm gone.* Mrs Stamp made herself a large pot of Earl Grey tea and sat down with it. Then she opened the cupboard again and took out *Pete Burns' Seafood Kitchen.*

Pete Burns. Or whoever he was. What an extraordinary interlude. She started to smile at a number of things. The puppy Pete Burns had said he'd saved when he lost his hair; the way Pete Burns was – supposedly – too intelligent to go to school; the way he'd caused that rumpus at the pool, seemingly without meaning to; the way he nursed Holly so carefully and mended her dolphin mobile when it broke; the way he took everything so literally, you had to be careful what you said. It really was too silly. Valerie Stamp wiped her cheek. Was she laughing, or crying? Certainly Pete Burns had been very strange indeed. The funny thing was, she missed him.

On impulse she called her son in. "Jack! Fancy the Mixed Seafood Risotto tonight?" She showed him the colourful picture on page ten of the *Seafood Kitchen*. "That was Pete Burns. Ringing from Greece. He's met his parents and they're fine."

"Greece. That's great." Jack Stamp eyed his mother. "Seafood Risotto looks good."

"So." Valerie Stamp straightened and brushed back her hair. "I don't know how he got there. I'm not even really sure what's happened. But it seems there's no need to worry, after all."

"You worry too much, Mum," Jack told her. "Sit down and finish your tea." He took the cookery book off her. "I'll make Seafood Risotto. It looks pretty easy, don't you think?"

Mrs Stamp let Jack steer her into her chair. She hugged him before he got away. "Did you know you were heavier than Holly when you were born?"

"How heavy was Holly?" Jack asked.

"Seven pounds, twelve ounces."

"And how heavy was I?"

"Eight pounds, ten ounces."

"Was Dad glad when you had me?"

"Your dad? He was over the moon." Jack seemed to tower over her somehow. She was comforting him. He knew it. She couldn't quite get through to him. Something was stopping her – what?

"I'm going to be nicer to Holly in future." Jack smiled. He was making a gesture. Saying, I know what you're doing, and thanks. "I'll come back when it's time to start cooking, OK?"

"OK." Mrs Stamp smiled. But something about Jack chilled her. His knowingness made him cold. At least he was going to school. *Things'll settle down now I'm gone.* Perhaps, with time, they would.

Valerie Stamp finished her tea. Then she got up and took a pack of Atlantic prawns out of the freezer. She brought out some rice and washed it. Then she dialled Rubytown Constabulary.

"Hello? Police? Yes. It's about a missing person. The

young man calling himself Pete Burns? We registered him the other night. The thing is, I've just heard from him, and – Mrs V.A. Stamp. Gough Street. Yes. No. Pete Burns. It seems he's with his parents. That's right. *He isn't missing any more…*"

# Stealing Time

MapHead smelled the air. The late night stroll to the Stamps' house had had a special quality about it. The air was still and sweet. Everything seemed to listen and lean – the cemetery yews excepted – to MapHead as he passed. The pelican crossing winked feebly; the traffic lights ordered Stop and Go down the long road empty of cars; the old soldiers guarding the cemetery walls popped up on cue, their ghostly faces spoiling as no one inspected their parade. MapHead wasn't about to. He had better fish to fry. All the same, it wouldn't do to get there too early. Not before he could be certain the Stamps had retired to bed. MapHead made it a rule.

The nuns' pond had looked sweetly cool under the moonlight. Frogs chirruped somewhere around it, probably glad he, MapHead, would never again sit on their tadpoles. The air had a quality of goodbye in it that made every second thing precious, like something you saw for the first – or last – time in your life. Turning the corner on Gough Street, MapHead wondered how much longer he would stay. Long enough to be certain Jack would watch over Holly. Long enough, at least, to give Jack his memories back.

MapHead registered the dirty white van outside Jack's house without much surprise. What *did* surprise him was the flickering torch-light inside the house. And the open front door.

Immediately MapHead entered the hall a large young man surprised him with the family Stamp's TV. MapHead stepped swiftly aside. In not allowing the large young man to see him, he would have time to work out what was happening. The large young man passed him closely with the telly. MapHead watched him take it down the steps and load it into the van. The steady drip of surprise was suddenly overtaken by a stronger feeling of suspicion. Something was occurring, MapHead felt sure. Not for nothing had he watched *Inspector Morse* and *The Bill*.

As soon as the large young man hopped up the steps and re-entered the Stamps' living-room, MapHead whisked the telly out of the van and carried it back to the house. He met the young man head-on in the hall with the family Stamp's VCR.

"I can understand why you're doing this," MapHead told the burglar. "You must have had a rotten life to have to do this. People don't understand you prob'ly don't have a job or any money. The thing is, they're not rich or anything. They've only got one TV."

The burglar looked at the telly. Floating in mid-air around waist-height, it seemed to be telling him it understood why he'd pinched it.

"Are you Rob?" MapHead went on severely. "Big Shout 2's big brother?"

*It even knew his name!!!* The VCR tilted in Rob's nerveless fingers. Something caught it as it fell. A deeply confusing moment passed. Then Big Shout 2's big brother Rob ran for his van like a man desperate for the toilet. He didn't know what it was that had happened, but whatever it was, he didn't like it. Something made him turn before he jumped into the van; something – a silhouette – up on the roof. It brought him up short with his heart in his mouth, what wasn't in it already. Someone standing up there like that. On the very edge of the roof. A person could get themselves *killed*.

"*Don't do it!*" Thoroughly spooked by the sound of his own voice, Rob Smith heard himself shouting. "Straight up, it isn't worth it! Do yourself a favour and get back inside again, matey!"

Expecting something else to go wrong every second minute, Rob Smith jumped into the dirty white van he'd "borrowed" from Rippon's Family Butcher and roared away. Maybe he'd pack it in for a while. This kind of stuff was too weird. If tellies could finger him now, *what could a stolen van do?*

MapHead watched him go. He coolly removed the

key from the door that Rob Smith used to get in with, and hung it back on its hook; Jack's key, he lost some time ago. He set down the VCR in the hall next to the rescued telly. Then he went out on the step and looked up. What had Rob the robber been shouting about? Matey? Where? Up on the roof. There *was* someone up there – wasn't there?

"Jack! Is that you? I said, *Jack!*"

It was – it looked like – Jack Stamp. Jack Bradley Stamp on the edge – the *very* edge – of the roof. With only the whole of the known world and a very hard pavement beneath him.

"Jack! Wait! Don't move!"

MapHead tore up the steps into the hall; up the stairs to the landing; through the door into Jack's room. The swivel-round Velux window onto the roof had been swivelled around, all right. Jack had got out onto the roof, all right. And stood there, all right, so far.

"So." MapHead swung out onto the roof.

"Rob Smith was taking our telly," Jack said, matter-of-factly. "But it doesn't matter to us."

"It doesn't?"

"No, because we're going any minute. You took long enough. I've been waiting here for ages."

"Stand back a bit, I should," MapHead advised Jack worriedly. How strong was the gutter? Jack was stand-ing, MapHead saw, in the very place he'd stood himself, not so very long ago – when he'd launched

338

off to visit the penguins, that time before he'd been outcast, when *joining in* had still been an option. "Jack. Stand back, why don't you?"

"Why?"

"You might as well sit down, if you want." He could see now, Jack's face had a fixed look. "We're not quite ready yet."

"Yes, we are," Jack said. "I've been ready a long time, me. I want to go where you go. Like when you saw the penguins? And now you're here at last."

"I'm here if you want me, but *please*, Jack Stamp, sit down." MapHead edged carefully towards him. Jack looked distinctly shaky. How long had he stood in the gutter with a wandering, half-puzzled look on his face and the whole dark world before him, and nothing at all except an idea of waiting for MapHead holding him back? Poised to leap off the roof, Jack Stamp had the look of a bungee-jumper. Only thing was, no bungee.

"It's you and me," Jack said simply. *"Just you and me together, OK?"*

"No! Jack Stamp! You can't!"

"It's too late to stop me now." Jack Stamp swayed out, swayed back. "I'm going places you go." He smiled. "In *travelling* time, all right?"

MapHead gained the chimney, swung down and around beside it and, reaching Jack, clipped his legs around Jack's. Jack smiled down serenely, as though MapHead's move were the last in a complicated game

339

plan designed to bring them together at the very point they'd arrived at.

*"Ready?"*

"No! Jack! *Don't!*"

Still smiling, Jack jumped off the roof. His legs tangled in Jack's legs, MapHead fell off the roof with him. Nothing much else disturbed the small hours. Outside a butcher's shop two miles away Rob Smith reversed a dirty white van back into its parking space, then legged it into the night. The front door of the Stamp house stood open on to the street. A cat wandered in, and then out again. The television sat blankly in the hall where MapHead had left it. The dog Weg slept dreamlessly in the kitchen. Mr and Mrs Stamp snored upstairs. Holly turned, too hot, in her cot, her blankets up over her head.

The moon shone; the garden settled; the green-winking night ticked and glowed. Nothing much more disturbed it after the complicated knot of arms and legs and bodies dropped silently off the edge of the roof and disappeared in a flash of light that died on the promise of morning.

# A Family Affair

"Wow!" Jack called, in free-fall. "We're going somewhere amazing, right?"

"We're not going anywhere at all." MapHead looked severe.

Jack Stamp saw a darkened bedroom from a point somewhere over the bed. "I'm floating. How am I floating?"

*This is subtle time,* MapHead seemed to tell him. *We can do anything we like.*

"But why can't we visit jungles an' stuff? I want to go places you've been, places with mountains and ghosts—"

"Jack Bradley Stamp." MapHead looked angry. He'd never, Jack realized, really seen MapHead angry. "I'm going to show you something."

The boy in the bed beneath them stirred. Somehow they seemed to dip closer. The boy in the bed was fair, with a radical haircut. His face was marked by the

341

deepest sleep, the deepest passing dreams. Posters looked down over his bed-head. A pair of jeans stood on the floor like he'd just jumped out of them. He could have been almost any age. It was hard to tell in the dark.

*"I'm strange. I'll always be strange."* MapHead whispered a subtle song straight into Jack Stamp's heart. *"This is my half-brother, Kenny. I can't know him. You've got two sisters. Be glad."*

"But why can't you know him?" Jack asked.

*"He'd change, the way you changed,"* the answer rang back, like an echo. *"I can't ever really know him. Because of what happened to you."*

Jack Stamp looked down on Kenny and wondered, What must it be like? A brother you can't ever know? He pictured Lois and Holly. They were pretty annoying sometimes. But they really weren't that bad.

The bedroom scene shifted and changed. This time the bed was a double, empty but for a fair-headed woman with silky-looking arms thrown wide over a rose-covered duvet. Jack dipped down. He smelled her. She smelled like—

*"This is my mother, Kay,"* the whisper ran on. *"I can know her only in dreams. You've got your mother. Be glad."*

Jack Stamp looked at Kay. Fairer by a mile than his own mother, she looked kindly, like her. And pretty.

Again the bedroom scene shifted. A large lady in a hairnet lay gently snoring in bed. Again MapHead whispered his song:

"*I'm strange, I'll always be strange. This is my grand-mother, Frida. I can't know her. You've got your dad. Be glad.*"

"But you've got your dad," Jack seemed to say.

"We've got each other." MapHead smiled.

The bedroom shrank and grew darker. Bold things rushed by in dreams. A light, Jack thought, came and went. Again they looked down on a bedroom. A bedroom much smaller, this time. No bookshelves decorated these walls. No friendly posters looked down.

"*No love no home this summer,*" ran the whisper. "*This is Big Shout 2. His foster home can't love him. His mother doesn't want him. He stays off school and spray-paints walls. He doesn't know what to do. He hasn't had a fair start. Not,*" ran the whisper, "*like you.*"

Jack Stamp looked down on Big Shout 2. His mind enclosed the lies he'd told, the lies Big Shout 2 had told, too. He'd pushed him around. He shouldn't have. The things he knew had made him mad for money – for everything – somehow. It didn't matter any more. What mattered most was family.

"*It's not his fault.*" It really wasn't. MapHead spread his arms. "*He doesn't fit in. Like me.*"

Jack Stamp felt himself nodding. "Can we go now?" he asked.

The poor bedroom shrank away. Big skies rushed down to receive them. This time the light flashed them high on a hill under the moon. The flower fields

343

skirting Rubytown lay like a bedspread beneath them. Away towards the distant north and west a brave line of wind turbines sticklebacked a ridge.

Jack could see his own house. "Wait! I don't want to go home yet!"

"Home," thrilled poor MapHead, "*home*."

Home. Jack sensed how much the word meant. "I'm glad I saw your family," he said. "Your mother looks really nice."

"My mother's human, my father isn't." MapHead almost broke down. "Now you know why I'll *never* fit in."

"You're special, not strange." Jack sat down next to him, touching him. "MapHead. You should be glad."

"I should be glad. I *am* glad. It's just, I have to get used to it. I'm going to be lonely a long time."

"Why would you be lonely," Jack said, "when you can always come and see me?"

MapHead smiled in a watery way. Then he smelled the air. "Thunder's coming. Feel it?"

"Purple," Jack said, "it feels – purple, somehow. I don't like it. Let's—"

"LET'S NOT!"

"What's that voice? Where's it come from?" Jack looked around him fearfully. A green hill. A thunderstorm. Something about to happen.

"MAPHEAD! STAY WHERE YOU ARE!"

"What is it?" Jack whimpered. "Is it God?"

"No." MapHead straightened. "My father."

# MapHead's Trial

*"Thou art so powerful..."* MapHead searched the sky, remembering the lines from *The Snow Queen* he read once, so long ago. *"Thou art so powerful that I know thou canst twist all the winds of the world into a thread ..."*

The night sky heaved and flashed. The brightest of lights alighted.

*"... and if the pilot loosen one knot of it he will have a favourable wind."* Powers stood before them in all his awesome glory.

"Dad."

"MapHead."

"This is Jack."

"Jack Bradley Stamp, I know. Excuse us, Jack? While we talk?" Powers placed a hand over Jack Stamp's face and Jack Stamp closed his eyes. Powers' suit flashed silver under the moon as he turned to MapHead.

"Dad –" MapHead raised a hand "– I know what you're going to say."

"MapHead. I don't think you do."

"You're going to ask me what I've done to Jack Stamp's mind."

*"What have you done to Jack Stamp's mind?"* Powers seemed to grow. His voice took on a dangerous note, his eyes a dangerous glow. *"Now is the time to account for anything and everything you've done, in this world or any other."*

"OK, Dad, the thing is I—"

*"You interfered. I warned you. You had no right."*

"I've learned, Dad. I know. I understand what I am." MapHead swelled, himself. "And I'm making it right without you."

*"You force me to intervene before seven years is up. Before seven weeks is up, you ask me what you should do. Is this the way you manage on your own?"*

"I know it doesn't look good, Dad. But I know what I'm doing now."

*"In every corner of every world you pursue me, calling for help."* Powers' teeth flashed. His body crackled with energy. *"MapHead. I must ask you. Is Jack Stamp's mind his own?"*

"Not quite yet. But it will be."

*"And have you understood?"*

"Understood what?"

*"What else? The nature of power."*

MapHead stared levelly at his father. It seemed a battle of giants. "The nature of power," he said evenly, "is such that it cannot be understood."

Thunder grumbled somewhere. Powers seemed to shrink. "Well and good." He smiled. "My dear and only son."

"It's lonely, isn't it?" said MapHead, after a moment. "Being us, I mean."

Powers nodded slowly. "Very lonely," he said.

Exchanging thoughts only they could understand they sat a while enjoying each other, like Arctic terns that range thousands of miles and only touch earth now and then.

"Was it you, Dad?" MapHead asked.

"Me, what?" murmured Powers.

"The man in purple. In Sparta."

"Sparta?"

"'It is better to travel than to arrive.' Come off it, Dad. The sage."

"Purple for wisdom. Choose your own way." Powers encircled his son with an arm. "You don't need me to tell you."

"Not now, I don't," said MapHead, flushing his scalp with happy maps of Rubytown.

Powers traced the outlines with his finger. *Well-Met Cross. Gladsome Lane. Heartslove Place. Rejoice-and-Be-Glad. Welcome Break. The Happy Shopper, Glee Street.*

"Did you see your mother?" he asked.

"I saw her. I didn't interfere."

Powers was thoughtful. "Maybe I'll look in myself."

After Powers finally flashed away on the wind with the time fixed for six years, nine months, one week, seven hours and forty minutes precisely until they met again, MapHead remembered Jack Stamp. Still mesmerized by Powers, Jack Stamp smiled mildly in subtle time. Subtle time that, suddenly, seemed to have an edge. *Hurry*, ran the vibe. *Hurry, for heaven's sake.*

MapHead took Jack's face in his hands and sucked away all those things he'd lent him – the pictures he'd smoothed in with Jack's pictures; the cave; the desert; the reading-day picnic; the big-sky country he'd grown up with. The memories flashed back faster as he remembered them, replaced by Jack's Stamp's own. My memories. My lifetime. My knowledge. MapHead pulled them back. *Remember it back to me.*

Jack Stamp opened his eyes. "Don't take it all away, will you?"

MapHead jumped, surprised. "I have to make you forget."

"No," Jack said, "I can handle it."

"Everything?"

"Some of it, anyway. *Please* don't make me forget. I want to remember—"

"Want to remember what?"

"You," Jack said, "I want to remember *you.*"

MapHead covered Jack's face with his hand in a gesture he rarely employed. When he pulled away his hand Jack was smiling. Some things Jack would *never* forget. MapHead smiled in the knowledge, too.

"It's good that's done, 'cos we have to hurry." MapHead smelled the vibe. "Can't you feel the pull?"

348

"What pull?"

The light built all around them. *Hurry. For heaven's sake.*

"There's something wrong. *That* pull."

"What d'you mean, something's wrong?" Jack felt the pull as it took him. Already he felt himself *travelling* as the light built quickly and engulfed them. "What is it?" Jack heard himself screaming as MapHead tumbled away into space towards a destination all his own. "MapHead, what is it, what's happening? *I don't understand! What's wrong?*"

Holly, drummed Jack's mind through space for the merest split-second of subtle time in the flash from place to place. *Holly. Hurry. For Holly's sake. Hurry. For hurry's sake. Holly.*

# Waking ... Shaking

"I don't understand!" Jack found himself shouting in Holly's room. "I don't understand! What's wrong?"

Where, for a start, was the baby? He felt around in Holly's cot, panic coursing through him as he did it. He tore off Holly's bedclothes. There she was, squashed, at the bottom. Very hot. Bright red in the face. *And not breathing.*

Jack scooped her up and shook her. What to do next? *Hurry, for Holly's sake, hurry.* He laid her on the floor. Covered her mouth and nose with his mouth. Breathed in quick, little breaths. Applied two fingers to her chest. Pumped them quickly up and down. Not too much pressure for a baby. Breathed little breaths. Pumped two fingers. Breathed little breaths. Pumped two fingers. Again and again and again.

He didn't know how long he did it. Suddenly Holly stiffened, spluttered – and wailed, a great, choking wail that died, came back, then quickly climbed to a full-on scream of annoyance. Feeling slightly sick, Jack held Holly to him, enjoying her struggling body, her irritable legs, her sticky-feeling chin and everything else about her. Close call, or what? A big hand for *Dr Gillian's Cyclopaedia of Childcare*. Some shreds of it had jumped across. Good thing MapHead read so much. How else had he known what to do?

Jack was still shaking when, holding Holly closely, he cradled her bravely next door. His parents' room stood open. The clock told a quarter to seven.

"Mum. Dad. Here's Holly." He laid her on the bed.

His parents were stirring already. Valerie Stamp hit the clock. "Jack. Is she wet, or something?"

"Probably." Jack kissed her and smiled. "Who cares?"

"You look flushed. Are you all right?"

Jack Stamp looked down on his early-morning mother. A million thoughts rushed by him. He could have said, No, I'm not. Holly almost died. It had been a pretty strange night. He'd dreamt – had he? – he jumped off the roof. It had seemed pretty real, but it couldn't be. Else he wouldn't be standing here in his parents' bedroom.

He rubbed his head. Then he said, "I sleepwalked into Holly's room. I dreamed she couldn't breathe." A little knowledge was a good thing. Way less threatening, this way. "She's too hot, Mum. You should get rid of that duvet. Put her to bed so her feet touch the bottom of the cot? That way she can't wriggle down and get overheated."

Valerie Stamp sat up. "You're absolutely right. That's what they said on that programme. That programme the other night? I was thinking about it, anyway. I should've done it before." She scooped Holly up in her arms and fed her, warmly, in the folds of her nightdress. She reached across and squeezed Jack's arm. "Thank you, Jack," she said.

Jack Stamp relaxed at last. He had the feeling – certain, somehow – that Holly would be fine. It wouldn't happen again, because his mother would take steps to stop it. Through him, she would know. Through MapHead, *he* knew. The danger had been averted. MapHead, in his own – a *MapHeadish* way – had guarded Holly well.

"Jack." Jack's father stirred and sat up. "Time to push the boat out. Happy birthday, old son."

"I'm not having any birthday," Jack said mechanically. "I've got to see Ada Leary instead."

"Ada Leary!" Jack's father lay back and changed colour. "Of course! He's got to see Ada Leary!" Strange hiccups shook the bed. "Ada … Leary … instead!"

"For heaven's sake, get on with it." Valerie Stamp kissed Jack. "Happy birthday, love."

"He's got to see … Ada Leary!" Jack's dad roared. *"You'll have a job! It's Saturday, you twonk!"*

"Oh," Jack said. "Then what—"

"Lift that sheet up. That sheet over there." Alan Stamp gestured weakly in the general direction of a large, sheet-covered lump in the corner. "Yes. That sheet. Go on."

Jack went over and lifted it. When he saw what was under it he felt kind of sick and *overblown*, somehow. It was too much. He'd been such a pain. Hadn't it been sold, already? How much had it cost, anyhow?

"Dad," he said, "you shouldn't have."

"I know, but I did it anyway."

"It was you." Jack stared. "When Starkers came to tell me they'd gone. Ben Pringle's brother only sold 'em to *you*."

"I knocked him down a bit." Jack's dad grinned. "You'll have to earn it, mind."

Jack Stamp swallowed hugely. When he saw the whole kit – the twin decks plus mixer – his dad *had gone out of his way* to make sure that he, Jack, had on his birthday, his chest filled with the knowledge that his father loved and understood him – *had* loved him, of course – all along. There would always be Lois and Holly. But love and attention wasn't divided like a cake at a picnic. However much got eaten up, there would *always* be enough to go around.

"Dad, you're *brilliant*. I can't believe you did this. Not after—"

"All the aggro you caused? Not half so much as I did, when I was your age."

"You did? I mean – make some hassles?"

"No excuses. But I was no angel. And you're worth three of me."

"I am?"

353

LESLEY HOWARTH

Jack's dad nodded slowly. "Underneath. I know."

After they'd hugged each other quite a while Jack held out his hand. "Hey, Dad," he said, "gimme five."

Alan Stamp grinned. He slapped his son's hand with his. "I'll give you ten if you'll get that thing out of here by tonight. We've lived with it in the bedroom so long, I practically kiss it good night."

"It's cool, Dad. Really the best." Jack Stamp struck a pose behind his twin turntables: "This is DJ BlackJack, Prince of the Mix, givin' out hardcore, techno, dance-zone, rap. Check it out. With the most – the coolest – sounds around, can you afford not to?" Jack popped his knees and grinned. "I'll make it pay its way, Dad. I'll do parties when I'm good. Rappin' Jack Stamp. Who could resist?"

"I could, for starters."

"I'm sorry. I know I've been out of order. I think I've been a bit mad."

"Loud music'll do it to you. Want me to jam the volume on that thing?"

"I mean it, I'm really sorry." Jack came over and sat down. "I did some bad things, I don't know why." The signs of strain stood in his face. Good and bad had fought in Jack Stamp. But the outcome had not been in doubt. "Nothing so bad I can't put it right, though. I think Pete Burns thought I took things. One time when I went up the multi? I *wish* I'd found that door key."

"You could have dropped it anywhere. No sense in

worrying about it now." Alan Stamp climbed out of bed and clumped his way downstairs. "I'll put the kettle on. No," he called back, "it's no trouble. I didn't want breakfast in bed."

"Aw, Dad..."

"Only joking!" Dad called.

Dozy with milk, Holly looked up. Valerie Stamp set her down. "It's like you've been away." She looked at Jack, then hugged him. "I can't tell how, but you're back."

"I really am," Jack said, both eyes shut really tight. "I wanted to like, do stuff. Stuff like travel around? But everything I want's right here."

"You'll want to get away some day."

"Some day's plenty of time."

"Jimmy-Jack Stamp, you're a strange one." His mother hugged him some more.

"Enough, already." Jack looked mock-severe. *Mappers*, he thought, *can you see this?* "How can I keep my cred with everyone *hugging* me all the time?"

Released from the kitchen, the dog Weg bounded upstairs and greeted them sloppily. Lois' bedroom door banged. A howl resounded downstairs. Alan Stamp's voice rose on an anguished note:

"WHAT'S THIS FRONT DOOR DOING OPEN? WHAT GENIUS LEFT THE VIDEO RECORDER IN THE HALL? WE'RE DAMN LUCKY NO ONE'S PINCHED IT!"

"STOP SHOUTING!" Lois shouted crossly, coming

around the door with a present for Jack in one hand and a toothbrush in the other. "EVERYBODY'S ALWAYS SHOUTING IN THIS HOUSE!"

"I wish I knew what was going on. I SAID, I WISH I KNEW WHAT WAS GOING ON. DID YOU KNOW THIS MISSING KEY'S ON ITS HOOK? ANYONE KNOW HOW IT GOT THERE?"

"I love this family, you know?" Jack threw back his head and allowed himself to laugh. "I wouldn't want any other."

"Business as usual, then." Valerie Stamp smiled. "Happy birthday, Jack."

# House of Tomorrow

*Power is lonely. Power stands apart.*

MapHead worked it out slowly. Round and round, in circles. The reason he wouldn't fit in.

*Power stands apart. I have power. Therefore, I'm lonely.*

The wind blew keenly over the Sierra Nevada. The plants on the patio of the house called Casa Mañana knocked softly together as it reached them. Sheltered by the wall around a small pool bright with inflatables, the girl on the patio pulled on a coloured robe and turned the page of her book. The holiday hacienda had been neatly tucked into a fold in the hills. The scrub land reminded MapHead of his one-time home in Arizona. In fact, it was southern Spain. Somewhere near Granada. MapHead had crossed a mountain or three before he'd found the house.

He watched from the hillside opposite as a tanned boy crossed the patio with a tray of tall pink drinks. He set the tray down on a table. The girl sat up and took off her sunglasses and laughed at something the boy said. The pool threw lights on her dark blonde hair. "Perry," she called, "I'm warning you." She threw a cushion at Perry. He threw the cushion back, not in anger at all. The girl pushed him. She laughed a lot. They knew each other well.

A middle-aged woman joined them and laughed a lot at them both. Perry picked up the tray and held it out. "Here, Mum – have a drink."

*Casa Mañana.* It meant House of Tomorrow. MapHead shifted on his rock. He watched the girl on the patio thoughtfully. Close enough to hear what she said, far enough to feel the separation in time and space, he wasn't about to break Future rules or any others. Here, at least, there were clear boundaries, and he, MapHead, meant to stay inside them. He would enjoy the scene while he could. No hint of his presence must escape. The House of Tomorrow must never feel his footstep on its threshold, a footstep that, as yet, couldn't – hadn't – ever been there. MapHead sighed. Future rules were complex. Along with love, responsibility, knowledge, friendship and just about anything *else* you cared to think of.

"Holly – don't – get off! Careful, you'll spill your drink!" The boy Perry straightened, panting, a cushion ready in his hand, should Holly hit him with hers.

"No chance." Future Holly plumped down on a sun-bed, laughing. "Too good to waste on you." She eyed the surrounding hills over the top of her long pink drink. As the level dropped, she quietened. "It's funny, I—"

"What?"

"Oh, nothing. I just thought of something, that's all."

Future Holly would be sixteen or seventeen at this stage, MapHead decided, from his hillside perch looking down on her. If only Jack Stamp could see his sister. Enough, for the moment, that *he* could. Enough that she was safe and well – and would be throughout her childhood, now that he could *see*, beyond doubt, she'd come through it.

"What sort of something?" Perry wanted to know.

"Oh, just this thing when I was small," Future Holly said, reflectively. "These stickers I had in my room? I spent ages and ages staring at them every night before I went to sleep, and I can still remember *every single sticker*, you know? And the light always seemed to be pink. I had a pig eating a chocolate eclair, a Father Christmas, a toothy snake, a one-eyed monster – an alien, I think – in a spaceship, just about everything you could think of on my white chest of drawers, and I used to, you know, think they were *magic*, or something. And once my brother told me—"

"Your brother told you what?"

"Oh, it's just my brother. Once he told me that they *were*. Magic, I mean. 'Specially the frog. Surfer Moe – isn't it silly?"

Perry raised a cushion and an eyebrow. "Did I say anything?"

"And now they're all gone, but it still makes me sad, you know? Like, when you're little it's another world or something, and you can't go back there *ever again*, no matter how much you want to." Future Holly searched the hillside. MapHead – invisibly – met her eyes. "I don't know what made me think about it. Jack's going to laugh when I tell him."

"When's he coming?"

"Next week. They're bringing *piles* of stuff for the baby. I'm an auntie now, you know. The baby's called Boothe, he's gorgeous. Jack says he's teething now, so I might stay on to help out."

"Auntie Holly. Do me a favour." Perry threw his cushion.

Auntie Holly. Future Jack. With – *baby Boothe?* – and all the family. MapHead quailed. Too much knowledge, too soon.

"No! Perry! Don't!" Future Holly dodged, shrieking, round the pool. Perry pelted after her. In moments they were splashing in the water.

MapHead watched the fun. Future rules had a kind of logic about them. It was good that he wasn't supposed to see too much. All he had to do was stick to the rules. Somewhere, Future MapHead waited. But not even Powers could look into his own future. MapHead would have to *live* it.

"I'm getting out! Perry! It's cold!" Future Holly swatted Perry with her towel. MapHead approved. With her berry-bright eyes and her rich laugh, Holly had the crackle of a real live wire, one that would never be dampened by anything life might throw at it.

What would Jack Stamp – the Jack Stamp he knew – have made of Future Holly? MapHead wondered. Hey, he'd have said, Is she good for a loan? Are we ready to make some dosh, or are we ready? Maybe he'd've made her a special Jack Stamp Rap – "Holly With the Lolly", who knows? MapHead smiled, remembering. He pictured Jimmy-Jack Stamp lovingly reunited with his family, hugging them all in turn, his family hugging him back. He pictured Jack Stamp fitting in, and it didn't hurt at all for some reason.

*Sorry I mixed you up, Jack Stamp. I won't be back for a long time. And then maybe only in your mind. I'm just so glad we saved Holly. Holly makes up for everything.*

Holly was the silver lining. Family life, relationships, you name it. It all boiled down to much the same thing, in the end. These were the things that were important. MapHead watched as the laughing girl on the patio pulled on a sweater and disappeared into the cool gloom of Casa Mañana with her friend. The wind had picked up quite a bit. Probably he should be going. A beach-ball blew on the pool. The plants knocked gently together. *I see you, Future Holly. I know you don't see me.* MapHead waited, but she didn't come back. Still he felt OK. *I have knowledge to understand. I'm lonely, but not alone…*

*I see now. I understand.* Suddenly MapHead rose. *Dad! My task! I am it! I know how to choose between right and wrong, and Jack, my friend, helped me learn. My power and choice. My future.*

Anything was possible. MapHead's unimaginable future stretched away in front of him, its every moment boundless. The choice was his. No limits. Anything he wanted to be.

For a while, he'd been Pete Burns. What was the real Pete Burns like? MapHead wondered. Probably he liked a stiff drink while he was cooking. Probably he was wild-haired, with eyebrows that met in the middle and bits of fish in his beard. Probably he could make Turbot Terrine or Salmon Mousse or Fried Excalibur Bananas. But could he wizard the future? Make the mountain come to Mohammed? Be all the things he wanted to be, and *still* have room to learn?

MapHead glowed with satisfaction. He might not be a seafood chef who could whip up a Herring Supreme, but in or out of the kitchen, there were other fish he could fry. In full possession of his kingdom, MapHead looked down and knew. Half-human but with power he knew what to do with, truly terrifying, his own best creation was himself.

*Hey, Jack Stamp. You and me. This is goodbye for now. Thanks for showing me what families do. I learned more than you ever did. I used to be Boothe. Then Pete Burns. Who will I be next?*